HOKEE WOLF IV

THE VISION QUEST

CLARK VIEHWEG

Black Rose Writing | Texas

ISBN: 978-1-68513-603-1
PUBLISHED BY BLACK ROSE WRITING
www.blackrosewriting.com

Printed in the United States of America
Suggested Retail Price (SRP) $21.95

Hohee Wolf IV: The Vision Quest is printed in Garamond Premier Pro

*As a planet-friendly publisher, Black Rose Writing does its best to eliminate unnecessary waste to reduce paper usage and energy costs, while never compromising the reading experience. As a result, the final word count vs. page count may not meet common expectations.

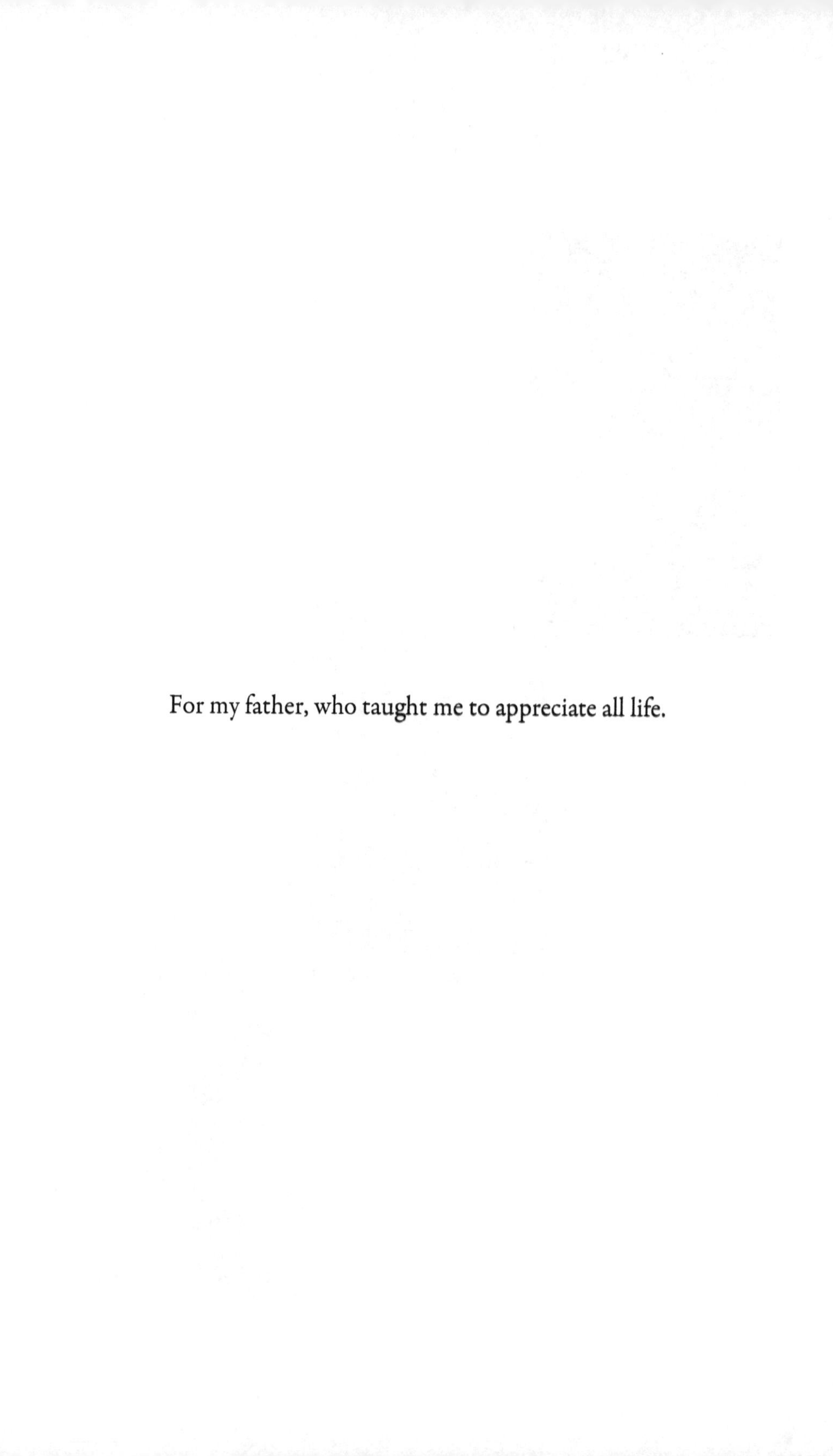

For my father, who taught me to appreciate all life.

Notes

The threat A.I. poses to humanity is mainly unreported. There are daily reports about the wonders of A.I. with pictures and videos showing fantastic breakthroughs in every field. For example, in medicine, there are robots performing operations. In entertainment, there are robotic singers and vaudeville performers. Unfortunately, there are also A.I. impersonators capable of mimicking any voice, a development used by con artists.

The Vision Quest is my attempt to shine a light on the problem this fantastic technology presents. I hope for the sake of humanity there is a Myron alive someplace.

WE HAVE REACHED SINGULARITY

At this point, it is impossible to predict the future

"Artificial Intelligence (A.I.) is the greatest threat to humanity."
–According to many leading scientists, including Elon Musk

HOKEE WOLF IV
THE VISION QUEST

The eagle was killed by an arrow made with its own feathers.
–American Paradox

CHAPTER ONE

Midnight in Idaho, then

A beautiful young sixteen-year-old Navajo girl was sleeping alone by an irrigation ditch to stay cool on a hot summer night. The white farmer she worked for discovered the nearly naked girl while making a midnight water change. Unable to resist the temptation, he raped the girl. When a baby boy was born, the farmer called the child a half-breed and sent the mother and baby back to their homeland in Arizona. Arriving back on the reservation, nobody wanted the unwed mother and child. With no family and feeling abandoned and unloved, the mother jumped from a towering cliff with the unwanted baby in her arms, planning to kill them both. During the fall, her body twisted midair, landing on the sharp rocks below, killing the young mother instantly. The unwanted and unloved baby landed on her stomach and survived. Passed around from hogan to hogan, the tribe grew tired of tending the half-breed. When the boy was six, they left the hungry, ragged boy near a seldom used Arizona road at noon in the scorching desert, unconcerned with the boy's chances of living.

Mormon missionaries going home to Idaho spotted the barefoot waif in ragged dirty clothes standing in the shade of a saguaro cactus by the roadside. With their teaching about Jesus and his admonition to love everyone fresh on their minds, the missionaries stopped to see if the child needed help. They gave water to the parched boy and asked why he was alone in the heat without water or shoes. The boy said they named him Hokee, meaning abandoned and unwanted. Arriving back home, the missionaries left the boy with the Fort Hall Indian reservation medicine man, a shaman named Way-ay'-looh.

Way-ay'-looh educated the young boy, raising him in the shaman tradition, hoping his informally adopted son would follow in his footsteps. Later, as a young man, Hokee nearly died crossing an immense lava plain on a vision quest before discovering a hidden underground river at the back of a cave that later became his home. Earth Mother shined on Hokee, giving him two animal guide spirits, an eagle and a wolf. Hokee then chose Wolf as his last name. A disappointed Way-ay'-looh gave his son a young gray timber wolf named Shila (brother) to keep him company when he decided to become a private investigator instead of a practicing medicine man/shaman.

Pocatello, now

Golden afternoon sunlight flashed through the open office window, casting rings around the room from the shine on Hokee's polished black Tony Lama boots resting on his desk. He was reclining in a custom-made Factory Furnace office chair, enjoying a warm breeze wafting through the window while thanking the universe for a chance to relax. Shoulder-length raven-black hair was secured with a white headband. With frosty blue eyes and lightly colored skin, inherited from his unknown father, Hokee could pass as a Caucasian, but he persistently emphasized his half-Navajo heritage.

It was early June, meaning the University of Idaho in Pocatello was in summer school recess, which accounted for Hokee's grateful lack of activity. This meant no young people being kidnapped, requiring Hokee's services. As Idaho's most famous private investigator solving crimes that stumped law enforcement officers, Hokee's primary interest was locating missing people, especially abducted university students. Hokee always found the person he hunted. Many of those responsible for the abductions vanished, but they all faced unhappy consequences.

Having recovered from being butchered last year by Saudi Arabia killers, Hilda, his secretary and office manager, knocked on his office door, interrupting his quiet time. Today she wore a gray long-sleeved vee neck tee shirt to hide the white knife scars on her arms. Her hair had grown back, and cosmetic surgery restored her pretty, smiling face to its natural beauty.

"Hokee, you have a male visitor," she announced in a soft, contralto voice. Since being cut up and tortured by mercenary thugs from Saudi Arabia looking for the whereabouts of Hokee, Hilda stopped flirting with her boss. Hokee gently helped her recover, and during the process, Hilda reluctantly came to understand her boss was off limits.

"Okay, thanks, Hilda, send him in." Hokee did not change his posture, he continued to relax with his feet still on the desk.

"You should read about him first," she responded. "I've downloaded his information to your computer." They both use *WhatsApp* to retrieve information about individuals, the same service used by the FBI.

"Thanks, give me a few minutes. I'll buzz you when I'm through."

Putting his feet on the floor, removing sunlight rings from the office walls, Hokee opened his computer browser to read about a potential client.

Myron Whittleman, PhD
Age 25
He earned his Ph.D. at age 16 in Computer Science at the Massachusetts Institute of Technology and is now a full professor at Idaho State University in Pocatello, Idaho. Dr. Whittleman is also the founder and CEO of SINGULARITY INC., a wealthy start-up computer company specializing in Artificial Intelligence.

The computer screen referenced several additional pages devoted to the history and accomplishments of Dr. Whittleman, including several lucrative patents, making him one of America's wealthiest individuals. He also held memberships in several scientific organizations and is the current chairperson of the <u>Association of Information Technology Professionals</u>. After scanning a few pages, Hokee had all the information he required to host his visitor. On the telephone, he told Hilda it was time to introduce his guest.

As she stepped in, Hilda said, "Dr. Whittleman, meet Hokee Wolf. Hokee, this is Dr. Myron Whittleman." Giving Hokee a smile and a big thumbs up behind Myron's back, she left the office.

Hokee stood up to shake hands with his guest. "It's a pleasure to meet you, Dr. Whittleman. Please have a seat," he said, motioning towards a soft-brown padded guest chair in front of his desk. As Myron was getting settled, Hokee appraised his visitor.

He would have guessed Myron's age at about eighteen based on his youthful looks. The handsome young man had a cherubic face riding on a slender five-foot-eight body topped with a mop of curly, sandy hair. His hazel brown eyes had a few light-yellow streaks radiating from the pupil, giving him an owlish look enhanced by a cupid's grin. Wearing white sneakers below blue trousers and a white polo shirt with an Idaho State University logo, he looked more like a high school senior than a wealthy college professor.

"Would you like some coffee or hot tea? Hilda makes a great green tea."

"No Thanks. I'm good." Myron seemed nervous as he fidgeted in his chair.

"What brings you to my office, Dr. Whittleman?"

"It's just Myron, Mr. Wolf. The doctor thing is primarily for my students." He smiled self-consciously while squirming in his seat, clearly uncomfortable with the situation.

"And you can call me Hokee," responded Wolf. He waited for Myron to answer his question. Hokee only said what was required.

Myron waited for Hokee to speak. He was used to admiration and flattery from the people he met, and Hokee's impassive, quiet demeanor surprised him. Understanding that the man across the desk was waiting for him to speak, Myron shifted in his chair as he answered self-consciously, "I'm here to see if you will perform a vision quest for me." The self-conscious smile appeared, and his body shifted nervously in the chair.

If his request caught Hokee off guard, there would be no sign of it from the absence of expression on his face. Hokee asked Myron what he knew about vision quests.

The professor relaxed a little in his chair, as he had prepared an answer to this question. "I researched the topic in our university library. I understand Indian nations practice different traditions, all having different techniques for achieving a supernatural experience. The quest can involve sacrifice and extreme difficulty." Myron was a little smug after what he considered a scholarly answer

"During your research, did you discover any evidence suggesting that certain quests have the potential to be fatal or lead to the loss of one's sanity?" Hokee remained expressionless.

The question flustered Myron, who resumed shifting around in his chair. "No. I never ran across a reference to dying on a quest. My reading suggested that the quest is an extraordinary event, providing one with an interesting and highly informative experience.

"Before I get into specifics regarding the potential risks, tell me why you are seeking a vision quest."

"It's about my work," Myron responded, sitting up straight in his chair as though this answered the question.

"Most people who have jobs and never seek a vision quest," Hokee responded quietly. "What about your job inspires such a dramatic request?"

"I started a company, Singularity, Inc., two years ago. With our backgrounds in computer science, my associates and I have achieved what is called singularity. A singularity occurs when an event happens in which humanity's future cannot be predicted. A.I., artificial intelligence, has the potential to be a singularity event. With advanced mathematics, we discovered there becomes infinite separations in time and space, a breakdown of our present three-dimensional reality where the future is unknowable. A.I. advancement is a pivotal moment in our existence as homo sapiens. Depending on protocols written into the subroutines of advanced computers implanted into humanoid robots, these robots have the potential to overcome our society. There are no governing bodies to oversee and regulate this development. Unethical programmers might unleash on humanity robots capable of destroying all human activity. Presently, I alone possess the answer to what everybody in the A.I. race will call the *breakthrough formula* and software."

If this statement perturbed Hokee, it didn't show in his demeanor. "I have read about A.I. and the prospect of a singularity event. I am aware that A.I. experts like Stuart Russell and Max Tegmark consider this development seriously. How does this situation lead you to desire a vision quest?"

"Large corporations and several foreign countries have discovered our achievements. I buried our achievements until controls are established to control A.I. programming. Several entities want to own this technology. Countries, corporations and individuals. There is one primary algorithm that I hold. Recently I have been subjected to intimidating threats and I don't know how to proceed. I hope a vision quest will provide me with insight into the future and direct my actions.

Hokee sat in silence for several moments while he considered Myron's plight. "Do you drink coffee?"

The question surprised Myron, and he looked at Hokee with questionable eyes. He pondered the connection between this and his situation.

"Black, okay?" Hokee asked.

"What? I mean... yeah. Blacks just fine." Myron had a puzzled look on his face.

Picking up the handset, Hokee buzzed Hilda. "Two black coffees, please, Hilda."

"Coffee can help clear the mind. Now, what specifically do you wish to discover on your quest?"

CHAPTER TWO

Tahiti

The cloying scent of frangipani floated like quiet, loving whispers of life, suggesting beauty, and many happy tomorrows. The fragrant white star-shaped blossoms with brilliant yellow centers grew among three types of orchids along the Tahitian forest path upon which the newlyweds strolled. Dressed in new blue Gucci shorts with yellow Louis Vuitton sleeveless tee shirts and wearing Christian Louboutin flip flops costing $350.00 a pair, the handsome honeymoon couple looked like any other extremely wealthy honeymoon couple. Not that there were other highly affluent couples in the vicinity. The man was a solid six-foot-four with dark, curly hair, smoldering gray eyes, and a movie star face resembling Tom Cruise. The bride's beauty put her at the top of the fashion model profession, which was, in fact, her occupation and the reason for the couple being in Tahiti.

A few months earlier, while Hokee was battling thirst in the Sahara Desert, Gene Olsen married Rashida Hassan, the beautiful model who used the name Opal Nevada in her profession.

Rashida's father, an unscrupulous Egyptian contractor in competition with the Olsons, had coerced his daughter to spy on the Olsons and get their bids for billion-dollar contracts to underbid them. Hokee was hired by Gene's father, Grant, to find the person leaking their proposals and was surprised to discover that Opal, Gene's fiancée, was Rashida Hassan, the daughter of Olson's competitor. After this discovery, Hokee met with the Olsons and Rashida. He dropped a briefcase with one hundred million dollars of Hassan's money on Grant's lap while explaining who stole the company bids. He left their home to let the family deal with the information.

The Olsons subsequently learned that Rashida had been living in fear of her father. She changed her name to Opal Nevada to model to avoid being killed by her father's security thugs. While paying lip service to his Muslim religion, her father objected to his daughter displaying her body. Opal stole Olson's bid to appease her father while hating herself for betraying her fiancée, but she couldn't find a way out of the situation. Hokee solved the mystery while freeing the girl from her father's grip.

The wedding announcement arrived in Hokee's office while he was out of the country, trying not to get killed. After returning to Pocatello and discovering that Gene and Opal were married, he sent the newlyweds an appropriate gift, a pair of handmade leather moccasins for each. They didn't hurt for money.

Surrounded by a green forest of palm, coconut, and chestnut trees, among which grew the Orchids and frangipani, the happy couple on their delayed honeymoon talked about their schedule for the next few days. While it was their honeymoon, albeit considerably delayed, they were on the Islands because Opal was engaged in a photo shoot modeling an exotic Tahitian wardrobe.

Opal was talking as they walked. "The work will only take a few days, my love. Afterward, we'll have three weeks to relax and enjoy Tahiti."

"Yeah, I'm aware," Gene grumbled while squeezing his bride's shoulder affectionately, "I just hate the delayed honeymoon part."

"Yes, lover, as do I, but you can attend all of my shoots," Opal had one arm around Gene's waist and gave him an affectionate squeeze in return.

Neither one had any premonition of the disaster ahead.

CHAPTER THREE

Tahiti

Ugla Hendrixson, a great-great-great-grandson of the Island's first Protestant missionaries, long ago abandoned his Christian heritage in favor of the Island's primitive religion, Oro. Ugla was a handsome man. His mixed-blood legacy gave him typical Tahitian light brown skin and dark flashing eyes. The Dutch protestant missionaries produced the golden hair he wore tied back in a ponytail.

Oro, the ancient Island God who ruled for centuries, had been replaced throughout the Islands by the God of Moses.

In the distant past, approximately four thousand years ago, Oro was a peaceful, loving God. This God wanted joy and happiness for his people, who lived beautiful, happy lives. Throughout the year, many festivals and celebrations existed for those who sang, danced, and paid homage to the God Oro.

The time came when Oro priests (administrators) desired greater power, as they still do, and power corrupts.

Over time, Oro became a wrathful God, demanding obedience and human sacrifices. The priests had temples constructed with altars three tiers high so that the people could witness their gift to Oro. Like a wedding cake, priests constructed altars of layered stones filled with dirt, The sacrifice had to be a young, beautiful virgin with large, pointed breasts. This image of naked Tahitian virgins can be purchased today in any island gift shop.

While everyone watched, the seven priests deflowered the virgin, slit her throat, and let her blood seep into the dirt floor of the altar. Over the centuries, the altar grounds became black with the blood of sacrificed virgins.

When the Protestants came to the Islands with their loving God, the natives were more than happy to dump Oro and the despicable priests.

Ugla lusted after the lost power of those Oro priests. He wasn't into religion, but loved the idea of fucking beautiful young virgins. Over time, several other young men longing to exercise their manhood were converted to Ugla's new version of Oro. With the help of his converts, he developed unique ceremonies to celebrate Oro, although sacrificing young virgins was not one he practiced. However, he and his followers were happy to deflower any young virgin they could entice into their web.

Many old Oro altars still exist on temples throughout the Island forests, and it was on one of these altars that Ugla and his men violated the willing young beautiful girls. The girls didn't need to have pointed breasts. Using the same altar Oro priests used became part of the new Oro experience. Ugla and his men were careful not to disturb the altars, which were historical monuments and tourist attractions.

Unfortunately, the production manager for Opal's photo shoot chose one of these old, abandoned altars as the primary location for Opal to display the new revealing Tahitian wardrobe.

Chapter Four

Pocatello

"I am seeking guidance for my actions," Myron answered, seemingly more relaxed as he sipped Hilda's black coffee placed on the desk in front of his chair.

"Can you be more specific?" Hokee encouraged.

"Look," Myron grew agitated, shifting in his chair like ants were crawling in his shorts, "people want to kill me or torture me for information. I lack knowledge of what actions to take.

"Myron, I take your request seriously. Relax. Drink your coffee. Let me describe the nature of your quest."

"Okay. I'm calm." He said, trying to make his words reality.

"Typically, vision quests are sought after by young men and ladies seeking to discover their totems or animal guides. These vision quests are weekend events providing guests with an eventful, entertaining experience. The vision quest you desire is difficult, lonely, and dangerous." Hokee sat back and drank his coffee while thinking about what to say.

"I had a similar quest many years ago and almost lost my life. Please comprehend that there is a possibility of death in your pursuit or a risk of losing your mind. Either outcome is a possibility."

Myron looked confused.

Hokee said, "Seriously."

"Losing your mind might be worse than death," he continued. "And finally, after undergoing the sacred rituals and ceremonies and subjecting yourself to the demands of your search, you may fail to establish a connection with your guide or totem and remain unclear about the future."

"I need something, Mr. Wolf; I mean Hokee. Please help me. Without direction or guidance, I can't continue. What are the chances of failure in my quest?"

"Without knowing more about you, what pushes your buttons, that is impossible for me to say. Should you choose to proceed, I will have a better understanding of your prospects in a few days."

"A few days. I thought we might do it tomorrow."

"That's one problem with getting your information from a book, Myron. The nature of your specific quest cannot be accomplished in one or two days. A real sweat lodge is not meant for amusement or to give the curious a bucket-list experience, which is what books on the subject describe."

Hokee thought for a minute before continuing. "A person should familiarize themselves with the ceremony before undergoing the experience, but book descriptions cannot possibly evoke the ingredients for a successful vision quest. Unscrupulous individuals with little understanding of vision quests exploit the unwary. These weekend facilitators have their subjects shed their clothes, douse them with a sage smudge, then put them in a sweat lodge for an hour while mumbling some meaningless incantation. Followed by a cold shower to rid themselves of perspiration, those who pay for this encounter often experience a profound sense of achievement. For an authentic transforming experience, someone experienced in conducting such ceremonies must guide the required preparation. Your guide must have experienced such journeys to facilitate another person's quest. These weekend fakers lack the knowledge and experience to provide a proper vision quest."

Myron looked sick. He appeared as someone lacking the ability to swim, desperately seeking a life vest.

"Usually," Hokee continued, "the serious young man or woman seeking a simple vision quest can be prepared and complete their quest in two or three days. This holiday type of vision quest does not entail any significant sacrifice. The journey you seek is far more complicated and dangerous and will take ten days and nights."

"I can't possibly take ten days out of my life for this." Myron seemed agitated and angry.

Hokee stood up and pointed to the door. "Stop wasting my time; please leave."

"Ba, ba… but what about my vision quest?" Myron stammered.

"Your journey will last ten days, including the proper preparation. During your quest, no one else will lay eyes on you besides me. You will not speak out loud for nine days during your quest. You will spend most of your time meditating and making lists. Your diet will be strictly vegetarian. You will be permitted only tea and water for the last two days, no solid food. Those, dear Myron, are the parameters of your vision quest. You may leave my office now unless you are prepared to commit to this program."

Myron slumped in his seat, defeated. "Oh God, I never expected this. Let me think a minute."

Hokee sat back down and took another drink of his coffee. His countenance was as impassive as the granite faces on Mount Rushmore. He made no more comments after giving Myron a brief smile.

"I'm sorry about this," Myron said. After my studies, I thought it was possible for us to complete the entire thing tomorrow. Can you give me a couple of days to arrange my affairs?"

"Sure. While arranging your affairs, ensure you have a tent, air mattress, and sleeping bag if you want to proceed with your quest. You will live outdoors."

"But what if it storms or something?"

"Then that will be part of your quest. After starting on this journey, the road may take many unforeseen turns. Once your quest begins, everything that happens for the next ten days will involve your journey containing clues to your quest. Everything that happens has meaning and relates to the answers you are seeking."

"Have you performed many vision quests, Hokee?"

If the question troubled Hokee, it wasn't apparent from looking into his eyes. "Myron, I thought you had reviewed my qualifications. Now is a terrible time to request a resume. Yes, I am experienced. I have not enacted many requests for experiences like the one you seek. I am too busy to engage in quests of this nature. And I don't participate in meaningless quests just to discover whether someone's spirit animal is an owl or a rattlesnake. Unless the supplicant has a demanding story like yours, I am uninterested. I must also devote time preparing myself for the type of journey you require. I rarely see anyone with a serious request, such as the one you propose."

"People on campus speak highly of you. How much do you charge?"

Myron, you are unfamiliar with me, so your question does not offend. When someone requests my shaman training, it is an honor to be of service. There is no charge. I am uncertain about your financial resources, but I can assure you they are insufficient to compensate me for the journey you are seeking. Think of it as Mother Nature's gift, from who you will receive your lessons and the answers to your prayers."

"Wow! I have no idea what to say. You keep springing surprises on me."

"Dear Myron. Your surprises have barely begun. Call Hilda when you get your schedule worked out. Your first day will start at eight a.m. Be here with your sleeping bag, mattress, and tent."

While Hokee performed few serious vision quests for others, his thousands of hours in a sweat lodge provided him a deep understanding of human nature and man's relationship with the infinite. Watching Myron leave his office, Hokee wondered if this quest would kill them both. Unfortunately, his thoughts were premonitions of a major upheaval in both lives.

Chapter Five

Tahiti

About eight miles northeast of Papeete, Mount Orohena rises over eight thousand feet above Tahiti. Between the mountain and Papeete are many other high, green-covered cliff-like ridges. Although composed of lava, lush green plants cover almost every square inch of the island, including the cliffs. A rectangular opening called the Window to Heaven is high on one of these narrow ridges. The Orchid-dotted Garden path Gene and Opal strolled along was oriented to provide excellent views of this sacred mountain and heaven's window. At least the mountain had been holy when Oro ruled.

Gene bent over, nuzzling Opal's neck before kissing her on the cheek. "What do you say we get a ride and do some touring before you begin modeling tomorrow?"

"Great idea, honey. The agency provides a special bus and local tour drivers for our personal use."

Opal models for Désirée Ines Model Agency in New York City, the exclusive house of exotic models. Désirée's agency does designer clothes but does not provide models for those ridiculous runway walks. She is not interested in delivering models to flaunt their bodies while flattering the latest must-have rags. Désirée models specialize in fashion shoots at far-off exotic locations, the dream vacation spots for those who can afford high-end designer clothes and travel. When they are not at exotic locations showcasing the latest high-end fashions, her models often parade around new car releases or openings for a new high-end gated community, paying models one to two hundred thousand dollars for one day's work. At the high-income end, with million-dollar paydays, are fashion shoots for the top designers and their must-have wardrobe for the ultra-rich. Opal only did million-dollar shoots where the agency ensured their stars received preferred attention.

"On yeah, I forgot," Gene said with surprise. "Let's go back to the hotel and grab a ride. We've walked along beautiful flower paths long enough; I'd like to see what the island looks like away from the city."

"You've got it, my love. Let's go find a driver."

Terilmana Mareva owns Island Tour Buses with her husband Otahi, an ordained Protestant minister. Terilmana drives the bus, providing her passengers with awe-inspiring sites, while during the week, Otahi prepares his Sunday sermon and books island tours for his wife. When Désirée's models are in town, Terilmana is booked exclusively by the agency.

Terilmana does not share the images of Tahitian women depicted on those coconut-wood-carved figures sold in souvenir shops. Weighing 140 pounds and blessed with a large-boned body, she looks like a coffee-colored image of a youthful Rosie O'Donnell. Otahi has a slender body and large hands he used as a young boy to carve bamboo flutes. Besides his ministry, Otahi is an expert on the old ORO religion, giving talks to tourists at fancy hotels.

When Gene and Opal walked into the open-air reception hall of their 5-star motel, the Hilton Hotel Tahiti, they found Terilmana behind the travel agency desk. She looked fetching in a sleek floral pantsuit, the standard driver's uniform bearing the company logo with her name embroidered in white nylon thread on a sky-blue cotton patch.

"Good afternoon," Gene said to the lady behind the counter. "Could we get a tour of the Island?" he asked.

"Most certainly. I'm here to provide information and tours for all Désirée's people."

"My husband is eager to visit one of the old sacrificial temple sites," Opal explained with a roll of her eyes as though this was the most ridiculous request in the world.

"I usually stop at one or more of the old temple sites on my tour," Terilmana smiled. "One of the best-preserved sites is only five miles from here on the sacred mountain."

"I don't recall reading about a sacred mountain here in Tahiti," Gene said puzzledly.

"Well, our modern population does not consider it sacred, but at one time, the mountain was the holiest place on the island and had the most prestigious sacrificial altar.'

"What made that mountain holy?" Opal wondered out loud.

"The Window to Heaven is at the top of that mountain," Terilmana explained. "I'm sure you've noticed the mountain top behind us with the large opening. Even in our modern guidebooks, that opening is named the Window to Heaven."

"We noticed that opening in the mountain during our strolls through the gardens," Gene mentioned. "Opal commented it looked like a *window to heaven.*"

"My husband is an expert on the old Oro religion responsible for naming the mountain," Terilmana informed the handsome couple. "He gives a lecture on the Oro religion at the visitors center once a week for the tourists. If you are interested, I can provide you with the details."

"That would be an interesting lecture to attend," Gene said. "Let's see how Opal's schedule works out during the next few days."

CHAPTER SIX

Pocatello

For the next two days, Hokee worked around his house stocking firewood for the sweat lodge and walking the lava fields with Shila. These treacherous walks were Hokee's way of meditating on complex subjects. His meager knowledge of singularities qualified the topic as a difficult subject. The ramifications of machines equaling and surpassing the mental powers of humanity were frightening. How does one conduct a vision quest to make this scenario real for a man?

Hokee would love to have his old mentor Why-ay´-looh nearby to provide encouragement and infinite wisdom, but this was a task for Wolf alone. He had been taught everything he needed to know to help Myron with his quest. Sadly, the outcome of a serious vision quest is unpredictable. In the quest where Hokee almost lost his life, he found his future home. If mathematics could not answer this singularity's development, how could Hokee find the answers in the cauldron of heat, sweat, and sapient-producing herbs?

Hokee wore moccasins today instead of his high-topped leather boots with thick rubber soles he usually put on for his meditative walks. The moccasins put him more in touch with planet Earth, but in lava fields where there are thin shells that easily break and slice through the thin leather, Hokee had to be especially vigilant with each step he took. Safety required surrendering conscious control to his subconscious mind. By forcing himself to use his brain in this fashion, Hokee had the clarity of thought necessary for advanced problem-solving. Conducting a vision quest regarding singularities qualified as a serious problem. Shila accompanied Hokee on these walks, unerringly leading his master on a path he followed without conscious thought.

Myron called Hilda and arrived at Hokee's office at 8.00 a.m., three days after his initial visit. The camping supplies Hokee suggested were in his car.

Hokee's visitor was waiting in Hilda's office. "Good morning, Myron. Are you ready to begin your quest?"

"Good morning Hokee. Yeah, I guess so. I hate to be out of touch for ten days. Is there any way we can cut the time down?"

"No. As we get to the end, extending the time a day or two may even be necessary."

"Oh, God. I'm not sure I can survive this Hokee. The wolves are circling like crazy. Excuse the homology. I didn't mean to slur your name."

Hokee laughed out loud. "Hell, Myron. If I let such a thing bother me, I would hang up my moccasins."

"Thank you. I'm just nervous. I've done nothing like this before. Unless it was science, I wasn't interested."

"Myron, you will experience more science in the next few days than in all your previous studies combined. It will not be your Ph.D. textbook science, more like the science of existence."

"Sounds perfect. Existence is what this vision quest is all about."

"If mother nature and the universe honor your request, you may find your answer. Please get your supplies and wait for me downstairs. I'll see you in a minute." Hokee explained to Hilda that his schedule will be hectic for the next few days and to avoid disturbing him unless it was an emergency.

Myron parked his Cadillac Escalade across the street from the bank building housing Hokee's office and he was waiting by the stairway when Hokee hit the street.

Leading the way, walking down the street to where he parked his Explores, Hokee said, "You will ride with me to my home. You'll be staying at my house but living outside. I'll have someone bring your car to you later."

"I don't get this living outside business. Why is that necessary?" Myron sounded somewhat peevish.

"You'll see," was all the response he received. They picked up Myron's supplies from his car and drove to Hokee's house.

Myron was stewing about the necessity of sleeping outside as Hokee turned onto his ten-mile-long private driveway across the desolate lava desert. You live way out here?" Myron asked, the question even sounded stupid to his ears.

"Nah, I drive here for the beautiful the scenery." Sarcasm was not Hokee's long suit

When they finally dropped over the edge of the lava plain going down towards Hokee's house, the sight of a giant wolf running towards their vehicle scared Myron "Whoa. Do you notice that wolf? He pulled his knees up to his chest, appearing in a fetal position.

"No. What wolf?" Hokee could not resist puncturing holes in Myron's balloon.

Recognizing that he was being played with, Myron mumbles, "Sorry, I hope that monster isn't hungry."

"I think he's waiting for someone with a little more meat on their bones, but if he's hungry enough, he'll even eat university professors." As Hokee drove down the slope to his home, Myron was speechless at the sight of a magnificent fountain in front of a beautiful Mediterranean house.

By now, they were stopped, and Hokee stepped out, giving his wolf a big hug. "Hello, Shila, we have company. Go say hi

As Myron got out of the front seat, Shila stood on his hind legs with his front legs on the car roof, straddling the frightened man, waiting for a head scratch. Myron flopped back across the seat, frightened out of his mind.

"Come here, Shila. I guess our guest needs a little time to get acquainted."

Hokee and Shila entered the house, giving Myron time to calm his frayed nerves.

When he regained his composure, Myron unloaded his camping supplies onto the wide front Spanish veranda under a beautiful red geranium plant hanging from the center of a Spanish Arch. He was still standing there five minutes later when Hokee came outside carrying two mugs of black coffee.

"Come take a seat," he said, indicating one of the two handmade easy chairs with an end table for their coffee. "Let's talk briefly about your agenda for the next few days."

"I'm sorry to be such a boob about the wolf; I never expected to be this close to one that is alive."

"Oh, that's all right. I don't think Shila even noticed," Hokee almost smiled. "Before your journey ends, you and Shila will become best friends."

"I'm going to risk sounding stupid and say that Shila is the wolf's name." Myron had a self-conscious smile on his face.

"Shila is the Navaho word for brother. After completing my vision quest and training, he was my teacher's gift."

"I've never been around animals and have no experience from which to extrapolate, but I'm sure I have never read about a tame wolf."

"It is an unusual companion for humans, but Shila is not the first wolf to become friends with a man. Well, let's get started. You will live outside on this property until you complete your quest or die."

"You don't believe in foreplay, do you?" Myron's self-conscious smile did not appear.

"Never understood the purpose." I'll show you where to pitch your tent when we finish our talk."

"Will the wolf be outside with me?" Hokee was irritated that Myron didn't use Shila's name but let it pass.

"Shila usually lives outdoors, although sometimes we share a bed inside. You will be grateful for his presence before long. He will scare away the night creatures and provide guard duty around the clock. I rarely get human visitors; few people are aware this place."

"He won't sleep with me in the tent, will he?" The thought of a real live wolf roaming around at night worried the professor.

"You won't even be aware of his presence unless an improbable disruption occurs."

"I never slept outdoors before. I'm not sure I'll be able to get any sleep."

"Oh, you'll sleep all right. I can promise you that. I will be surprised if you don't have the best rest of your life after the first few nights. Now, tomorrow is the last day you may talk. You will then remain mute until it is time for the sweat lodge. I'll provide you with a checklist of your assignments tomorrow."

"Are ten days necessary to have my vision?" Myron seemed to think twice about his rash decision to ask for a vision quest. Living outdoors, having a live wolf sneaking around, and Hokee's mention of disturbances was unsettling.

"Myron, you came to me. My time means something to me, and I don't want to waste it on a complaining, uncertain twit who doesn't know what he wants. Are ten days necessary? Hell, it could take twenty, but you wouldn't last that long. I will try to end your journey in ten days, but I already told you it might be eleven or twelve. If you don't want to make this commitment, say so now and spare me the agony of pulling your insecure ass along a treacherous path."

For Hokee, this was a long speech, and he was already tired of Myron and his insecurities.

"I'm sorry, Mr. Wolf, I mean Hokee. Yes, I want to proceed. I'll be a good little boy and take my medicine. What's next?"

"Get your gear, and I'll show you where to set up your tent." Hokee led the way around his fountain towards the towering lava wall surrounding his two-acre oasis. The wall he inched down with bleeding feet and bloody hands years ago while dying of dehydration to discover his cave and the water that saved his life.

Chapter Seven

Tahiti

The new Mercedes tour bus was a shining two-toned ride, providing seating for ten. The bottom half was painted a bright silver lacquer between tall windows so riders would have fantastic island views. Painted sky blue, the vehicle's upper half also featured a sprinkling of silver stars. Inside there were five rows with large, wide, sand-colored soft leather seats you see in an expensive private airplane. One seat on each side of a wide aisle. Gene and Opal were the only occupants and chose to sit directly behind Terilmana to make communication easier.

"Tahiti is the largest of the French Polynesia Islands," Terilmana told the honeymooners while suggesting a 70-mile drive around the island. "It's a three-hour drive, not counting stops we may make," she told them, but it will give you an authentic flavor of Tahiti."

"That sounds great, doesn't it, Opal? Gene asked, looking at his bride.

"Sure, honey, let's go around the Island." When Opal spoke, Terilmana put the bus in gear and started the drive.

Tahiti, the island where the sea and land harmonize like no other place on earth, is magical, and the drive around it is breathtaking. They drove through Papeete, the Capital city, and stopped in Papenoo Valley to view the magnificent waterfalls. After going through the Maraa Grotto, they stopped at the Marae Arahurahu Temple, where Opal will model the clothes she will wear for the photo shoot. "This temple is the best-preserved site from the old Oro religion and features a three-tiered sacrificial altar at one end," Terilmana informed her passengers.

The couple left the bus to explore the grounds and familiarize themselves with the location. There are no walls for the temple, just a wide-open spot in the jungle surrounded by beautiful trees. Why this pile of dirt is called a temple befuddled Gene. The temple is a raised dirt platform, about 100 by 80 feet two feet high, surrounded by black lava rocks. The ten-by-fifteen-foot altar, comprising three tiers, extends six feet above the temple grounds. Gene and Opal climbed up to the altar for the view and the experience. The soil on top of the altar was dark, and the couple was convinced they saw remnants of the blood from the hundreds of girls sacrificed by the Oro priests over the millennia. They didn't notice the men watching them from the forest's edge.

Chapter Eight

Tahiti

The Marae Arahurahu Temple is where Ugla and his followers bring the girls they ultimately seduce. Their religious ceremonies were always conducted after dark when they wouldn't be bothered by tour buses or visitors.

Ugla admired the Oro worshiped long ago when the people lived in peace and joy. Ugla's brand of religion included many parties called *festivals*, where they drank copious amounts of the local Hinano beer. He provided rum mixed with pineapple juice for the girls who didn't like beer. Young people love to party, and it wasn't difficult for Ugla to entice young men and girls to join his new religious version of Oro.

Worship services were held on Saturday nights, so Oro's crowd would not alarm or threaten the Sunday church-going community. The new religion's primary meeting house was an abandoned banana packing shed three hundred yards up the canyon from the Marae Temple. Ugla and his followers cleaned out the bird shit, tacked up colorful cloth banners, and made coconut wood benches for the audience. A brief ceremony comprised Ugla extolling the virtues of his brand of Oro religious practices, followed by drinking and dancing to a boom-box. Once the girls experienced a sense of liberation, the boys led them down a path to the altar, where garments were removed, and the sexual festivities started. The men set tiki torches around the old temple for light and to ensure the rocks around the temple and altar remained untouched. Many on the island still consider the ancient temple a sacred site. Ugla spent part of each religious ceremony warning his worshipers to be careful and not disturb the rocks or leave any sign that they used this place to have sex. Part of the thrill was to fuck where the ancient priests deflowered virgins before slitting their throats.

The island grapevine was full of information about the photo shoot at the old temple. Ugla and his men concealed themselves in the forest close by as Terilmana escorted the Olsons near the temple. Listening to Opal and Gene discuss the ancient ceremony made Ugla's blood boil. The foreigners had no right to be here, especially on the altar. When thinking about this woman parading around his altar in decadent clothes, he vowed to make them pay.

They will pay for their blasphemy.

CHAPTER NINE

Pocatello

Hokee made his way to the lava wall, where he planned for Myron to set up his tent. A shovel was leaning against the wall.

"You will pitch your tent here," Hokee said, pointing to the shovel. "You may want to dig up the soil where you will sleep and break up the clods. Your mattress will remove most of the rough spots, but soft dirt underneath helps."

"You want me to dig up the dirt where I sleep?" Myron asked with a frown.

"That's entirely up to you. This is where you'll sleep for the next few days. Dig it up or pitch your tent on the hard dirt. Your choice."

"Are you familiar with the process of setting up your tent, Myron?" Hokee asked after watching Myron struggle with the shovel.

"No, I assumed it has instructions in the package."

"Probably not. After you get the ground broken up, I'll help you with the tent."

"May I ask why I'm sleeping outdoors in a tent?"

"Yes."

Myron gave Hokee a puzzled look until he realized his question had been answered. "Okay," he said with a grin, "why am I sleeping out here in a tent?"

"You must experience many aspects of life to accomplish your quest." Hokee didn't elaborate, and Myron looked disappointed.

"I cannot perceive how sleeping out here on the ground will aid me in grasping what to do with my singularity," he pouted.

"You will."

When Hokee didn't say anymore, Myron shook his head and continued to dig a spot for his mattress. When he had the soil turned and broken up, Hokee helped him set up his tent and put his air mattress and sleeping bag inside. Myron blew up the mattress by himself as Hokee went and sat on his porch.

After Myron finished with his tent and bed, Hokee showed Myron where to dig his latrine.

"You mean I have to do my business out here in the open?" Myron looked sick. "But what about privacy? I can't do it in a place where people can observe me." It amused Hokee that the professor didn't say shit or defecate, but it didn't show on his face.

"Are you able to observe a gathering of individuals around her, Myron? Only five individuals are familiar with this place, and they have never arrived without an invitation. Your privacy is secured unless you count Shila," who was standing by, grinning like he was getting a kick out of Myron's discomfort.

"But you will be here," he said with a pout.

"Not much until the last few days. I want you to be alone. And when I am around, you will rarely glimpse me."

"Think of it as bonding with life. Sort of a relationship with our cave-dwelling ancestors. At least I provided you with a soft toilet paper." It was perplexing to understand Myron's look. Somewhere between *'are you serious?'* and *'thank God.'*

Following this exchange, Myron joined Hokee on the porch.

"Until we complete your vision quest, you will eat vegetarian," Hokee said, starting his instructions. "This refrigerator," he said, pointing to one standing on his veranda, "is stocked with carrot and mixed vegetable juice. You may drink all the juice you want and, of course, water. Also in the refrigerator are packages of lentil soup, vegetable soup, bean soup, and lots of bread. Over here in this corner," Hokee got up and walked to the other end of his porch," is an electric burner, pots, and eating utensils. You may eat all you want, when you want, but only the food I have stocked for you. The refrigerator also has a few rabbits for Shila; leave those alone."

"Why am I only eating vegetarian food?" Myron asked, feeling like he was about to enter a convent or monastery.

"To raise your vibration. Meat is a wholesome food; if you survive, I'll cook you a substantial meal with meat. But meat is heavy; it lowers your vibration." Myron was perplexed and unhappy,

Hokee stood up, said, "Follow me." He led Myron around the house to the woodpile and sweat lodge.

"Here," he said, pointing to the wall-mounted showerhead, "you can shower whenever you desire. Towels and wash clothes are in the cabinet next to the house."

"What? I'm also supposed to shower and clean up outside?" Myron looked like he wanted to change his mind about the entire experience.

"Yes. You will live out here under the sun, the moon, and the stars."

As the instructions continued, Myron's pale complexion turned white.

"Now we learn to build a fire."

"I can't build a fire!" Myron almost shouted in despair, overwhelmed by so many new experiences.

"Sure, you can. I'm going to teach you how right now. You will build a small fire daily and stare into the flames for thirty minutes with the questions you want answered."

Hokee proceeded to the woodpile he had stocked earlier and grabbed a small log. He placed the log on a large cutting block, pulled a hatchet from the block where he stuck it earlier, and chopped small kindling. "Watch this, Myron, because this will be your daily chore."

Handing Myron the hatchet, Hokee gave a lesson in building a Boy Scout fire. It took over thirty minutes, but eventually, Myron chopped the kindling and started a small fire in the sweat lodge fire pit.

"Good job, Myron, do this every morning before your breakfast. If it rains, which I don't expect, I'll help you rig a tarp to keep you and the wood dry. Since you now have a fire, sit here for thirty minutes, stare into the flames, and ask the universe to answer your questions. Ask your question, then clear your mind and stare into the fire."

Myron stood for a minute contemplating all he was being asked to do, then questions Hokee. "Hokee, can you tell me why I'm sleeping outside, building fires, and spending time alone? I would like to understand the big picture."

"Sure, Myron. To experience your vision quest, you must get in touch with life. Your inquiry concerns every living thing on this planet and every aspect of nature. The program I have devised will help if you experience life with only the basics while living alone with your actual real mother, Mother Earth."

"Okay. Thanks. I think perhaps I understand. I'll now watch my fire."

"Come find me when you finish." Hokee left Myron to his fire and took Shila inside to fix a meal for himself.

Chapter Ten

Tahiti

The first day of the photo shoot arrived with a glorious shining sun bringing life and color to paradise. A colorful red and green parrot perched on the branch of a Bougainvillea tree greeted Opal with a loud squawk when she left her room with Gene to eat breakfast. The couple squawked back and then laughed as they wandered down the hibiscus-lined path. The jasmine trees, interwoven with several other species, infused the air with their cloying scent. Life was beautiful, and the honeymooners couldn't have been happier.

Today's breakfast was a communal affair with the entire photoshoot gang, including the lighting men, makeup ladies, costume fitters, and hair stylists. Also included were the wardrobe custodians, cameramen and wardrobe ladies, Terilmana with the other bus drivers, plus the production manager. A surprise visit by Désirée Ines delighted everyone, especially Opal, who had a daughter/mother relationship with the model agency's grand madam.

A breakfast buffet table included every delicacy the island offered, much to the chagrin of Opal, who had to watch her diet. She chose a small bowl of yogurt to eat outside on a picnic table with Gene. Knowing how much his wife would have loved to feast on the dates, figs, bananas, and pineapple,

Gene selected a breakfast sandwich to avoid providing temptation, a gesture Opal appreciated.

"Are you excited about your shoot?" Gene asked.

"Oh yes, especially with Désirée here. She rarely leaves New York."

"I'm delighted to witness you model at last," Gene expressed. I feel deeply honored.

"You should. No outsider is allowed to watch a photoshoot. Everyone needs to focus on their jobs with no distractions. Since this is our honeymoon, Désirée is making an exception. Plus, I think she is curious about my husband." Opal couldn't resist chuckling at the thought.

"I'll try not to be a distraction," Gene responded with a grin.

They were waiting for the others to finish breakfast when Terilmana approached, looking fetching in a blue jumpsuit with her company logo and name stitched in red silk thread across one shoulder. "Are you guys ready to experience paradise?" she asked, eager to get everyone moving. "The boss wants to see the temple and get to work."

"Sure, we're ready," right honey? Opal answered, nudging Gene softly in the ribs with her elbow.

"Whatever you say, darling. Let's go dazzle the island's God with your beauty."

Terilmana led the couple out front, where everyone was getting onto the buses. Men hired for their muscles loaded several oversized cases containing the agency equipment for the shoot onto a large flatbed truck. Helpers loaded a separate truck with the clothes Opal will model. A special bus, equipped with a dressing room for make-up and clothes change, was positioned behind the trucks. Opal and Gene got on Terilmana's bus, taking two seats behind the driver. Désirée sat behind Opal, happy to get the shoot underway.

Fortunately, the large parking area at the temple had enough room to accommodate the buses and trucks. The local men set to work unloading the cases under the direction of Majorie Zoller, the production manager. Marjorie dressed like a boot camp drill instructor with green khaki pants and a camouflage design sleeveless tee shirt. Her brown hair was clipped in a buzz cut, emphasizing the military look. That's where the military appearance ended: she had a smooth baby face and was soft-spoken. However, you didn't want to piss her off; she could make that soft voice crack like a whip.

Lights and reflectors were placed with much fuss under the photographer's direction. Steps for Opal and the photographer were discreetly placed by the temple and altar so that they wouldn't trip and disturb the rockwork. Gene stood far off to the side under the shade of a giant banyan tree, watching everything with interest. He struggled to envision how a straightforward photo shoot required so many individuals and such a complex production. Gene was completely unaware of the distinction between a Loro Piana and an Armani, not to mention the House of Bijan, who funded this production to showcase their new South Pacific summer styles. As much as Gene thought about such things, he assumed that the House of Bijan was a Chinese restaurant. Fortunately, this was a thought he kept to himself.

The photographer shot his first five hundred pictures before a lunch break, and Opal sat down for a minute to rest her legs and get a retouch on her makeup. Désirée wanted Opal to model the swimwear after lunch as she sensed an urgency to return to New York and was curious to see the swimwear designs that the House (her term for their clientele) had created for their affluent customers.

When Opal appeared in the first outfit in the afternoon, Gene couldn't fathom how anyone might consider a pair of shoelaces to be valued at eight thousand dollars. Okay, they were fancy colored strings with sequins or something shining woven into the threads, even so, just a pair of shoelaces. The Olsons were far from paupers, but even with their billions, the prices for these clothes seemed outlandish to Gene.

Opal's dark complexion and stunning beauty made one forget about the price. Of course, that was why she commanded such a hefty fee. Opal's beauty emphasized the high-priced strings that rich woman wanted for themselves. Hopefully, the strings would have the same effect on them.

Hiding in the trees well back from the photoshoot, Four of Ugla's most brutal followers watched the nearly naked woman parade around on the altar like a queen. To Ugla, watching from a nearby thick grove of Dahila and Traveler's Palm trees, she was an abomination defiling the ancient sacrifices. This interloper had no business on the altar, and her near nakedness only inflamed his anger. He didn't see a perfect body or a beautiful woman; Ugla only saw a half-naked harlot strutting around on a sacred altar. The irony of him using the same altar to deflower virgins escaped his mind. His was a religion. A gift to Oro. This slut needed to be punished.

Later in the afternoon, nearing the end of the first day's work, Opal was returning to the changing bus alone when someone grabbed her from behind, clasping a hand over her mouth so she could not scream. When Opal didn't return to the altar after a few minutes, Marjorie sent a runner to find out what was delaying their star. The runner returned with no Opal. Their model wasn't on the bus, and no one had seen her in several minutes. The agency personnel started an immediate search, and upon noticing the commotion, Gene departed from his shady tree to discover the source of all the fuss.

Something terrible happened, and nobody knew what to do. Gene sought Terilmana as she was the only native who seemed to understand how they conducted business on the Island. Terilmana had already called the gendarmes when Gene located her standing by the tour bus. She said it would take fifteen minutes before the gendarmes arrived and suggested organizing a search to discover potential clues.

The night and darkness crept into Gene's soul. Opal's whereabouts remained a mystery. A few locals knew about the ancient virgin sacrifices and thought the sacred altars might be haunted. They put forward the idea that something beyond our understanding might have taken place, but their suggestion was dismissed.

Gene called his father with the sad news.

Chapter Eleven

Pocatello

Hokee was relaxing on his porch, scratching Shila's ears, when Myron came around the house looking for him.

"I've studied the fire Hokee; now what?" He sounded petulant.

Hokee handed Myron a large spiral-bound notebook and a ballpoint pen.

"You will begin making lists and adding to those lists every day."

"What lists?"

"I will not provide you with the names of all the lists you will make, but I will help you get started. Your first list should be, WHY DO I WANT A VISION QUEST?"

"I already told you why I want a vision quest," Now Myron sounded pissed.

"Look, Myron, you can fight me or fight yourself. I am familiar with the information you provided me. Your desires are not simple and do not warrant a quick one-line answer. Consider the reasons driving your desire for this ceremony. Make a list and add at least one additional reason every day. This exercise will make sense later."

"What if I can't think of anything to add to my lists?"

"Then we'll go get your car and you can go back to the university. I have nothing to offer you."

"All right, I'll do it. What's next?" Now he sounded like a whiney child.

"List why others may not want you to have this ceremony."

"Boy, I can think of a million reasons they don't want me to get any help."

"Great, make a list. Next, make a list of your enemies."

"That shouldn't take me long." Myron sounded more confident.

"Remember, you must add to every list each day. For your next list, write the names of everyone you consider friends who want to help you succeed."

"Okay, I can do that. What's next?"

"Oh no. I've got you started. Think about the peripheral issues regarding your work, your dreams, and what you wish to accomplish. Think about the hardships and trials you've endured and those you face. What are the benefits of your work, and what are its disadvantages? Make lists, Myron. Create many lists, add to them daily, and start new lists."

"Is this all I do for the next several days, make lists?" He sounded petulant again.

"Not even close. You still have your fire ceremony every day, and starting tomorrow, you will begin getting in touch with nature."

"I thought I did that by sleeping outside in a tent and eating rabbit food."

"That's a start. Tomorrow you will spend the entire day in front of a fire. I want you to study the flames until you observe yourself reflected in them. Gaze into the fire until your invention becomes visible. Study the flames until the faces of your enemies become visible. Everything in this universe is in those flames, Myron. Come to understand fire as an elemental force. Fire is a fundamental element of nature."

"This sounds like a lot of work, Hokee."

"Yes. I told you it will not be easy. Your quest touches on every aspect of life and involves the nature of our universe. You are standing on a giant precipice, about to change humanity. Surely you would want to be in touch with the world you live in today. It will not be easy, and we are only getting started."

Myron looked sick. When he decided to seek a vision quest, there was no thought about the physical aspects of the ceremony. The original plan was a few hours in a sweat lodge. Perhaps taking up to half a day.

"Master's from antiquity to today teach us that life begins with the sun," Hokee lectured. "Without the sun, there would be no life. The earth depends on energy from the sun to produce the essential ingredients for all living matter. These ancient masters named our sun the father and our earth the mother. Your fire is our earthly representation of the sun."

"I've heard references to Mother Earth; I never thought about it that much."

"The day after tomorrow, you will get in touch with mother earth. No pun intended, as I meant literally. You will get undressed and spend all day lying, walking, and sitting on bare ground. Take the shovel and dig yourself a soft place to lie down. Earth is the womb that produces our life. You must understand this to proceed with your quest."

"I'm supposed to lie down naked on the ground?" Myron was unable to believe what Hokee just described.

"It won't kill you Myron, and you might learn something to put into your lists."

"But what if I get sunburned?"

"I said you can also sit and walk barefoot. I'm sure you will find shady spots to practice omphaloskepsis."

"My God, you sound like a philosophy teacher."

Ignoring this, Hokee continued, "Your third day is water. You will sit in the driveway fountain or under the shower by the sweat lodge. Our bodies are about 60 percent water, which is essential for humans. Spend an entire day thinking about and living with water. Why are we water beings?"

"Fire, Earth, and water, I suppose the next day is air?"

"You got it, Myron. Walk up the driveway with Shila to the lava plains and watch the wind blow on the sage and grass. Watch how it moves and shapes the clouds? Experience the air as it enters your nostrils and lungs. Taste the air on your tongue. Live with the air an entire day until you understand the contribution air makes to our lives."

"What's next, the spirit?" Myron sounded petulant again.

"Yes. The spirit. This exercise will be your most challenging task of the five. You might count this as a day of meditation. Do you believe we have a spirit? How about animals? Are plants immune, or do they also possess a spirit? And what is this thing called a spirit? What does a spirit have to do with spirituality?"

"Suppose I am an atheist?"

"Good question. It doesn't matter if you believe in God. Do organizations have a spirit? How about a community or our country? Live with the word and concept until you understand the world of spirits."

"Okay, that's five days. Then do we have our vision quest?"

"Not quite. After getting in touch with nature, you still need to get in touch with your quest. You are to spend the sixth day meditating on your inquiry. Remember, you have been making and adding to your lists every day towards this end. Focus all your thoughts and energy on this one question. What is the purpose of your vision quest?"

"Oh lord, Hokee. This whole affair sounds like one hell of an assignment."

"Yes, and then you repeat the earth and water days. Getting back in touch with the earth just before our vision experience is essential. If everything works perfectly, we will finish the next day, but it may take two. I won't know until we get to that point."

"At that point, one extra day won't mean a thing." Myron sounded discouraged.

"Cheer up, Doctor. It won't be that painful, and when you finish, you will be a different person."

Before Myron had a chance to reply, Hokee's phone started ringing. His number was private. He used a special private service that prevented nuisance calls, so it had to be the office or one of only four people with his number. It was a call he must answer.

"Hokee."

"Hokee, it's Grant. I need you, man."

Chapter Twelve

Tahiti

Désirée canceled the photoshoot, booking return seats for everyone on tomorrow's flight. Gene offered a one-million-dollar reward for the safe return of his wife. The House of Bijan matched Gene's offer as soon as they learned about the kidnapping from Désirée. Unable to sleep, Gene paced around the hotel gardens, numb with worry.

Terilmana called her husband Otahi, asking him to come to the hotel. His expertise as a minister and the old Oro Religion would be welcomed.

The local gendarmes blocked access to the temple grounds and started a thorough search of the surrounding forest. They ultimately found the spot where Ugla and his men had been hiding behind the thick undergrowth, watching the photo shoot. Unfortunately, they found no clues about the watcher's identification or where they had taken Opal.

After a sleepless night, Gene watched buses leave, taking the agency's people to the airport. Désirée arranged for the FBI's elite K&R, kidnap and ransom, team to help recover Opal. Although no ransom demands had been made, it was widely assumed that the purpose of the kidnapping was to seek a ransom. The FBI team was scheduled to arrive tomorrow. Meanwhile, Gene paced the hotel grounds like wounded like a tiger.

Otahi, Terilmana's husband, conducted a meeting at the hotel, discussing the Oro religion and the importance of the sacrificial altars at the temple site. The old religion did not involve kidnapping, and Otahi couldn't help in the current situation.

The handsome Ugla sat in one of the lounge chairs in the hotel's beautiful open lobby, listening to Otahi and the local gendarmes discuss the kidnapping. He wore a colorful Hawaiian shirt, white shorts, and brown leather sandals on his feet, looking like the other hotel's wealthy guests. When he learned about the two-million-dollar reward offered for the safe return of Opal, his brain went into overdrive figuring out a way to collect the reward without getting caught.

In the meantime, they held Opal in a monkey cage at the old packing shed. Ugla threatened the other kidnappers with severe punishment if they damaged their captives looks. While Ugla wanted to punish the harlot for her sacrilege on the ancient altar, he entertained the thought of offering her as an old-time sacrifice to Oro, but his greed kept him from inflicting any physical damage until deciding her fate.

News about the kidnapping swept the islands like a secret gets distributed in a small town. Within hours, tourists heard about the event and began making flight reservations to leave immediately. Since no one knew what happened, everyone assumed the worst and planned accordingly. Hotels around Tahiti emptied as tourists left in droves. If they could not access a plane, they quickly secured a boat capable of safely taking them away. With no one in a position of authority able to provide answers, the hotels were unable to halt the tourists exit stampede.

Chapter Thirteen

Pocatello

After listening to Grant's problem with the missing Opal and learning that she was in Tahiti, Hokee agreed to leave immediately but warned Grant that it would take him at least two days before arriving on the Island.

"Listen up, Hokee; I will get you to Tahiti in eight hours."

"Come on, Grant, not even God can get me there that fast."

"There will be an SB-1 helicopter at the Pocatello airport in 45 minutes. This helicopter will get you to the Mountain Home AFB within another 45 minutes. You will be dressed in a G suit and fly in an F-15E Strike Eagle, which will have you in Tahiti in less than four hours. With a few minutes to dress you and provide orientation, the whole thing will take seven to eight hours maximum.

"What, you just have these planes available, and the military will fly my butt to Tahiti?"

"Yeah, I do, and yes, they will. There are 10 F-15E's stationed at Mountain Home and a dozen SB-1 helicopters. The general at the base owes me big time for the work I've done at Mountain Home, and I'm collecting. Can you make it?"

"For you, Grant, almost anything. I'll be at the general aviation terminal within 45 minutes."

"Great, don't pack any luggage."

"Can I bring a toothbrush?" He asked half facetiously

"No, just your phone," sounding strictly business. "I'll talk to you when you're on the helicopter."

"Okay." But Hokee was talking to the airwaves. Grant was already gone.

Hokee glanced over at Myron, who had listened to Hokee's side of the phone call.

"It appears your vision quest and the unexpected experiences in store for you begin now, Myron. You have your instructions. Should you have any problems, call this number." Hokee wrote Curly's phone number and name in Myron's notebook.

"Curly is a deputy sheriff and a friend. I'll have him bring your car here tonight. You should not need any help, but in case, he will immediately respond. If I'm not back in three days, throw a rabbit from the fridge to Shila. I will return before it's time for the last few days of your vision quest." The gravity of the situation struck Myron as he looked into his eyes and heard his voice.

"What, you're leaving me here alone?" Myron looked sick before, but now he appeared physically ill.

"It's only for a few days, Myron. The universe seems to have something special in store for you. Your quest appears to have an importance beyond what I have presently perceived. I'll meditate on the subject before our next meeting. In the beginning, I said you will spend several days alone.

"Damn it, Hokee; I expected more professional treatment from a man with your reputation."

"Myron, I've put up with your whining, sniveling, and uncertainties for several days. I've outlined a course for you to follow to achieve your goals. If the program I have outlined is too much for you, please leave and bother someone else. If you decide to stay, complete the assignments I've given you, and I'll see you when I return."

Hokee left Myron in the yard going into his home. He returned in two minutes wearing a pair of brown moccasins instead of cowboy boots. Calling Shila, he ruffled the hair on the wolf's head, telling him to take care of Myron. Waving to Myron, he got into his Explorer and left for the airport.

Myron stumbled around the yard, looking like a lost soul searching for a body. He experienced an overwhelming urge to cry, shout, or pack up and depart. He could contact someone to retrieve his car. After stewing for a couple of minutes, Myron regained control of his emotions and, recalling his purpose for being there, the professor eventually proceeded onto Hokee's covered porch and, sinking into one of the handmade chairs, began making lists.

CHAPTER FOURTEEN

Tahiti

Fortunately, when they grabbed Opal, to provide relief from the sun, she was modeling a wrap covering the tiny bikini with a modicum of modesty. The nearly sheer bright, yellow-colored wrap barely achieved either goal, but it was visually captivating while providing the viewers with a tantalizing glimpse at the beautifully proportioned body it covered. As Opal sat on a stool in the monkey cage, she didn't experience any sense of sexiness and was scared by the hungry stares of the six men working on their church building gawking at her. The men were calling the shack a church, but it looked like a dilapidated rust-stained ruin to Opal.

Besides the men, three young ladies hovered nearby with faces reflecting feelings of envy and hatred towards Opal while expressing delight at the beautiful clothing. Opal couldn't resist contemplating what these gals would think if they knew the ensemble she was wearing had a price tag of over twelve thousand U.S. dollars.

Her kidnappers restrained Opal until they had her safely stowed in the back of a windowless van resembling an old bread truck. She could scream inside the van, but no one outside would hear, unless they were close. However, before that could take place, the van was already moving. When people at the temple noticed their missing star, the van was five miles away, leaving a false path away from Ugla's church a few hundred yards away.

Many years in the past, someone built the monkey cage prison with heavy gauge wire fencing, which is observable surrounding prison yards. This openness meant no privacy when Opal's bladder signaled a desire to be emptied. Besides the short three-legged stool she was sitting on, the only other item in her prison was a dirty, rust-streaked, galvanized five-gallon bucket. The two choices were to wet herself where she sat or to squat on the bucket. Models grow callouses over the inhibitions most people experience, and for Opal to piss in the bucket was no big deal. She missed some toilet paper to wipe with but could live without that. Eating was a whole different non-experience.

The wire cage had a small three by six-inch opening for feeding monkeys. Opal recalled reading in a flight magazine that poachers in the past used to capture and sell Japanese Macaques because they were highly sociable and full of facial expressions. The hunters tossed bananas through the opening, but that was about the extent of the monkey's diet. Opal decided that if they offered her bananas, she would not eat. She could regain weight if she lost a little before being rescued. She never considered that being released might not be on her kidnapper's agenda.

Where in hell was Gene?

Where were the damn police?

This fricken island isn't that big. Surely, they would rescue her before she starved to death.

She was back on her stool when a handsome man wearing expensive clothes entered the prison shack; they called a church. He had a contagious smile and was charming with the other ladies before introducing himself to Opal.

"Hello, harlot. I'm Ugla. I planned on offering you as a sacrifice to old Oro, our ancient island god, but damn if they aren't offering an insane reward for your overused pussy. Two million U.S. dollars. God damn. I so want to waste your harlot's face and sweet little ass after an appropriate sacrifice to Oro, but it's hard to turn down that much free money. But hey, don't get your hopes up. Unless we can figure out a foolproof way to collect the ransom without getting caught, I will still give ole Oro a gift to remember us by. For damn sure *we* will remember it."

It was difficult for Opal to reconcile the man's looks and charming manner with his vile expressions and indifference to her plight.

"Well, Mister Ugly, you have no understanding of the woman you have abducted." To you, I am just some harlot model. Before this ends, you will either be dead or wish to your God Oro that you were."

"The name is oog, lah, slut. And what, your tall, handsome, worthless husband will beat me to death? Any man who lets his woman strut around in whore clothes is a jackass, nothing more than a worthless pile of monkey shit." With that, Ugla laughed, and the others joined in the merriment.

"Oh no, you **fucking jerk**!" Opal stood up with fire in her eyes. "From the moment you grabbed me, your lifespan became a matter of a few days, if not hours. And the same thing goes for your merry band of sick, twisted helpers. The people who will search for me are the nastiest, meanest, cruelest, most vicious people on earth."

"Why don't I kill you now and bury your body? No one will ever be aware. Ugla Sneered.

"Do you *really* think so?" You can only wish? Sadly, you, the true jackass, will never have such luck. If they must, my people will bury this whole fucking island in bodies until they have your ass. And if I am dead, your death will be a long, painful process. If they find me alive and unharmed, they may spare your life if I intervene on your worthless behalf. You lack the slightest notion of your captured person's importance."

"Why don't you tell us, princess?" He snickered, appearing as though what she said had not even been worth considering. "What makes you so special?" While showing how little concerned he was with Opal's words, his bowels were clenching. The harlot seemed so damned confident. *Is there a chance she is right?*

Opal stood looking at Ugla in the eyes, wanting him to witness her face and the truth she expressed. Although he tried to laugh it off, she saw her words worried him.

Finally, one of the other men spoke. "What if we turn her loose in the jungle, Ugla. Let her wander around until she dies or gets rescued."

"What? And give up two million dollars? I don't *think* so. Let's collect the ransom, then throw her body off the mountain."

Opal sat back down, confident that what she said was the truth, although she couldn't fathom how anyone would locate her in this jungle. She hadn't yet considered the thought that Hokee Wolf, her husband's family shaman, would show up.

CHAPTER FIFTEEN

Pocatello - Tahiti

Hokee was standing on the tarmac 50 feet from the General Aviation terminal when the Sikorsky SB-1 Defiant helicopter swept in from the north. It isn't easy to impress the shaman, but the Sikorsky was something out of a Mr. America movie.

The long, green, sleek, smooth body resembled a high-end minibus. On top of the body were twin stacked rotors, with four blades turning in opposite directions. The tail assembly featured stabilizers resembling those on a trimaran sailboat with a vertical propeller between the struts. With the helicopter hovering a foot off the ground, an Air Force major jumped out, waving at Hokee to join him under the spinning rotors. You don't need to duck under the blades while running towards the helicopter, but it's nearly impossible not to duck, knowing the guillotine is just a few feet above your head. When Hokee got near, the major stepped inside, holding out his hand to help their guest passenger enter.

Before Hokee could sit down, the door closed, and the helicopter rose. Inside, the noise level was equivalent to that experienced in a commercial jet. After he was seated, the major began Hokee's orientation.

"I don't know who you are, cowboy, and I don't want to know. Somebody somewhere thinks you're important enough to spend several thousand dollars to get your ass to Tahiti. Have you ever flown in a supersonic airplane?"

"No."

An E-9, Chief Master Sergeant of the Air Force, held out five white aspirin-looking tablets to the major with a bottle of water.

"Here," the major said, handing the pills and water to Hokee. "For nausea."

Hokee almost objected, but the major's gaze silenced him.

"You will experience several G forces and periods of weightlessness. Everybody gets sick the first few times. If you throw up inside your helmet, you will drown."

"Okay. I'm taking the pills." Although he tried to be pleasant, it wasn't easy to project friendliness when doing something you hated and felt was unnecessary.

"Have you ever worn a G suit?

"No."

"Okay. The folks on the base want us to give you a briefing on your way to Mountain Home so you can be in the air as soon as possible after we get you there. Someone thinks your ass is gold and wants you in Tahiti yesterday." The major didn't look happy. Besides the gold leaf on his shoulders showing his rank, he wore no name tag, giving Hokee had no opportunity to address him in a personal manner.

"This is a G suit," the major explained, indicating what looked like a jumpsuit on the deck. "Air bladders in the legs and across your abdomen keep blood flowing to your brain in a high-G environment. We were unaware of your size, or else we would have brought yours so you could suit up.

Hokee was sitting quietly without expression, which seemed to fluster the major.

"Hey, cowboy, are you getting this?" he asked, sounding almost angry.

"Yes, I understand the concept of a G suit."

"Great. You're familiar with what they are, even though you've never worn one, correct?" Disgust oozing from the major.

"Correct." Hokee knew the major wanted him to be impressed, stunned, or show signs of anxiety, but sharing his feelings or thoughts wasn't his nature. To Hokee, this was simply a ritual he was required to experience to help Grant find his missing daughter-in-law. He planned to spend the flight in his shaman's mind, outside of his body.

"All right then. The airmen at the base will help you suit up and get you plugged into the plane's operating system to pump air and keep you warm. They'll fit you with a helmet and connect you to the captain's mic. When you reach Tahiti, you must clean the crap out of your suit and helmet." The major was convinced Hokee would foul his suit by expelling liquid and solid matter in the high G environment.

Hokee did not respond to these instructions and commands, further angering the major. At least this civilian should show a little appreciation and act halfway alive.

"Questions?" barks the major.

"What is the flight time to Tahiti?"

"My God. It lives and breathes." The major couldn't resist a little sarcastic smile. "The flight takes around three and a half hours."

"Thank you for the briefing and information." Hokee favored the angry major with a genuine smile to show there were no hard feelings.

A little over four hours later, Hokee stood at the Tahiti International Airport, not experiencing sickness, nausea, or a soiled suit. It's a shaman thing. Gene met Hokee at the terminal building and was surprised the detective arrived on site so quickly.

Addressing the startled young man, Hokee said, "Perhaps your father pulled some strings or bribed somebody, or both. Although it might have been his stunning personality," he added with a grin.

On their way to the hotel, Gene briefed Hokee on Opal's disappearance.

"Skip the hotel. Show me the temple and altar where Opal disappeared," Hokee suggested.

Gene's rental was a red Talbot Matra, a four-wheel-drive vehicle similar in appearance to a Jeep Wrangler. Twenty minutes later, Gene parked in the temple parking lot, and they got out of the Matra.

"Please stay here," Hokee suggested. Gene looked confused, as he had never seen Hokee at work before. Wearing his moccasins, Hokee climbed up on the temple and then the altar. He shut his eyes and slowed his breathing rate, allowing the feelings of the temple and forest to inhabit his body. Before long, he kneeled on the altar and picked up a handful of the black soil, holding it to his forehead before letting it drift from his fingers back to the altar. "They should never have presumed to shoot a commercial on this site." After a few more minutes, Hokee adds, "Others have also defiled this sacred spot."

Hokee descended from the altar and temple and, standing with his eyes closed, allowed the forest to speak. In a few minutes, he unerringly walked to where the kidnappers had hidden while watching Opal model the agency clothes.

Gene stood by the vehicle, watching Hokee in amazement. How did he find the hidden spot so easily? Not witnessing Hokee work before, he was unaware of his ability to feel the earth through his moccasins.

Hokee followed an invisible trail from the woods to the vehicle where Opal was abducted. He then ran down the road almost a half mile before stopping at a wide spot where it was possible to park another vehicle. It was like watching a bloodhound work using his nose to follow scents humans are incapable of sensing.

After a few minutes at the clearing, Hokee hiked back to the temple parking lot and joined Gene. "There were five men. They put Opal in a vehicle, probably a van. She was unconscious but unhurt when they put her inside. The temple has been violated before. The men have been using the altar to seduce young ladies. Let's go back down the mountain."

"I understand why my dad had you flown here, Hokee. I wish you had been here yesterday."

"Please take me to the hotel. I want to meditate in my room for a few minutes."

"Sure, Hokee. It's only about fifteen minutes away."

As Gene drove back down the mountain, Hokee closed his eyes, visualizing the abduction, making sense of the situation.

CHAPTER SIXTEEN

Myron

Once he began making a list of the reasons for his vision quest, Myron forgot about being left alone in the middle of the desolate black lava flats. A.I.'s importance and potential impact are staggering. The potential exists for the end of human civilization. What exactly was Myron's role in this situation? He had the potential to sell his development for maybe billions of dollars and retire to some desolate island, anticipating the downfall of humanity. Or was it possible for him to take a significant role in policing the release of A.I. on humans?

Moving a page in the notebook Hokee left, Myron began listing the people he could rely on to help him contain the threat. The more he thought about his 'friends' and associates, the more unsure he became. It suddenly dawned on the professor the importance of this exercise. He now had a glimpse of what Hokee wanted him to perceive.

Who were the people trying to steal his company's development?

Was it even possible to return the genie to the bottle at this stage without losing his life in the process?

Can A.I. benefit the world without machine domination? Without controls, humanity holds no value to superior intelligence. Isaac Asimov, the writer who invented A.I. protocols, where are you when we need you?

"Okay, Myron, list the benefits of A.I. for the world." He found it easier to concentrate while talking to himself. He missed Hokee and wished the shaman was around to lend support. As he worked on his lists, the day slipped away, and before he knew it, the sun was dipping toward the horizon. Glancing upwards, he noticed Shila grinning at him, displaying white teeth in a wolf smile. *"It's a good thing that fellow likes me,"* he thought.

Dinner was vegetable soup with two of Hokee's homemade biscuits. As the sun left and it became dark, Myron was happy to crawl into his tent. It appears he had a greater sense of security under the canvas compared to sitting outside. Intellectually, the doctor acknowledged the thin canvas walls of his tent would not keep harm at bay, but outside, Shila was keeping watch. Before long, the day's trauma won out, and he fell into a peaceful sleep.

The next day was fire day. "Oh god, I've got to stare into the fucking flames all day." Myron rarely used profanity as it represented a weak mind, but his animal nature took over at times like this. After an oatmeal breakfast and a quick shower," *damn, but that water is cold,"* he started his fire-watching.

During the first few hours, he restlessly moved, wriggled, struggling to find comfort, and faced the challenge of thinking constructive thoughts, but eventually, the dancing flames entranced him. In the fire, he witnessed the dawn of humanity, the cave dweller, and all his superstitions. Like those ancient ancestors, Myron sat before the flames wondering how life worked. For the cave dweller, the disappearing sun was a mystery; for Myron, it represented the force of life.

As the day went on, Myron witnessed civilization emerge from the flames in his fire, transforming it into a tool for cooking food and strengthening the wooden spears of the cavemen. Later, mankind used fire to shape spears out of metal. In his mind, Myron was able to hear the blacksmith's hammer forging plows to till the earth. Myron was no longer cursing the flames as they consumed his entire attention.

Myron saw stars explode, creating our universe like a fiery ball. He momentarily lost his trance as the thought arose, *"Good lord, I had no awareness of the extent of knowledge one could gain from a fire."* The spell returned with a vengeance as though it didn't appreciate his loss of attention. The destructive power of fire is frightening. For ancient man, a large forest fire was often deadly; the same is true today. Rarely did a fire in a cave get out of control; if it did, the humans escaped by going outside. Modern apartment house fires often prove fatal to one or several human beings, as an escape is often impossible.

Suddenly the fire flared up as flames appeared eager to reach out and consume everything nearby. It was then that Myron caught sight of the lightning. In his mind, he heard the thunder and felt the ground shake. It was even more frightening that superior beings were artificially creating the thunder and lightning. As the sun set, Myron witnessed fire controlled by A.I. It would be devastating if a superior mind unleashed flames upon humanity.

Gazing upwards, Myron witnessed Shila's smile, then the wolf licked tears from the professor's face.

CHAPTER SEVENTEEN

The Chinaman

The Chinese embassy in Paris, France, is a large (football-sized) classical Georgian-style building made of white granite. Their high-walled embassy grounds, which includes a Chinese-owned hotel, the Hotel-deMontesquiu, occupies an entire city block between Rue Monsieur and Bd des Invalides. Surrounding buildings and grounds for several blocks in every direction are government agencies and other private enterprises with similar stunning architecture. Walking or driving through the area evokes a sense of insignificance, encompassed by towering, white, imposing, grandiose buildings. It's a similar sensation that arises when standing in a serene grove of ancient giant redwood trees.

In embassies around the world, military intelligence personnel (spies) occupy staff positions with innocuous names, such as International Organizations and Economic and Business Affairs, two actual titles in the Chinese embassy. The Chinaman, named Feng Cheng, a representative of the Business Affairs delegation, was China's premier secret operative responsible for killing nineteen enemies of the state while acquiring several advanced scientific inventions for China that were developed in other countries.

Three other top spies working in China's State Central Military Commission report to Feng. Their working titles are Ding Dong One

(DD1-being Feng) and DDs 2, 3, and 4. Ding Dongs (which means wrath) earn their status by demonstrating superior ferocity in early assignments. It takes ten years to earn DD status. In the Chinese language, the number one is yi. When operational, Feng Cheng is known as DDyi in coded communication with the leaders in China. When visiting other countries, Feng's status is superior to the resident Chinese Ambassador. If the situation warrants, Feng orders the Ambassador to do his will.

Countries developing A.I. are in a mad race to be the first to build an A.I. with above-human intelligence. Every country with the capability and every high-technology company around the world is engaged in this activity, and they use spies to monitor the status of their competitors.

Myron's progress is known by almost everyone in the A.I. race. China was the first to field a team commissioned to acquire Singularity Inc's work and Myron's triumphal development by any means possible. Their team leader is the Chinaman.

CHAPTER EIGHTEEN

Tahiti

When they arrived at the Intercontinental Tahiti Resort & Spa, Hokee proceeded directly to the front desk. "Does this hotel feature a sauna?" he asked the attractive young lady behind the counter. Dressed in black denim pants and a black long-sleeved tee shirt with brown moccasins stained with black earth, the tall man with long black hair held off his face with a white headband did not look like a hotel guest.

"Are you staying with us, sir?" The young lady asked.

"No. My friend is," he said with a gentle smile, waving an arm in Gene's direction. The clerk recognized Gene, who nodded his head affirmatively.

"Well, yes, we feature a sauna for registered guests." The young lady smiled while assuring the strangely dressed intruder that the sauna was unavailable to anybody who walked in off the street.

"I wish to use the sauna for several hours and do not wish to be disturbed," Hokee informed the clerk.

"Why, that would not be..." she was interrupted by Gene, who stepped forward and said, "Please accommodate my friend. He is helping to find my wife."

"Yes, certainly Mr. Olson. I'll inform the spa personnel to prevent anyone else from entering the spa." While such decisions were beyond her pay grade, seeing the Indian appearing man and the handsome guest together, the young lady was sure management would not object.

"Gene, please ensure the sauna is hot and prevent anyone else from using it until I return," Hokee requested, before turning and walking toward the rear entrance.

Gene and the registration clerk exchanged confused looks before Gene left to do as Hokee wanted.

Hokee found the trail Gene and Opal used on their daily excursion while admiring the beautiful scenery. Finding an overgrown path taking off up the mountainside, Hokee left the main trail climbing up, occasionally stopping to pick a leaf from one of the plants. He sniffed the leaf before biting a small sample, which he tasted with his tongue. Finding a familiar taste and smell, Hokee pulled it from the ground, shaking soil from its roots. Wiping off the residual dirt, Hokee tasted the root to be sure he was not mistaken. Within a few minutes, he returned to the hotel with a handful of leaves, roots, and bark from several plants.

The sauna was hot, and Gene ensured no one was using the facility. There were a few minutes of daylight remaining before the mostly orange ball glided into the Pacific and most hotel guests were out and about without wanting to sit in a hot box, making Gene's job easy. When Hokee arrived at the sauna, he separated a few leaves and roots from those in his hand, handing them to Gene.

"Please take these herbs and make a tea concoction. Boil a cup of water in the microwave, then put the herbs in hot water to seep for ten minutes. Bring the concoction here to the sauna to finish steeping. Advise the spa manager to keep everyone else away from here. I am not to be disturbed."

To Gene's credit, he did not question Hokee, but immediately left to do his assignment.

Hokee undressed, and using a towel to cover up, for Gene's benefit, sat on the floor and began slow shamanic breathing. He was still lowering his heart rate when Gene returned with the hot herb tea.

"Thank you, Gene; now, please ensure that no one disturbs me until I leave this facility."

Fortunately, it was an electric-style Swedish sauna with rocks to be doused with water, creating steam. When ready, with the sauna at 180° Fahrenheit hot, Hokee's preference, he grabbed the rest of his leaves and roots, then entered the hot sauna, taking Gene's tea concoction. The session began with Hokee meditating for several minutes, getting into the Island and forest rhythms. After assimilating the energy in the surrounding environment, Hokee dropped the leaves and roots he had brought inside onto the hot rocks. The burning herbs produced smoke Hokee inhaled in long, slow breaths. Once he experienced the effects of the herbs in his system, Hokee dumped the hot herb tea concoction onto the rocks, producing intense steam. This rocketed him deep into the subconscious levels of non-local reality. In this space, he witnessed and encountered Opal's abduction. After being satisfied he would gain no more information from this session, Hokee left the sauna for a shower to wash away the sweat pouring from his body. A handy water cooler provided liquid to replenish that he lost in the sauna.

Leaving the spa, Hokee found Gene maintaining his vigilance in an outside chair. Glancing at his watch, Gene was surprised that Hokee had been in the sauna for nearly four hours.

"Gene, I need to talk with someone who knows the old history of the Island."

"I am aware of the person to consult," Gene replies. "Terilmana, our bus driver, it's her husband, Otahi, who appears to be acquainted with everyone on the island." Seeing the confusion on his friend's face, Gene quickly continued, "Terilmana owns the charter bus company that ferried us around the island. Her husband, Otahi, is a methodist preacher specializing in the old Oro religion prevalent in the French Polynesian islands before Christianity arrived."

"Let's locate Otahi and determine if he will aid us." There was no mention of eating. Hokee returned to the hotel lounge as Gene hurried to keep pace.

Gene led them to the travel desk where Terilmana was busy with her husband arranging more search parties. They both looked up as Gene approached with a strange man dressed for an outing in the desert, not tropical Tahiti. Gene introduced Hokee to Terilmana and her husband as the person his father sent from the States to find his wife.

"Mr. Mareva, are you acquainted with anyone who has knowledge about the historical background of this island?" Hokee wasted no time with the traditional pleasantries.

"Please call me Otahi, and yes, I remember just the man. Mr. Akamu Hauata is almost ninety and still very sharp. He knows the island's history better than anyone else I can think of."

"How soon can I visit Mr. Hauata?" Hokee asked abruptly.

It was Terilmana who answered. "I can drive you there now if you wish. He lives in Papenoo, about thirty minutes from here."

"Would he be home now, do you think, and could we just drop in on him?" It was apparent that Hokee didn't want to waste any time.

Now Otahi answered. "Old Akamu rarely leaves his home these days and loves visitors. However, it is practically dark, and Mr. Akamu goes to bed with the sunset. I'm afraid we cannot visit him before tomorrow morning."

"Damn, I hate wasting these hours. Hokee's impatience was showing despite his attempt at civility. He was tired, stressed, and eager to find Opal now that he had a lead on her prison. With Gene leading the way, the other three followed him to the hotel restaurant for a late dinner.

Chapter Nineteen

Opal

Looking out from her prison, Opal sensed the fear inspired by the previous comments she made about her rescuers. Ugla and his followers were in a serious discussion regarding their actions. Ugla still argued for a way to collect the ramson, but the men and women surrounding him wanted to release her somewhere near Papeete. Still, it was hard to dismiss two million dollars.

"Hey, princess, tell us more about the people you believe will rescue you."

"Are you familiar with the concept of a shaman?" "Or what a billion dollars in reward money will do to this island? And not from just one source, but at least two different men equally powerful. And my father's men do not play by rules. They cut the hands-off thieves, and for torture, there is no one more cruel and violent. If they must, they will torture and kill their way around the island until they find someone who will give you up. You are certainly not so ignorant as to think that there are no other people on this island who are unaware of your foolish church. Your best hope for survival is that the shaman finds you first, and even then, I cannot vouch for your safety."

"What a scary little speech. It's too bad I don't believe one word you said." Ugla tried to sound positive, but Opal picked up on his concern.

"Well, Ugly. It will be your funeral. Perhaps you don't do that here. Just throw the corpse on a pile of wood and light a match. Hell, my people will even pour gasoline on the wood to help it burn faster,"

"Who is this bitch," Ugla asked. "Does anyone have any information?"

One man who helped abduct Opal spoke up. "That was an expensive setup at the temple. Many serious people. They had several busloads of folks with many cameras and lights. I observed a truck packed with clothes for this chick to flaunt her body. Whoever she is, she must be important."

"Yeah, and did you notice they had a hairstylist and makeup artist?" Another kidnapper added.

"Shit. What if the bitch is right, and she has a fucking army on the way to rescue her slutty ass?" Ugla didn't sound like he believed that was possible, but threw the question out to gauge the response.

"We've already kidnapped the lady," another man spoke up. "If what she is asserting is true, I see limited benefit in allowing her to go free. The people she mentioned will still search for us."

"Yeah, that's what I think," Ugla said. "We might as well collect the ransom. If she isn't lying, we can use the money to get us out of here."

"Yeah," Two of the kidnappers said in unison. Let's collect the two million bucks and leave here."

"All right," the other men responded.

"What about us?" One girl asked.

"You didn't do the kidnapping," one man responded, "so they won't punish you like the rest of us. We'll give you some of the money though, right, Ugla?"

"Yeah, sure," the handsome leader responded. But his words were not convincing.

Chapter Twenty

Myron

The day following his fire day, Myron built his early fire as the plan required, then searched for his shovel. Discovering it near the restroom from his earlier excavation, he brought it back towards the house and sweat lodge. Finding an excellent spot a few yards up the hill from the house and fire pit, Myron dug up the earth, making a soft bed. Once he arrived back at the house and veranda, he removed his clothes, carefully folding them on one of Hokee's handmade chairs.

Walking gingerly barefoot, the reluctant professor returned to the recently dug earth and lay down on the dirt.

"This is ridiculous," he said to himself. *"What am I supposed to learn laying here getting dirty,"* the thoughts continued.

As he had yesterday, sitting before the fire, he squirmed, fidgeted, and kept shuffling around, trying to get comfortable. Finally, remembering he was allowed to walk around on the earth and sit down, he got up and walked away before remembering he had no foot protection. "Shit!" He returned and sat down on the bare dirt. He dug his dirt bed close to the lava wall, allowing him to sit and lean back, increasing his level of comfort a bit. "Well, hell, these rocks are part of the earth, right?"

Alternating between lying down and leaning against the wall, the morning creeped by ever so slowly. Towards noon, he discovered he neglected to bring a water bottle and was forced to walk back to the veranda for one. The chairs in the shade on the porch were so tempting it took all his willpower to grab an energy bar and water and then return to his earthly bed.

It was the middle of the afternoon when he drifted off into a light slumber. In his dreams, he saw worms crawling from the dirt onto his body. Then some giant black bugs joined the worms crawling on his skin. This mini nightmare woke him before realizing it had only been a dream. Grabbing the water bottle for a drink, he slopped a few drops onto the earth. The water landed where he usually placed his hand, and without thinking, Myron laid his hand on the wet dirt.

The wet earth stuck to his fingers, which he rubbed on his bare leg, leaving a small spot black. "Wow, it's possible for me to paint my entire body in mud to avoid the sun." This minor revelation started the synapses in his brain to fire off, setting in motion a series of transporting images.

He observed the moist earth on his leg capable of providing substance to the plants growing in Hokee's garden. The sun and Mother Earth were giving life. *Oh, my god. The earth is our mother. The sun is our father. This dirt I am sitting on has the potential to sustain me if necessary. And think of all the different plants that grow in this soil. Many are beautiful. Plants we can eat like carrots or trees to provide shade and recreation. I've forgotten that early man dug earth caves to live in, and many cultures still make their homes out of the dirt. And well, the trees we harvest to build our houses today grow in the soil.*

Like the first, this day ended with Myron gaining a new perspective on life and Mother Earth. He then realized that an A.I. would not need or appreciate our soil. An A.I. has the potential to survive forever without soil. *Oh, man! It looks like my little invention is ultimately more destructive and powerful than I realized, and I already knew it was dangerous.*

The sun was low on the horizon before a humbled Myron Whittleman walked back to the veranda for his clothes on bare feet without giving the lack of shoes a thought. His experience with Mother Earth made him humble. A smiling wolf joined him on his walk.

CHAPTER TWENTY-ONE

Draco and The Chinaman

No one knew where Draco Vargas was born.

He never talked about his background or current illegal activities, which did not include drugs or prostitution. When approached by the Chinaman in Paris, the city of lights, no one would have thought their meeting unusual. People from all over the world visit Paris, a renowned international destination.

Draco, a fit swarthy man with a pockmarked face and sunken dark menacing eyes, looks at people with a chilling glare. He stands five foot eleven. His standard clothes are blue denim pants with black pioneer boots and a white polo shirt. A medical condition made his hair turn white in his early teenage years and, when combined with everything else about his appearance, makes him a person to be feared and avoided. How the Chinaman found him and knew of his character is not known. Neither did anyone have knowledge of how the Chinaman was aware of Draco's illicit actions.

The Chinaman stood five-foot 8 with a swimmer's body, powerful arms, a slender waist and sculptured body. He wears a dull cotton three-piece gray business suit with tailored pockets. Concealed in his clothing is a customized Walther 22-caliber pistol and a Dead Air Mask silencer. Based on a unique baffle design, the first shot through a Dead Air Mask is barely noticeable. As one of the world's premier assassins, the Chinaman only needs one shot. Only five inches long, the silencer is easy to conceal.

The Chinaman is a comely man, with fine cheekbones and full lips, women are initially attracted to him, but no one looked at Feng Cheng's white eyes, eyes that were almost unheard of in China. The eyes are frightening, with pupils so dark they look like the black holes of the universe.

On a warm sunny day, the Chinaman walked up to Draco on a Paris sidewalk and asked in flawless French, "Mr. Vargas, would you please join me for a drink at this outdoor cafe?" he asked while pointing to a nearby cafe with sidewalk seating. Draco nodded, didn't ask for a name, he didn't ask how the stranger knew his name, but followed him to the cafe where each sat on a red metal chair under a bright yellow umbrella with the name Tsingtao splashed in red letters. Whether it was an accident that these colors were pure Chinese or somehow planned by the Chinaman is unknown. They both sat, Draco had not said one word.

"I have a proposition for you, Mr. Vargas." The Chinaman began even before the server approached their table. Draco nodded but still said nothing.

Before any more conversation took place, if only one person speaking is conversation, the server arrived, dressed in the cafe's standard white tuxedo suit. "What would be your pleasure, monsieurs?" The server asked, his voice trembling slightly, as both men looked intimidating.

"I will have a serving of your Jasmine tea," the Chinaman ordered, speaking in flawless French, which was unexpected. The Chinese usually have trouble speaking the French language, much like they have trouble with the L in English.

"Desperados," Draco ordered softly, in heavily accented French. It was difficult for both the Chinaman and the server to recognize the accent.

The Chinaman looked at Draco expecting a comment on his opening statement. There was none.

"Are you amenable to a contract where you can earn ten million U.S. dollars?" The Chinaman asked.

"What do I have to do to earn your ten million dollars?" Draco didn't appear particularly interested.

"There are three tasks to this job. The first task pays ten million. The other two pay much more."

The server interrupted with Draco's Patron Tequila cocktail and the chainman's tea. Uneasy in the presence of either formidable-looking man, the server set the drinks on the table and then hurried away without speaking.

"Who do I have to kill?" Draco asked in his soft, dry accent.

"That is the second task of this contract. It only comes into play after you complete the first one." The Chinaman took a sip of jasmine while waiting for a response.

What if my interest lies solely in part one?

"No problem. But the next task pays twenty million."

Acting like it was no big deal, Draco took a long pull on his tequila, then said in the same soft, flat voice, totally void of emotion, "How did you figure out where to find me?" The look on his face was deadly. His deep black, frightening eyes radiated a piercing, deadly beam like a black-tipped arrow glistening in the sun.

The Chinaman was unfazed. "Come now, Mr. Vargas, don't pretend modesty. A man with your skills and experiences has earned a certain reputation, respected and admired in those circles where the dark arts matter."

"That does not answer my questions." Angry tone.

"You know more than anyone; money can buy anything."

"Yeah... that answers it." Pause. "What's the first job?" He was still displaying anger in his eyes and the tight squeeze of his fist wrapped around the Desperado glass.

You must steal a specific type of a large helicopter in Russia, deliver it to a safe designated spot in America, then locate an experienced pilot and crew with no morals."

"Sounds too simple. Why not buy your helicopter?"

"That is also something you know. Money leaves a trail. You might hide the trail for a while, but not forever." The Chinaman displayed no fear throughout this brief encounter, oblivious to Draco's intimidating looks.

And Draco was unfazed by Cheng's white eyes with evil black holes in their center.

"All right. When?" Draco responded to the offer without emotion

"Soon, however, there are conditions that account for the high-priced contract. Russia must not know who stole their helicopter, and it must be smuggled into America with no one in America knowing about it."

"Yes, that explains the large contract. What about money for expenses?"

"Our estimate is two million dollars for expenses. If that is too low, we will add to it in the future. You will be given two million for expenses and five million dollars for the first half of your profit. Another five million when the helicopter is delivered to the U.S.A. with your crew."

"Okay, what's next?" Draco's expression finally showed interest. Draco never asked what would happen if he took the first seven million dollars and disappeared. He knew the answer.

Pulling a burner phone from the pocket of his pants and sliding it across the glass-topped table toward Draco, the Chinaman answered the question, "We will call you within the next two days."

Picking up the burner, Draco drained his Desperado, then rose from the table, tucked the burner in his pocket and walked away, disappearing down the sidewalk, dodging other pedestrians, never looking back.

Chapter Twenty-Two

Hokee Tahiti

Early the following day, with Terilmana driving the bus, she took her husband Otahi, Hokee, and Gene to Papenoo, where the older man who knew the island's history lived. Papenoo is a beautiful town perched on the Pacific Ocean, surrounded by majestic mountains forming Papenoo Valley. The area's principal attraction is a stunning waterfall ending in the glorious blue of Papenoo Lake. Hauata's house in Papenoo near the river Papenoo is an old rock house about twice its primary residence's age.

Hokee knocked on the doorframe to attract attention. It took a few moments as island natives don't believe in hurrying through life. It is only the hustlers after tourist dollars that move fast.

In about two minutes, an elderly lady wearing a long blue sarong topped with a printed floral blouse came to the door and smiled a greeting. Hokee thought she looked like she was about sixty-five but might pass for forty-five. "It isn't often we get visitors these days, especially early in the morning," she teased in English with a pleasant French accent.

It was Otahi who responded. "Greetings Heiana; I hope this isn't a bad time to come calling."

"Oh, not at all, Otahi. Company is always welcome these days." The smile never left her face.

"Heiana, this is Mr. Hokee Wolf from America," Otahi said, pointing to Hokee, "and this tall, good-looking lad is Gene, whose wife has been kidnapped. They wish to have a few words with Mr. Hauata."

She smiled, her eyes lighting up, and said, "He'd love some company." Beckoning them inside, she led them through the house to a backyard adorned with gorgeous flowers of many colors and varieties. A withered elderly man with sparkling blue eyes sat among the flowers in a wooden rocking chair.

"Akamu, I've brought you some visitors," Heiana said with a lilt in her voice.

"Well, thank God. I've been dying to talk with somebody besides my minder." Although he looked ancient, Akamu spoke in a powerful baritone voice. He wore a plain white long-sleeved cotton shirt and black shorts, showing his withered legs. "She means well, but I'm tired of listening to town gossip, which isn't interesting even on the best days." Old Akamu chuckled while saying this.

Otahi, stepping forward, said, "I've brought Mr. Hokee Wolf from America, who wishes to have a few words with you."

"Mr. Wolf, did you say, like one of those gray timber wolves we read about?"

"The same," Hokee responded. My closest friend is one of those giant gray wolves. We live together."

"How amazing. I don't suppose that is how you got your name?"

"Well, it's sort of related. I didn't have a last name until my adopted father gave me the wolf when I started my profession, and needing a last name for business, I chose wolf. My wolf is named Shila, which means brother in my native language."

"What an interesting story," Akamu said. Would you like to go inside, sit down, and have a cup of coffee? There are no more chairs out here in the garden." Like Heiana, Akamu had a pleasing French accent.

"No, this won't take much time," Hokee responded. "I'm looking for information about the location of an old building near the highway, but up in the mountains. This building would be on the other side of Papeete."

"Oh, my. You're asking about ancient history. Well, maybe not ancient, but old, like me. When I was young, I spent a lot of time on that side of the island. There used to be a banana plantation somewhere near Fááä. On a Saturday night, my friends and I would get in a car and drive over there to steal bananas from a truck they parked near the road. Someone said they had a nearby packing shed a few hundred yards up the mountains, but I never climbed the mountain to see."

"Would you know anything about this shed you mentioned?" Hokee was reaching for straws at this point. He was disappointed that the old man didn't have more information.

"I can't tell you anything about the shed on that banana plantation, but they used to grow pineapples near here, and they had a packing shed. I worked there for a couple of years. Our shed was open on all four sides but had a roof to keep out the rain and sun. The banana plantation probably had a similar packing shed somewhere near the highway. If you like, I can show you where they used to park their banana truck."

"We will appreciate any help you can provide, Mr. Akumu.

"It will be my honor and pleasure. Does this have anything to do with that missing lady?"

"Yes, it does," Hokee answers. "I believe the kidnappers are holding the lady in an old building in the lower mountains."

"Okay, let's see if that old packing shed is the building you are looking for."

CHAPTER TWENTY-THREE

Ugla

The afternoon sun was brutal, making the kidnappers sweat as they huddled in the church. They couldn't wait to leave and get rid of the bitch.

"Let's take her down the quick way to the highway," Ugla commands. "We'll take her close to her fancy hotel and collect the ransom money. Then leave this God-forsaken Island."

"Well, we wouldn't want to hang around on the island anyway," one kidnapper suggested. "Sure as hell, they'd hang us from a big ole trees if they caught us."

"Okay, ladies. Get the bitch, and let's get out of here," Ugla said with a snarl.

Four church ladies in on the kidnapping released Opal from the cage, then tied her arms behind her back, ensuring the ropes were good and tight. They didn't want their payday to escape.

When the church ladies let Opal out of the cage, and she caught sight of the steep rocky path they expected her to walk down, she sat down on the ground and refused to move.

"What in the hell are you doing, bitch? Stand up and walk down the trail."

"I will walk down, or you can carry me down, but I am not walking on those rocks barefoot." It was evident to anyone that Opal was serious.

"Okay, ladies," Ugla said with a sneer. "Find something for the princess to put on her feet."

There weren't any shoes lying around, so the ladies found some old cleaning rags they wrapped around Opal's feet.

Leading the way, Ugla weaved down the banana trail growers used to haul their produce to the highway. The steep trail was the shortest route to the highway. Another longer trail was easier, but it required more time. The two paths inadvertently saved them from being snared by Hokee.

Ugla sent two of his men back down the easy path to get their vehicles and drive them to the old loading zone. Two old vans were waiting when the party with Opal reached the highway. The four ladies loaded Opal in the van resembling an old bread truck, following her inside. One man made his way to the driver's side while Ugla took the passenger seat to observe the ladies with their hostage. The rest followed in another van. Their ride to the Hilton Hotel Tahiti took only ten minutes, and they used another twenty minutes to select a place to hide their hostage. They located a spot two hundred yards behind the Hilton under a large coconut tree. After tying Opal to the tree, Ugla put a rag in her mouth, then wrapped an old dirty rag around her head to hold it in place.

"Okay," Ugla said, sitting on the ground nearby, "Everybody find a place to sit. I want one of you ladies to write a note."

"What sort of note?" Kahaia asked. One of Opal's minders, Kahaia, was a slender island girl with long black hair framing an Elizabeth Taylor face,

"A ransom note," he said. "It's almost three in the afternoon, and the banks are still open. If they're serious about the reward money, this should give them plenty of time to get the money, but not enough time to mark all the bills."

The kidnappers sat down and discussed the note for a few minutes before deciding on the preferred wording. Meanwhile, Ugla had another girl fetch hotel stationery and an envelope. When everyone agreed the message was perfect, Ugla asked Kahaia to write the note.

We have the bitch everybody is looking for. Have the two million dollars ready by nine p.m. tonight. If you do not have the money, the bitch dies.

Enclosed is a lock of her hair to prove this is not a hoax. We will update you on the arrangements for obtaining the girl when we are ready to trade her for the reward. Don't fuck this up.

After everyone agreed the note was perfect, Ugla used his knife to cut off a lock from Opal's hair. Hair and note were placed in the envelope. On the outside of the sealed envelope, Ugla had another kidnapper write the word URGENT in block letters. Another girl was sent to the front of the hotel to find a boy to deliver the message. There are always several young hoodlums hanging around in front to beg from hotel guests. Hotel security chases these pests away every few minutes, but they came back immediately after the guards return inside. Ugla gave the girl five dollars to give some boy to deliver the envelope to the front desk. The boy was to return outside immediately for another five dollars.

After regrouping, Ugla presented his exchange plans, the crucial moment in any kidnapping.

They will place Opal in a kayak one hundred yards from shore, tying her hands and feet. She will stand in the kayak, wrapped in a blanket, hiding the restraints, although observers from a distance will determine the girl is restrained, they cannot be sure what bindings hold her captive. Two male kidnappers wearing snorkeling masks will be in the water, one on each side of the kayak holding it steady. Should any issues arise on shore with the money exchange, the men in the kayak will overturn it, tipping the tied-up hostage in the water to drown. Ugla assumed people on the shore would have a spotlight shining on the girl. Any attempt to rescue the hostage from the shore will mean her certain death. Once the money exchange is successful, I will signal the men in the water with a flashlight to help the girl sit down so they can shove the kayak towards the shore. Its momentum will carry the girl to the beach and her waiting husband. The kidnappers in the water will swim out to a waiting boat.

As a plan, it seemed foolproof. The watchers on shore could see the kidnapped lady and verify that she was alive before releasing the ransom money. Once the cash had been counted and verified, Ugla will signal the men to send the kayak ashore. If there was a trick with the money, the girl would drown.

After making their plans, the kidnappers just had to wait a few hours before collecting the money. The group was practically giddy with excitement, believing nothing could hinder their plans.

They didn't know about Hokee.

CHAPTER TWENTY-FOUR

Myron

The third day began like the last two, with a fire ceremony. By now, Byron had made peace with the fire and, despite his reluctance to admit it, found pleasure in this time of meditation with the fire gods. The fire pit was next to the sweat lodge, so Myron crawled into the lodge this morning after his fire chore to get a feel for the enclosure. His first sensation was the scent. Hokee used several herbs and other items for his ceremonies. Although hot rocks consumed these compounds, the lodge had a powerful aroma of something exotic.

Myron lay down by the rock pit inside when powerful feelings within the lodge overcame him. He quickly crawled back outside, drawing a deep breath of fresh air. Any more sweat lodge experiences will have to await Hokee's presence.

Myron was informed by Hokee early on that he would spend time alone and wouldn't be seen often in the initial days, so his absence wouldn't cause any discomfort. While he missed seeing the man and feeling his comforting presence, he knew his isolation would not last much longer.

After the fire ceremony, he ate a bowl of raisin bran topped with strawberries from Hokee's porch fridge while thinking about his Earth Day, remembering how much he discovered about life by lying on a dirt bed.

Knowing the coming day will be torture, at least in the beginning, he lingered over two cups of coffee while working on his lists. Looking at his assignment for the day, he groaned and complained to Shila. "Dammit Shila, I've got to get naked and sit in the fricking water all day. It's almost enough to make me sick to my stomach." Shila just grinned that wolf grin Myron had come to enjoy.

Sitting in Hokee's chair on the big, shaded porch, he undressed and folded his clothes. With sandals on his feet, he made his way to the outdoor shower to rinse off the nighttime perspiration. Casting a brief eye towards the nearby fire pit and sweat lodge, he was almost happy to have a wet day, though he was curious about what he would learn from water. It was water time.

The fountain base was a black lava rock oval, four feet high and fifteen feet in diameter. Its interior was a tall polished aqua green rock pillar cascading downwards ten feet. Water flowed out of a tilted decorated red jug resting on the top pillar. While in Mexico, Myron admired a water jug with a Boho Chick design, one of the popular choices resembling the one on Hokee's fountain. The jug had a large round bottom with a narrow top. The painted Aztec style decorations on the sides certainly depicted a Mexican flavor. Water from the jug poured onto the green rocks, cascading from one pillar down to the next lower level, falling all around the fountain's base. Inside the fountain base, the water was two feet deep.

Myron sat on the edge, swinging his legs into the water. Fortunately for him, the sun made the water in the fountain several degrees warmer than the underground river, which was its source; still, it felt awfully damn cold. He sat with his back against the fountain's wall with his legs stretched in front towards the center. As he slowly grew accustomed to the water temperature, Myron closed his eyes and relaxed, listening to the fountain.

Before long, he wondered where all this water came from. No well was visible on the property, nor was there any sound of a pump motor. As he thought about the situation, he noticed a small current moving across his stomach, not from the fountain's splashing water. Aware of this, he found the current cooler than the fountain water. Curious, he used his hands finding its source. He discovered a small one-inch hole in the wall where cold water entered the fountain. This water kept the fountain full. "Great, Myron, you're a genius."

He returned to relaxing with his eyes closed, listening to the water cascade down the fountain. The wall of water falling on his legs reminded Myron of the rain and how it cleaned the air. And the rain helped plants to grow. *"Hell, the water made life on earth possible."* Myron had the sudden realization that an A.I. robot doesn't require water.

What is the maximum time a person can survive without water? He wasn't sure, but it seemed he remembered reading that three days was generally the longest a person could go without water, although five days were possible for specific humans. The cells run out of water first, meaning no fresh water enters the brain, which begins to die. Bouts of dizziness follow this, and then one loses touch with reality, soon followed by either a coma or stroke. That would be an awful way to die.

So, the body is roughly 60% water, although this varies from 45% to 75%. I'll settle on 60%. That's still a lot of water. Okay, we've got the sun for fire, which is necessary for life. Then we've got the earth, which we also need for life, and of course, we must have water, or neither of the first two have any meaning. A.I.s don't need those things to survive.

Needing a bathroom break, Myron left the fountain for his latrine. Despite having many choices, he opted for the privy he dug on his first day, showcasing his cultured side. As he made his way back to the fountain, he observed steam rising from the rocks he dripped water on earlier. This got Myron thinking about the various forms of water besides liquid. Not that one should discount the fluid we usually associate with water.

As a liquid, water is man's best solvent. Lakes provide fishing, boating, waterskiing, and other sports. Lakes and oceans provide shipping, sightseeing, cruises, and seashell collecting. *Okay Myron, you primarily think about water in its liquid state. But what about the other states?*

Since he observed the steam earlier, Myron was struck with the benefits of steam. The steam engine comes to mind. Used for centuries as the power behind several of man's giant machines, and today steam is used to clean clothes and carpets and cook certain foods. Ice is water. And man, do we use ice? Besides our cocktails, we use ice for entertainment, such as ice skating and ice sculptures. Ice lakes provide a surface for other activities, such as ice boating and festivals. And don't forget about ice cream, shaved ice, and food preservation.

"Oh my God, initially, I couldn't think of one reason for Hokee to put me in water for a day."

As the sun sank behind the Sawtooth mountains, a humbled man emerged from the fountain. Tonight, the clouds, another form of water, provided prisms turning sunlight into orange, red, yellow, and green rays. The entire western sky was a portrait Myron could watch forever. This observation made him think about A.I. and how scenes like tonight's sunset will be meaningless for a machine.

Hurry back Hokee, I need you.

As he had at the end of Myron's previous daily exercises, a grinning Shila accompanied him to the porch where he got dressed, and then man and wolf had an evening meal.

"Shila, ole buddy, thanks for keeping me company," Myron said I will be happy to spend my time with you. I never wanted a pet, but Shila, you have made me rethink that decision. An A.I.'s doesn't need or appreciate pets."

Shila grinned and thumped his tail against Myron's legs.

CHAPTER TWENTY-FIVE

Hokee

Following Akamu's directions, Terilmana drove her van two miles past Fááä when the old guide said, **"Stop!"** The other passengers, Gene, Hokee, and Otahi, looked around to see what attracted Akuma's attention.

Terilmana found a small grassy spot to stop just off the road.

"The banana trucks parked here," Akuma said. "This is where we stole their bananas. I believe the bananas were carried down the trail we see in front of the car. The packing shed must be up that hill someplace."

Hokee left the car to inspect the trail. He returned to the van after briefly examining the trail leading up the mountain. "I don't believe this is the primary access to the packing shed. The path is steep and shows little activity. A few people came down that trail recently, but no one has climbed up that steep gorge."

Akuma thought for a minute before responding. "Well," he spoke softly and didn't seem confident, "I believe we passed another parking spot a little back down around the corner. That may be where the main path to the old shed begins.

Driving back around the corner, Terilmana drove three hundred yards before Akuma said, **"Here!"** practically shouting and pointing off the highway to a small grassy grove. This is where the path climbs the mountain.

Without being asked, Terilmana drove into the grassy grove, where it became apparent that other vehicles had parked in the recent past. Hokee hastily left the van, hurrying towards the trail.

Returning to the van, he remarked, "The trail up this canyon has been walked on by a multitude of people for approximately two or three years." I'm confident that this is where they were holding Opal. I don't believe she is still there, but I want to check out the site."

"Why do you think Opal isn't there?" Gene questioned.

"If the person I am seeking has been in a place, I feel slight subliminal vibrations of that person. If it is someone I met previously, the vibration is stronger. Opal was here, but they moved her somewhere else."

'Okay, can I come with you?"

Sure, but I won't stay up there long. I only want to see if I can learn something about where she is now."

Otahi asked, "Is it okay if I come along too? Terilmana might remain here if she doesn't want to make the climb. That way, she could keep company with Akuma."

"I'll be happy to stay here and let Mr. Akuma protect me from the island's bad guys," she said with a smile. Terilmana felt relieved that no one expected her to climb a stupid mountain to look at something she was not interested in seeing anyway.

Hokee rapidly walked up the trail, trailed by Gene and Otahi. The top housed the converted packing shed, now The New Church of ORO. There were signs and pamphlets with this name stacked on a makeshift pulpit, made with three stacked square wooden boxes painted red and topped with a large square of plywood painted black.

"They held Opal in the cage over in that corner," Hokee said, pointing to the wire cage that had been Opal's prison. Gene and Otahi checked the cage, while Hokee headed to the trail's starting point, the one they checked out earlier from below. He returned to the packing shed shortly and met up with Gene and Otahi.

"The trail we first saw was too steep for climbing, but it would be easy to carry bananas down that canyon to the road or walk a prisoner." The other two men looked at Hokee to continue.

"I saw the tracks of eight or nine people going down the trail within the past half hour." Hokee said. "Opal made one set of tracks wearing padded bindings on her feet."

Neither Gene nor Otahi responded to his comment. Without another word, Hokee began walking back down the hill, trailed by the others towards their bus.

On the bus, Otahi began explaining to Terilmana what they learned from their visit to the church of ORO.

After returning to the bus, Hokee said, "We'll find a message waiting for us at the hotel desk." Addressing Terilmana, Hokee went on, "Could you please take Gene and me back to the Hotel while you and Otahi take Mr. Akuma to his home. We'll brief you on what we have learned when you return. Please don't fret, as nothing will happen for several hours."

Hokee didn't know how much time they had; he only knew it would be several hours from now.

Chapter Twenty-Six

Hokee

Terilmana dropped Hokee and Gene off in the Hilton Hotel Tahiti's portico before taking Akamu to his home in Papenoo. Hokee, followed by Gene, entered the lobby and a staff member quickly guided them to the reception counter. The receptionist was a beautiful island girl wearing a soft-white-blue tailored Mumu decorated with large orange flower petals and with a worried look in her eyes. Before Hokee reached the counter, the frightened young lady picked up the kidnapper's letter lying on the counter and held it out for Hokee to take. Sharing the letter with Gene, they read the Kidnapper's demands together.

When they finished reading the letter, Hokee returned it to the receptionist. Please make a copy of this. After giving a copy to Gene, Hokee led the way to one of the large orange lobby couches in a secluded corner. They sat together, rereading the letter for clues.

We have the bitch everybody is looking for. Have the two million dollars ready by nine p.m. tonight. If you do not have the money, the bitch dies. Enclosed is a lock of her hair to prove this is not a hoax. We will let you know the arrangements for getting the girl as we exchange her for the reward. Don't fuck this up.

"What is your opinion on this demand letter?" Gene asked with worry in his voice.

"I believe they are running scared, Gene. Opal has undoubtedly told them about your family and her father. The kidnappers didn't have any idea what sort of person they grabbed. The two-million-dollar reward must have them rattled."

"Do you think we can get the other million dollars from the House of Bijan before nine p.m.?" a concerned husband asked the shaman.

"There will not be any ransom cash, Gene, but we want the kidnappers to think we are working with a local bank to prepare the money they demanded. I seriously doubt the local bank has that much cash on hand, anyway. Since we don't know what any of the kidnappers look like, it's possible they have someone here in the lobby watching to see what we do. So, let's make sure our actions look authentic."

After thinking for a minute, Hokee said, "Let's talk for a few minutes until Terilmana returns from dropping off Akamu. We'll ask her to drive you to a local bank where you spend a few minutes with the bank manager. You explain what you are doing and get the bank's cooperation to act as though they are preparing the reward money. Have Terilmana drive you someplace to buy a large briefcase, which you will drop off back at the bank. The kidnappers may have someone who works at the bank, so the manager must act like he is serious about counting out the money. Once the bank closes and all the employees leave, the manager will pack newspaper in the briefcase."

Thirty minutes after Gene went with Terilmana to the bank, four intense-looking individuals entered the lobby in a rush disturbing everyone, including Hokee, who was enjoying a brief time-out with a cup of island tea.

The tall, thin man who appeared to be in charge wore a gray suit and starched white shirt with a red and gray striped necktie. His sharp-angled cheekbones gave his already intense demeanor a strict look of, '*Don't fuck with me.*' The man's blond hair was cut in a military flattop, and his cold, menacing gray eyes above a scowling face screamed for attention,

A striking blond lady and two large men dressed like the leader completed the foursome. They all wore the leader's cold, stern look. The lady appeared to be in her early thirties, while the three men seemed to be in their mid-forties. All four newcomers marched up to the receptionist, where the thin man talked with the counter lady, then almost immediately, the four newcomers turned and looked for Hokee. They angrily approached Hokee, who had been watching them with amusement. He realized who the newcomers were from the moment they entered the lobby.

Their leader stopped in front of Hokee. "Give me the letter!" He demands without greetings or pleasantries, just the mandate.

Hokee didn't appreciate their approach or their demand, so he decided to jerk their chains. He wanted to play with their superior attitude. "I'm sorry," he spoke gently with a smile, "were you speaking to me?"

"Yeah, I'm talking to you," yelled the leader. "Give me the letter."

Hokee took his time placing his coffee cup on the side table. "Who are you to come here and make demands?" His voice was soft and unconcerned.

"I'm FBI Special Agent Leon Wortmen in charge of this kidnapping situation. The receptionist told us you have the letter the kidnappers dropped off here in the hotel. Give me the letter." You are obstructing a serious investigation and could face charges unless you immediately comply with my demand."

"Well, Special Agent Wortman, we weren't expected to see you until tomorrow. Are there just the four of you to oversee this operation, or will we be seeing a whole busload of FBI agents and technicians scouring the island for the kidnapped lady?

"Look, mister," Wortman fumed, speaking loud and slow as though talking to a five-year-old, "Give... me... the... damned... letter... or I'll arrest you for obstruction. You are hindering a serious investigation."

Hokee stood and faced the irate agent. "First, Mr. Wortman, on this island, you have no authority to arrest me. You are here at the invitation of the Tahitian government to help locate the kidnappers and save the victim, but you do not have the authority to make those demands or arrest me."

"Second, your manners could use some help. If you had asked me pleasantly for the letter, I would have promptly given it to you with some suggestions if desired. But, when you march over here making demands as though you are God, it makes me resent you and your entire organization."

"Thirdly, you are unaware of the present circumstances or accomplishments, and your conduct is offensive to the only person on this island who possesses a comprehensive understanding of the immediate status. Now, here is the letter you demanded; take it," he said, holding his copy of the letter out for the FBI man. "Now, you stay the hell out of my way." As Hokee finished speaking, he had a fire in his eye while turning around and leaving the lobby.

Wortman grabbed the letter to read the kidnapper's demands.

Chapter Twenty-Seven

Myron

Myron sat on Hokee's porch, stroking Shila's back, thinking about his vision quest. "Your master said I'm not supposed to talk to anybody, Shila, but I don't think he meant you."

Shila thumped his tail on the porch deck as though agreeing with Myron's statement.

"Okay, I see now why Hokee has me getting immersed in Mother Nature. My gosh Shila, here I was feeling so smug about developing this advanced robot, and it could be the end of our civilization."

The wolf ignored this comment, satisfied to rest his stately head on his outstretched paws, giving Myron the wise old dog look.

Fire, earth, and water were the first three elements of life Myron investigated, and he already understood the danger his A.I. development posed for humanity. His machines didn't require those elements which they could destroy, potentially ending human life. Polluted air, water, and soil are not conducive to a healthy biological life. While he still had air and spirit days to experience, his heart was sick with the realization that he might not be able to put the Genie back in the bottle. Would this practically unknown shaman be able to help?

"Oh God, Hokee. I need you." Myron shouted his plea out loud, but only Shila heard his outburst, earning Myron a tongue lick on his troubled face.

CHAPTER TWENTY-EIGHT

Ugla

Ugla was sitting with his back against a coconut tree near Opal when he suddenly called his gang together. "We've got to give the hotel another letter."

"What?" "Why?" Two of the other kidnappers asked simultaneously.

"We don't have a foolproof plan to collect the ransom," he said. "We'll have to make the exchange tomorrow night instead. We don't want to push it too hard today, as making a mistake could be fatal."

"Okay," the other kidnapper chimed in. "Who will we write the new letter, Kahaia? She wrote the last one."

"No," Ugla responded, "one of these other girls. We want different penmanship on the new letter. Any volunteers?" Ugla did not give a reason two different writing styles were required. It was more than likely that he wasn't aware.

Poema, another of the deflowered virgins hoped to be noticed, said, "I'll write the note."

"Great," Ugla responded. "Here's what I want you to write."

Change of plans. Tonight doesn't work. We will make the exchange tomorrow night at 9:00 PM. If you don't want to see the whore gutted, don't rock the boat. We'll update you tomorrow night at nine regarding trade arrangements.

Everyone read the note, and all agreed it was genius.

"All right," Ugla said. "A man should deliver the note this time. Topoa, you're elected to deliver this message. No one knows what you look like but don't do anything to stand out. Please find one of those beggar kids and give him five bucks to deliver this note to the front desk. Promise him another five if he returns without speaking to anyone. Don't be obvious, but make sure the kid delivers the note to the front desk."

"Okay, boss. I'll be careful." Topoa picked up the envelope from Ugla and, waving goodbye, left to deliver the message.

After Topoa left to deliver the message, Ugla called a Council Meeting. He dubbed any gathering with two or more attendees with the grandiose title.

CHAPTER TWENTY-NINE

The FBI

Shortly after Hokee left the lobby, a red and white airport shuttle bus stopped under the Hilton Hotel's oversized portico, unleashing a dozen FBI agents with bags, cartons, and trunks full of special equipment. Watching their arrival and supervising their actions was Special Agent Wortman. Someone located the local police, government leaders, and hotel security, who conferred with Agent Wortman and his staff regarding the situation and their search for the kidnappers. They had little to report since they were unfamiliar with what Hokee was doing.

Wortman sent a team with a local police officer to examine the location where the kidnapping occurred. Another agent was sent to locate Gene Olson for his statement. The lack of Désirée Ines Model Agency personnel to interview was upsetting, but Wortman was unfazed. Setbacks were to be expected, but they would not be a deterrent. Since Gene was unavailable, the tall-thin leader sent another agent to bring Hokee back to the lobby. Since the Indian was collaborating with the husband, he will possess information. Why Gene asked a civilian for help did not please the FBI, but relatives of kidnapped victims rarely made excellent decisions. The sooner they interviewed this unwanted nuisance and got him out of the way, the easier it would be to conduct the search without interference.

The agent searching for Gene returned with the information that the husband will be back in about twenty minutes. Five minutes later, Hokee returned to the lobby, followed by the agent sent to bring him back. A functioning band stage was erected at the back end of the open-air lobby next to the walking path enjoyed by Gene and Opal. Hokee made his way over to the vacant stage and, upon spotting a wandering hotel employee, requested the young man to fetch him a stool. A gent found Hokee relaying the message that Special Agent Wortman wanted him to come and discuss his activities. Hokee responded by asking the agent to inform Special Agent Wortman that he, Hokee, was available to have a discussion whenever the special agent wanted.

A couple of minutes later, the agent returned and told Hokee that Agent Wortman wanted Hokee to come see him for an interview. Hokee instructed the agent to relay to Wortman that if he desires a conversation with Mr. Wolf, he can be found on stage at the back of the lobby. Before the FBI and entourage arrived, the hotel employee brought Hokee a tall stool. Half sitting and half standing, Hokee waited for the mob to arrive. Besides the FBI and the local police, the mob arriving at the stage included several government officials from the mayor to the president of French Polynesia, plus nearly fifty media personnel from around the world drawn by the tantalizing story of a stunningly beautiful woman who was the designer's leading fashion model kidnapped in the vacation paradise of Tahiti. The two-million-dollar reward didn't hurt the public's interest, either.

After holding another discussion with the police and local government officials, Wortman addressed the man on the stage.

"Mr. Wolf. The hotel staff tells me that the kidnapped girl's husband asked you to help find his wife. This kidnapping operation is being run by the FBI, and I am asking you to step aside and let us do our job."

Hokee had a thin smile on his lips, but not his eyes. Talking to the audience but addressing the FBI man, Hokee responded, "Leon, go do your thing. Check out the temple where the lady was kidnapped. Start your island search. Do your FBI things. Go run your operation but," with blazing eyes and the determined look of a warrior, Hokee said in a demanding voice, "STAY OUT OF MY WAY." When he is on a mission, Hokee's eyes appear black like his wolf's, and his fierce warrior countenance suggests pay attention. "I am responsible to the husband and his father for the successful return of Opal. I will handle the kidnapper's demands and arrange for the exchange. Under no circumstances are you to interfere. I will not tolerate interference from any agency or government representative. Things will go much smoother and easier if you stay the hell out of my way."

Agent Wortman, unaccustomed to such an address, was ready to explode at the civilian. However, one look into Hokee's eyes killed any response he had planned. Instead, he ducked his head and turned to his fellow agents.

The FBI huddled alone for about ten minutes; then they conferred with the entire contingent of police officers and government officials. It looked like they reached some kind of decision.

"Mr. Wolf," Wortman began speaking sternly but with a more respectful tone, "we have just been informed about your investigation and understand you have made significant progress. As you represent the husband who offered the reward and appear to understand the situation, please tell us who you are and why we should allow you to continue your activities."

Hokee's response was accompanied by a hint of a smile in his eyes. "I am a private investigator from Pocatello, Idaho, in the United States. The Olsons have used my services in the past, and I consider them family. My foremost business profession is finding and retrieving the missing. My formal training was at the side of a Blackfoot medicine man on an Indian reservation. The Olsons hired me because they knew I would bring Opal home safely. That is my business; that is why I am here, and I will not tolerate officious, meddlesome interference." Hokee paused a moment, allowing them to see his eyes.

"Things will be smoother and easier if you stay out of my way. I could use some police and FBI help if offered, but it will not be required." Hokee intentionally didn't mention Wortman's statement about 'allowing him,' to continue with his activities.

After making eye contact with the other leaders, Wortman addressed Hokee. And like Hokee, he also did not mention his earlier comment about 'allowing him' to proceed. "What could we do to help *you*, Mr. Wolf?" Wortman had a sneer in his voice but seemed ready to offer help.

"Nothing needs to be done now. We know where the kidnappers held Opal until an hour ago and suspect they are currently holding her nearby for the ransom exchange. In a few minutes, I will cover the activities we will undertake. I'm waiting for a word from the bank before proceeding. Please hold yourselves ready to assist, and you can recall the FBI agents and police officers you sent to the temple where the kidnapping occurred. Nothing can be learned from that site. If you wish to examine the location where Opal has been held, I will prepare a map, but that exercise will also be a dry hole. The kidnappers left no clues behind suggesting their present location. When they left their so-called church an hour ago, Opal was walking unaided."

Wortman held a brief conference with the other leaders by the FBI and police officers, then asked Hokee, "Where would you like to hold our management and planning meetings? This open lobby is not secure as you mentioned."

Hokee looked over the large audience in front of the stage. "Is there anyone here who can speak for the Hotel in this audience?"

A fiftyish man dressed in white like Mr. Roarke from Fantasy Island raised his hand and worked his way toward the front of the crowd. He had dark brown curly hair, a body like Tom Cruise, and a face like Val Kilmer. "I'm Valu Kahale, the hotel manager. How can I help?"

"Mr. Kahale, does this hotel have a private conference room?" Hokee asked.

"Why yes. We have a beautiful room overlooking the swimming pool with audio and video conference capabilities," Valu beamed, and his chest expanded as he described this room to Hokee.

"Would you make sure the room is vacant and please show us the way?"

"I'm not sure about the status, but if it is in use, we will boot them out. Follow me."

"Okay, thanks, Mr. Kahale. I would like the FBI, the Papeete mayor, and the Commissariat de Police to join me in the hotel conference room." As Hokee stepped down from the stage, Gene entered the lobby, followed by

Terilmana and her husband, Otahi. Hokee saw Gene enter, so he waited for him to wade through the throng before following Valu to the conference room. By the time Gene and Hokee met, the hotel receptionist came rushing through the crowd, yelling excitedly while waving a sheet of paper.

"Mr. Wolf... Mr. Wolf, we just got another kidnap letter."

CHAPTER THIRTY

Ugla

Standing up from the coconut palm tree he had been leaning against, Ugla spoke to his fellow kidnappers. "Let's get away from this bitch to do our planning," he said, waving his arm in Opal's direction. "There's a little clearing up this canyon a few dozen meters. Let's go there. "Koa," he said, pointing to one of the kidnappers, "stay here and watch the slut. Yell if you see anyone coming."

Leading the way, Ugla walked for about five minutes before coming to an open grassy area about the size of the average living room. Plopping down next to a thirty-foot Casuarina tree full of purple male flowers, he waved for his helpers to sit on the ground in front. "All right then," he began with a smile for the females vying for his attention, "we need to discuss our plans for tomorrow night." The young girls who received the smile almost swooned at being recognized by the handsome, charismatic leader.

"We are certain that the leaders searching for the slut and paying the ransom will attempt a double-cross. We must make sure they fail. How do we do that?" Ugla asked as he smiled at his small flock and seemed relaxed.

They exchanged glances, searching for a face with an idea. The faces all remained blank, or at least confused and uncertain.

"At nine o'clock tomorrow night, there will be no moon. It won't come up until after ten. That means at nine, it will be dark out on the bay. The bitch will be tied up, standing in a kayak three hundred feet from the shore in front of the hotel. Only when the shore's spotlight turns towards her will she be visible. We will wrap her in a blanket so she can stay warm and so everyone on shore can see that we have treated her well. If she appears in the Kayak half-naked, the good folks will get themselves all pissed off. It will go smoother if we don't aggravate their desire for revenge." Here he paused for a minute but didn't smile. Still, it was plain to see he was enjoying himself.

Two men with snorkels will be in the water, one on each side of the kayak. These men will be barely visible from the shore and will never reveal their faces. They will watch what is happening on shore. If they see a red-light waving, they will tip the kayak over, dumping the bitch in the ocean.. The men will swim back to the pickup location on the beach, about half-a-mile north of the hotel. If the men see a green light waving, that means we have checked the money, and we will take the next step. The men in the water will sit the slut down and give the kayak a big shove toward the hotel shore. The kayak should glide all the way to the hotel. After the Kayak is on its way, our water boys will swim to the pickup spot."

Ugla stopped talking for a minute to allow everyone a chance to process the information. "Now, we must plan the next steps with great care. Before waving the green light for the men in the water to swim away, we must get the money away safely and arrange our disappearance. I have a few ideas, but let's hear some of your suggestions first.

The followers looked at each other to see if one of them had any ideas. Ugla shook his head at the silence that followed.

CHAPTER THIRTY-ONE

Myron

The fourth day began with Myron sleeping in. He had tossed all night, wrestling with his conscience and praying that Hokee could help solve his problems. Around the time the sun lit up the peaks of the Sawtooth Mountains to the north, he finally fell into an exhausted, troubling sleep. At nine, Shila crept into Myron's tent and laid his head on the sleeping man's legs. Myron was startled awake, and when he realized it was only the wolf, he dropped back on his air mattress with a groan.

In what Myron thought was purely a coincidence, Shila started tapping his paw on Myron's stomach.

"Okay," he growled, "I'm getting up. Get off me." Myron meant to sound friendly and not demanding, but he was still groggy and not thinking well.

Instead of heading to the shower by the sweat lodge, he undressed and splashed in the fountain, where he spent considerable time yesterday. The icy cold water shocked him into full consciousness. While toweling, Myron started talking to Shila, who was sitting back on his two hind legs with his straight front legs holding his head and shoulders high. A grin on his handsome face. "So, you got me up," he said to a smiling wolf, " Was that what Hokee told you to do if I slept in?"

Shila thumped his tail on the ground.

"You are as smart as you look, Shila."

Shila just grinned and thumped his tail.

Myron had an oatmeal breakfast with some strawberries. He worked on his lists, then did the fire ceremony. The moment arrived for him to confront the air. For the life of him, he couldn't imagine what he was going to do all day with air. Hokee suggested that for his air day, Myron might want to walk up to the driveway to the lava plain, find a rock, and study the air.

"Hey Shila, want to walk with me up to the lava plain?" He was startled to realize how much he enjoyed the wolf's company. '*And I started out afraid of Shila. What a change,*' he thought. Grabbing a bottle of water, he started up the long driveway and had to smile when Shila bounded past him toward the rim.

He only walked a short distance down Hokee's ten-mile-long driveway when he found a large black lava rock with a flat top. Plopping his butt on the rock, Myron shut his eyes and felt the subtle breeze as it played with his mop of sandy hair.

After a few minutes, he felt Shila return and sit by his feet. "Well, buddy," he started, speaking to the wolf, "what do you make of this air business?" Myron's eyes opened, but Shila paid him no mind. The wolf was focused on something in the distance, a vast, dark plain that stretched beyond sight. With Shila occupied by something Myron couldn't see; he decided to study the air.

He knew air is mostly nitrogen, with over twenty percent oxygen. Myron took chemistry classes, but his focus was primarily on computers, their design, and programming. After studying air in his mind, Myron remembered that besides oxygen, we also needed nitrogen to live. The development of our DNA involves nitrogen, and without DNA, we wouldn't be alive.

'So, okay, our bodies need air, but what else is the value of air?' Well, Myron reasoned, in the winter, we need air circulation to help heat our houses. Air provides a home for clouds and helps move them around in the sky. Clouds then provide rain. Airplanes need air to fly; air gives fires the oxygen they need to burn and turns wind turbines, creating electricity. Our hearing requires air to carry sound vibrations, which stimulate our eardrums, sending signals to our brains. Air carries scents to our nostrils, which is another of our prime senses.

"Shila," Myron said, getting the wolf's attention, "this air business your master has me experiencing is like the "other elements I've studied; we animals need air, but my AIs, not so much. Let's go make a kite and play with the air. Okay?"

With a big smile, Shila began jumping in excitement. He was familiar with the word PLAY.

CHAPTER THIRTY-TWO

Hokee

Hokee read the letter with Gene, then handed it back to the receptionist, asked her to please make ten copies. Wortman was unhappy to be second fiddle, but Hokee was clearly in charge. "Well, Mr. Wolf," he said in a condescending tone, "what does the letter say?"

"The kidnappers want to do the exchange tomorrow night instead of tonight." Hokee ignored the tone in Wortman's voice. "There are some interesting nuances in the letter. When our receptionist returns with the copies, we'll hand them out and follow Valu to the conference room."

Hokee and Gene joined the invited participants in the conference room five minutes later. Hokee took the floor, "Read the letter, then let's talk about what is going on."

Change of plans. Tonight, doesn't work. We will make the exchange tomorrow night at 9:00 PM. If you don't want to see the whore gutted, don't rock the boat. We'll update you tomorrow night at nine regarding trade arrangements.

It was a colorful assembly in that conference room. Wortman and the FBI agents wore conservative blue suits, white shirts, and neckties. The Papeete mayor, Puati Wong, wore a brilliant yellow, short-sleeved shirt with white seashell buttons, long-legged red trousers, and brown leather open-toed sandals. Their Commissariat de Police, Mr. Tane Richmond, wore a dark blue long-sleeved shirt and white tie with black pants and shoes. Valu Kahale, the handsome hotel manager who stayed after leading the group to the room, was in an all-white linen suit, white shoes, and a pink necktie. Gene wore a hibiscus-flowered Hawaiian shirt, red shorts, and dirty, grass-stained, white leather sandals. Hokee was in the same clothes he wore back in Pocatello, a black V-neck tee shirt, black denim pants, and brown leather moccasins. A white leather headband held his black shoulder-length hair in place.

Hokee said, "Let me begin by telling you what I think is happening and what actions I believe we should take. I would then like you all to comment freely and make suggestions."

"Why are they delaying the exchange for twenty-four hours?" Hokee asked, but didn't want or expect anyone to respond. All he wanted was for them to consider the question.

"I believe they realized the difficulty in planning a successful exchange of their prisoner for the money. They want the reward money but know they won't take possession of it until we get the girl. And the girl must not be harmed. That is a big problem." Hokee paused for them to consider the problem.

"What are their options?" Hokee asked, but again, he didn't expect an answer.

"If they bring Opal in a car, where could they put her in a vehicle without being caught? The police will block all roads near the hotel starting at about six tomorrow night." He glanced at the police chief, Commissariat Richmond, to see if he concurred.

"Yes. I believe that would be wise. We could use some help from the FBI."

Wortman nodded his head. "We'll provide all the support you want, chief." Like Hokee, he wasn't much into island politics. The pronunciation of Commissariat was not part of his PC training.

"That just leaves the water. They can't put her in the air. I think they will put Opal in a boat three or four hundred feet out in the bay. With no moon until after ten, it will be dark, and Opal will only be visible in a powerful spotlight. The kidnappers will not release the boat with Opal until they have inspected the money and are ready with their planned exit. Looking at their last letter, the phrase, 'don't rock the boat' is telling.' Why that wording? If my hypothesis about the water is correct, that was a subliminal message. They intended the threat to be read as 'don't make any trouble.' They were thinking about putting Opal on a boat, so the language slipped out. Does anyone have other ideas?"

The room erupted in several conversations with FBI agents talking to each other; Wortman huddled with Richman, and Mayor Wong engaged Kahale, the hotel manager, in a spirited conversation. Ideas were tossed around the table and abandoned. After a lengthy five minutes of considering and dismissing other options, Wortman spoke up on behalf of the group. "The water option is their best hope to make a secure exchange. Opal in the boat and the money here on shore. What are your thoughts about how to proceed?"

Hokee looked over the group, assessing their reaction to the plan he was about to propose, but first, he continued with his speculation. One or more kidnappers must be on shore to inspect the money. Then the kidnappers must get the money somewhere safe before releasing Opal. Her safety will be most at risk during that time. My guess is they will have Opal tied up in the boat with someone there to tip the boat over and drown Opal if we interfere with the money. Given all the situational constraints, I don't see them making other arrangements, do you?"

When no one responded, Hokee laid out his plans. Like many plans, it went to hell immediately. Discovering that would take officials some time.

CHAPTER THIRTY-THREE

Gene

Gene had been quiet since entering the conference room, but after Hokee laid out his plan, Gene asked to speak with him alone.

Hokee had Gene take him to his room so the two could be alone. There was nothing for either of them to do tonight. Gene began, "You didn't explain what we do with Opal once the boat hits the shore. How certain are you about the water-based exchange?

"I don't want anybody else to know our final plans, Gene. I'll tell you what I think we should do, but first, to answer your question. What I have felt and seen about the kidnappers from my sojourn in your sauna, the boat, and the water are both somehow involved. Are my conjectures accurate? I have no idea. The actions I proposed in the conference room are my best guesses about how the kidnappers will arrange the exchange. I want the FBI and local authorities to follow the plan I proposed. Do you have other ideas?"

"No, I'm only interested in understanding your strategy when Opal makes it to the shore."

"Gene, I haven't told the others that there will be no money in the briefcase you will be carrying. There will be no money exchange. However, everyone must believe the exchange is real, so when you leave the bank, you must behave as though the briefcase is full of money. Only you, the banker, and I will be aware of the briefcase's true nature. Did you make arrangements with the bank?"

"I have. The bank manager is fully on board."

'Okay, that's great. When you pick it up tomorrow night, everyone in the bank will believe the briefcase holds the ransom money. We don't know if the kidnappers have anyone in the bank or here in the hotel lobby, so the police and FBI must believe we will pay the ransom. The only way we can succeed is to make everyone else believe the exchange will be real."

"God Hokee. What if you're wrong?"

"I promise you that nothing bad will happen to Opal that hasn't already happened. The kidnappers cannot afford to do any permanent damage. Our large ransom offered almost immediately has them rattled. They have got to be wondering who this woman is they have kidnapped. Why was a large reward offered almost immediately? I'm also sure that Opal has been feeding them stories about you, your dad, maybe me, and probably her father. At this point, the kidnappers are aware that they have captured someone incredibly important and that if any harm comes to Opal, there is nowhere in this world where they can find refuge. Their only option at this point is to exchange her for the ransom. I want everyone involved to believe the exchange will be real. The bank manager is the only other individual permitted to have knowledge that the briefcase will contain newspapers.

"Opal is my life, Hokee. I want her back safe and the bastards who kidnapped her punished."

"It is only appropriate that you be the one to rescue Opal and whisk her to safety Gene. This is how we'll make it happen.

CHAPTER THIRTY-FOUR

The Plan

Later that night, Hokee had Gene and the hotel arrange another sauna session for him. He gave Gene more roots and leaves for fusion while he meditated alone in the hot tub. After Gene brought him the herb potion, Hokee spent three hours in the sauna communing with his spirit guides. He then crashed in Gene's second bedroom until late the next morning. By the time Hokee finished breakfast at about ten, those government officials in charge of organizing the kidnapper program, like road closures, the spotlights, and the money transfer, were having fits getting everybody's cooperation.

The city refused to close the streets, even briefly. While most tourists fled the island, those staying, plus the city inhabitants, wanted the roads open. Tahiti is supposed to be vacation heaven. Businesses wanted traffic for business. The few remaining tourists wanted to shop and roam around the city, and residents didn't want to be inconvenienced. In Papeete, road closures were not on the agenda.

Gene was having trouble at the airport. Hokee wanted to have the Olson jet airplane parked by the departure lounge for thirty minutes to an hour starting at nine p.m. Twelve airlines service Papeete Airport with three scheduled departures and two arrivals after nine p.m., so the airport controllers would not allow Gene his parking spot.

Since this was Sunday, banks were normally closed. The Tahiti Island Bank was no exception. No matter who called the bank president, he was unavailable. As the morning grew old, government officials were panicking. This was the bank that was supposed to provide the ransom money. Hokee had not shared his ransom exchange plans with them, and Gene alone knew how to contact the bank president.

Traffic control was planned and agreed upon by the police and FBI; however, absent Hokee, all parties were wrangling about road closures and the hostage-for-ransom exchange.

After finishing breakfast, Hoke asked the server to inform the hotel manager to call everyone involved in the kidnapping back to the conference room. Hokee stood at the table's end as everyone found the seats they used yesterday.

Like yesterday, it was a colorful assembly. The hotel manager, Valu Kahale, stood out in his all-white Mr. Roarke assembly; Papeete mayor Puati Wong's royal blue silk shirt patterned with white hibiscus blossoms was a brilliant contrast.

Commissariat de Police, Mr. Tane Richmond, looked almost casual in a red short-sleeved Polo shirt. Puati Wong, the Papeete mayor, wore a neon green short-sleeved button-up shirt with pearl buttons. The FBI men ditched their jackets, wearing short-sleeved white shirts and black neckties as the female FBI agent, Carole Mendenhall, broke a hundred-year-old FBI tradition by wearing a flowery blue and yellow silk pantsuit. Carole didn't think the dress code mattered because they weren't in the U.S.A., and no one in Tahiti cared about her appearance. Besides, she told herself, if she didn't look like an FBI agent, she could freely mingle and perhaps pick up some useful information. Gene was in a sober blue V-neck T-shirt, while Hokee looked the same, although refreshed. It's wonders what a decent sleep and a substantial breakfast will do for a person. Everyone saw and felt Hokee's intense energy that radiated like hot sunlight filling the room. Supreme confidence radiated from every cell in his body.

Hokee waited until everyone stopped talking before beginning. Looking at both FBI Special Agent Wortman and Tane Richmond, the

Commissariat de Police, he asked, "Have the police and FBI agreed upon road closure assignments?"

It was Richmond who responded. "We have agreed upon our allocation of manpower but are having problems with the road closures. There is considerable pushback from many sources."

With no hesitation, Hokee said, "Forget about the closure. Providing manpower at key intersections to control traffic and identify vehicle occupants is all that is required. Have the police and the FBI identified the individuals belonging to that church we discovered?"

Agent Wortman responded. "The church is called 'The New Oro,' and its leader is Ugla Hendrixson. We have pictures of Mr. Hendrixson and several of his followers. Copies have been made and will be given to all personnel assigned to control the intersection. That should accomplish the desired goal of forcing the kidnappers to use the water."

"Okay," Hokee continued, "the kidnappers will have Opal in a boat, out in the bay, several hundred feet from the hotel." Hokee spoke with the confidence of someone who sat in on the kidnapper's planning session. No one questioned this quiet pronouncement. He continued with the same confidence, "Their leader, whom you identified as Ugla Hendrixson, will come to the hotel lobby at nine o'clock, as promised in his note, to handle the money for the hostage exchange. I want the Commissariat de Police, Mr. Tane Richmond, to be our representative."

"But I don't know any of the exchange plans," Richmond complained.

"I am now going to walk you through this evening's plans." Hokee cracked his first small smile. It appears like he was smiling at his audience, which he was, but also because the ending was going to be shocking.

CHAPTER THIRTY-FIVE

The Kidnappers

Ugla was disappointed but not surprised that no one else had suggestions for the money exchange. They were followers.

"We need to steal a kayak with an outrigger. I want Tane and Hina to take our white van several miles past the airport up near Tata'a to find a kayak. We can't afford to steal one any closer. The men must get the kayak around seven-thirty after it's good and dark, then meet us at the AUAE beach by eight thirty, where we will hold the slut." Like the rest of his gang, Ugla could not wait for this mess to end.

"Topoa, you and Kana have the best snorkeling gear, so you will be the ones in the water with the slut. She is our ticket off this island, so your tasks are critical. I will enter the hotel and begin negotiations to get our reward and give them the bitch. Now for the girls."

"Melia, you and Onaona will go to Arue and rent a boat big enough to hold twenty people. The rest of us will join you between nine thirty and ten o'clock. Uhila and Vala will stay close to the hotel with the rest of the girls to count the money. Once they produce the money and its counted, I'll join you while signaling Topoa and Kana to send the kayak toward the hotel, when we're safely away. While everybody is waiting for her boat to reach the shore, we'll sneak off with the money and be off to Arue."

Kana, the brightest one, asked, "What if the money count is not correct?"

"No problem, I'll signal you to dump the whore in the ocean, and then you and Topoa will swim to safety. Probably back to this site. The two of you and the girls in Arue will be safely away from the areas of interest. The rest of us may have to fight and could be killed. However, don't anybody panic. I'm sure the officials will not risk the woman's life by giving us less than the full two million."

Surprised there was a possibility of being killed, Uhila balked at staying behind to count the money. "Hey boss, how about me trading places with Tane after he steals the kayak?"

"What's the matter, Uhila, afraid of dying? I'll be there counting the money right with you." The handsome leader had a smile on his face, closely resembling a sneer.

"Does anybody have a question?" Ugla scanned the group, searching for any frowns. Almost everybody either smiled at him or seemed comatose. With a forced smile and attempting a cheerful voice, he said, "Let's go get the money."

CHAPTER THIRTY-SIX

Myron

Myron had never built a kite but thought, how hard can it be? A few sticks, we've got plenty of those. Paper? I've got my writing pads. So okay, it'll be a small kite. String? Oh, that could be a killer. I have a blanket, shirts, and can make a string. I need string to tie the sticks together, anyway. Anything else? No, that about does... oh shit! How do I stick the paper to the sticks? No glue. No tape.

Myron considered raiding Hokee's house, where he was sure there would be both glue and tape. Hokee never invited Myron inside, which made him wonder if the house was forbidden. No, it was only his honor. Nothing stood in his way. The house was not locked. But his quest included nothing in Hokee's house. He even had to sleep outside. To enter the house meant leaving his vision quest. That couldn't be faked or rationalized. His honor and desperate plight to save himself made him drop the kite idea. He needed this vision quest.

"Well, Shila ole boy, I'm afraid the kite is out. Let's play chase. I'll run, and you chase me; then you run, and I'll chase you. Okay?" And Myron started running.

Hokee never ran on his long driveway, although he often walked it in all seasons of the year. Small rocks on the road are not a problem when walking.

Unfortunately, or perhaps fortunately, a small rock changed the shape of Myron's quest.

He started out running slow, then gradually built-up speed until he was running full out and loving every second. Taking a quick look behind to check if Shila was pursuing him, he failed to notice the small rock beneath his foot, throwing him into a lava field where his momentum propelled him several feet across the rough black terrain. He finally stopped, turned around, and grinned at Shila back on the driveway as though saying, *yeah, that was stupid,* and in his next step Myron's right foot crashed through one of the thin lava bubbles.

Fortunately, it was a small bubble, only twenty-eight inches deep, and Myron's leg fell in slightly above his knee, but going down, a jagged lava edge tore a long hole in his calf muscle almost from his heel to his knee. He landed on his face against the rough lava bed, which cut a gash above his left eye. Bloody and dazed, in his head, he heard Hokee say, *"Once your quest begins, everything that happens for the next ten days will involve your experience. Everything that happens has meaning and relates to the answers you are seeking."*

"Damn," he said, looking up at Shila. "What's this fucking lesson?" As these words left his mouth in his head, he heard the words *focus and concentration.* He wasn't sure if someone spoke or if he imagined the sound, but it caused him to think about Hokee and wonder where he was. Hokee warned him he would be left alone for a few days.

It took all of Myron's concentration to get his leg out of the hole without tearing more skin or muscles. With blood falling in his eye and filling his shoe, Myron crawled across the jagged lava to the driveway, dragging his right leg. He pulled his t-shirt off, tearing it into strips, and used one to wipe blood away from his eye. Only then did he dare to glance at his leg. A long-jagged tear in his skin and muscles looked horrid, with blood flowing onto the gravel driveway. Using the strips from his shirt, Myron, wincing in pain, wrapped his calf several times, pulling the wrap tight to halt the bleeding. Blood kept running into his eye, so he wrapped the last shirt strip around his head to stop that bleeding. Only then did he consider the problem of getting back to his tent and the first aid kit Hokee had given him, 'just in case.'

He couldn't crawl back to his tent; it was too far. His hands hurt. The pain in his head made him dizzy, and his leg throbbed. He searched for a suitable crutch, but found nothing long enough. No one ever drove down Hokee's driveway, so there would be no one coming to his rescue. Now how in the hell was he going to get back to his tent? He pushed himself up onto his knees, nearly crying from the pain. Waiting for the pain to subside, he once again heard Hokee speaking in his head, *"everything that happens has meaning and relates to the answers you are seeking."*

Surely, he was not meant to spend a day or two lying on the hot driveway waiting for help. Without a shirt, his skin will sunburn, and without water, his mouth and throat will swell up, making it impossible to swallow. *Everything has meaning.*

"Okay, Shila," Myron groaned. "Come over and help me stand up?"

Without another prompt, the wolf came over and stood quietly by his side. Myron could swear he saw sympathy in the Shila's eyes.

"Okay, boy, don't let me fall over," Myron said, grabbing a handful of long hair on Shila's back and using it to help him stand, putting a lot of weight on the wolf's back as he stood up. His head was still ringing, but he was no longer dizzy. Using the wolf as a crutch, Myron made his way back to his tent and found salvation.

"Thanks, Shila," he said with pure adoration. "You are one smart friend. I may have to fight with your master when he returns to let me possess you. You are the most surprising part of my vision quest."

Myron drank water for what seemed like an hour before beginning to doctor himself. As he worked on his leg, Myron wondered what the lessons were from this experience. *Everything has meaning.*

CHAPTER THIRTY-SEVEN

Hokee and Gene

Hokee next provided everyone with the details of his plan, feeling resistance from almost everybody in the room except Gene, who knew the actual plan. "Gene will pick up the ransom money twenty minutes before nine o'clock. He will bring the money in a briefcase to the hotel lobby and give it to Mr. Tane Richmond, who will be our negotiator for the return of Opal."

There were mummers of dissent, but Hokee ignored the squabbling. "We expect mister Ugla Hendrixson to be in attendance for the negotiations. No one will do anything until Hendrixson produces Opal; at the very least, we must see her and know she is safe and will be delivered unharmed after Hendrixson is happy with the money and believes his plan to escape is intact."

"What happens after Ugla gets the money?" Wortman asked.

"I expect there will be other kidnappers in the lobby who will count it and verify there are no tricks like hidden trackers. They will undoubtedly ditch the briefcase, believing it to have a hidden transmitter. Once they are satisfied with the ransom, someone will call Ugla with an all-clear message. The counters will take the money to Ugla who will signal him men to release Opal, sending the boat with her to the shore, where we will be waiting. Ugla and the other kidnappers will leave as Opal is coming toward the shore. He will not expect any action from us until we verify that Opal is uninjured and alive."

"If the money and kidnappers are somewhere out of our control, how are we going to capture them?" This question is from Puati Wong, the mayor.

"Mr. Wortman will have FBI agents hiding along every highway. The kidnappers will not feel safe anyplace close to the hotel or Papeete. With three or four FBI agents spaced three or four miles apart along every route the kidnappers will take driving to a spot where they feel safe. Probably someplace along the shore where they have a boat stashed to escape the island. The FBI agents will be able to find out where they stop."

"What about Ugla?" asked Carole Mendenhall, the female FBI agent.

"He will join his companions where they feel safe. When they are all together, you and your mates will move in and make the arrests."

"How will Gene get the ransom money from the bank?" asked the finely dressed hotel boss It is closed today, and no one has found the bank manager, Valu Kahale.

Without hesitation, Gene responded, "Mr. Kahale, I have been in touch with the manager, and he has agreed to meet me at the specified time. The ransom money is already counted and in a briefcase, ready to be picked up."

Being informed that Opal's husband had been in contact with the bank manager while everyone else anxiously searched for him without success didn't sit well with the group. In their thoughts, they were aware that it was his wife who had been kidnapped, and he was under a lot of stress, but concealing his relationship with the bank manager while they were experiencing anxious episodes was still unacceptable.

Gene and Hokee both felt the group's silent anger but ignored it.

With a quick look at Special Agent Wortman, Hokee asked, "Do you have enough personnel to police the roads?"

"No, we want to have agents here in the lobby to monitor the situation and ensure we retrieve Opal safely, but Chief Richmond, the Commissariat de Police, has provided me with enough police officers to watch the roads and help us find the kidnapper's escape spot."

"I think that about covers it. Are there any more questions?" The group was silent, and Hokee wondered why no one asked what he would be doing. He had a brilliant Wolf answer ready that would satisfy the question while saying nothing.

CHAPTER THIRTY-EIGHT

Going home

At seven-thirty, six selected FBI agents and 10 police officers left the Hilton Hotel Tahiti to locate their hiding spots along the highways. They left one at a time at discrete intervals so the kidnapper's spies would not be suspicious. By eight o'clock, the mayor and governor joined Special Agent Wortman and police Commissariat Tane Richmond in the hotel lobby, waiting for the kidnappers to show up and begin negotiations for the release of Opal. Gene left the bank at eight-thirty with a briefcase full of money in case the kidnappers were watching. Conspicuously absent was Hokee Wolf, although no one seemed to notice. Satisfied that the ransom money was now in the hotel lobby, Ugla Hendrixson, dressed in white denim pants and a flowery Hawaiian-style shirt, entered the lobby at nine p.m. Movie star handsome, he looked about as unlikely a kidnapper as Shirley Temple Black.

Just after dark, wearing a swimsuit and scuba gear, Hokee swam out in the bay, waiting for the kidnappers and Opal to arrive. If Hokee was wrong in his assumptions about the kidnapper's plans, he was going to look ridiculous while risking Opal's life. Only Gene was aware of Hokee's success in the sauna, which eliminated the risks. Tane Richmond met Ugla to begin the negotiations.

While Richmond was conversing with Ugla, Gene slipped out of the lobby and crossed to the shore. He held a flashlight with a blue lens, which he turned on and waved. Two senior police officers employed by Hokee handcuffed Ugla, placing him under arrest for kidnapping Opal Olson. Pandemonium erupted with government officials, including Wortman and Richmond, yelling at the two officers to release Ugla immediately.

Hokee waited for the kidnappers ten feet below the ocean's surface. He was uncertain about the distance they would hold Opal out into the bay, but it would have to be in a direct line of sight from the hotel. This uncertainty had Hokee swiveling his head, looking up at the ocean's surface, watching for a boat and the kidnappers. When he finally spotted two men wearing swim flippers and snorkeling gear a few yards to his left and on the surface, Hokee took his first relaxed breath in several hours. From his vantage point, Hokee could not tell exactly what kind of vessel the kidnappers were escorting, but the boat had narrow pontoons. *More than likely a canoe or kayak,* he thought. Hokee surfaced thirty feet behind the kidnappers, waiting for Gene's signal before beginning his rescue of Opal.

When he saw the rotating blue light, Hokee swam underwater to one side of the boat and then stabbed the man holding onto the kayak in his thigh with a hypodermic syringe full of a powerful homemade tranquilizer. Grabbing a rope tied around his waist with a slipknot, Hokee lifted the kidnapper's head above the water and then tied him to one of the kayak's outriggers. He repeated this same maneuver with the other male kidnapper, tying him to the other outrigger.

Opal was standing precariously in the kayak when Hokee surfaced and helped her sit down. Cautioning her to be silent, Hokee began pushing the kayak with its prisoner and two unconscious kidnappers towards Gene and the shore. When he was close enough with the kayak's momentum to carry it the rest of the way to the shore, dragging the kidnappers, Hokee ducked back under the water's surface and swam a few hundred yards up the beach toward the airport.

Opal was still wrapped in her blanket when the kayak reached shore. Gene immediately bundled her in his arms, carrying his sobbing wife to a conveniently waiting limousine. They stopped along the highway to pick up Hokee on their way to the airport and Olson's private jet. While airport controllers would not allow the plane to be parked at the terminal, they allowed it to stand by on the apron. Olson's pilots started the jet engines burning hi-octane fuel at precisely nine p.m. When the limousine arrived a few minutes later, Gene and Hokee hurried to get Opal aboard and the plane started moving towards the runway before airport officials could prevent the plane from departing.

Back at the hotel, Wortman and Richmond were fuming with righteous anger. They had no victim to question, no anxious husband, and no Hokee to answer for their actions. With Ugla in restraints and the two kidnappers tied to the kayak's outriggers in custody, they believed it was only a matter of time before they apprehend the other kidnappers. When they finally discovered the briefcase was only full of newspapers, the outraged *officials* would have gladly cut the Indian's throat if they could have found him.

On board their airplane, Gene carried Opal to the rear bedroom where they could have privacy for their reunion. Tired from his recent activities, Hokee grabbed a blanket and sacked out on a couch in the main cabin.

When the plane touched down in Boise, Hokee was out of the plane and into the lounge before Gene or Opal emerged from the rear cabin. Having been called by Gene during the ride home, Grant was waiting for them in the airport lounge. Hokee and Grant shook hands, but before Grant could get all emotional, Hokee excused himself for a minute. Exiting by the side door, Hokee grabbed a taxi and headed for home before anyone could detain him. Hokee knew Grant, and his grateful son, and a stunned wife, would insist on a proper reception and emotional show of gratitude lasting several minutes, after which they will insist on dinner and drinks. Hokee knew they would forgive him for ducking out. He had the taxi driver take the four-hour drive south to the Pocatello airport and his Explorer.

He was concerned about Myron, having experienced a dream where Myron was covered in blood. He was injured and in pain, his face distorted by fear.

It was time to check in on his frightened guest.

Chapter Thirty-Nine

Myron's Vision Quest Explodes

It was early evening when Hokee drove toward the driveway slope leading down to his house and Myron's tent. Shila heard the car several minutes before it arrived with Hokee and was waiting for him at the head of the slope. Hokee stopped the Explorer and opened the door as Shila stood on his back legs, putting his front legs on Hokee's thigh and licking his face with a big smile and bright, happy eyes.

"Okay, big boy, I'm happy to see you too."

Shila jumped over Hokee into the passenger's seat and rode with him down the driveway to the house. Before going into his house, Hokee looked for Myron, as it was still daylight. Not seeing him, Hokee walked over to his tent.

Moving the flap aside, Hokee looked inside. One look at the bloody bandages on Myron's leg and head Hokee had him break his vow of silence. "Myron, what happened? I am aware you're not supposed to speak for a few more days, but given the circumstances, talk."

"Oh Hokee. My God, but I'm glad you are here. I've been wondering if you forgot about me?"

"You were told you would be alone for a while; what did you do to your body? Allow me to examine your injuries while you explain what happened."

Then, seeing the gash in Myron's leg, Hokee spoke before Myron could respond, "I see you fell into a lava hole."

"Carelessness and lack of focus. I think those are the lessons," Myron replied in a groan. "Although I'm unsure how they relate to my quest." While saying this, Myron pulled the wrap from his head so Hokee could see what was required in the way of a proper dressing and bandage.

"We will address the lessons later. It looks like you have treated the wound proficiently. Ordinarily, I would insist on taking you to an emergency clinic and having your leg stitched up; otherwise, you will carry a nasty scar, but that would destroy your vision quest. You must decide."

"Hokee, if nothing else, the past few days have shown my absolute need for this quest."

"Alright then. Are you in much pain?"

"I took some aspirin which helps but doesn't take it away."

"I have something in the house which will numb the pain and not interfere with your concentration. Did you use a disinfectant on your wound?"

"There was some disinfectant gel in my first aid kit."

"Gel is good for many skin abrasions, but not a deep gouge and tear. I have a better disinfectant, a spray. Would you like an alcoholic beverage?"

"Will it interfere with my vision quest?"

"Under the circumstances, I think that is exactly what you need. Let me get the pain meds and disinfectants, some more bandages and your drink. Be right back."

Hokee backed out of the tent, and followed by Shila went into his house. After getting the supplies for Myron, he fixed himself a straight scotch and grabbed a beer for Myron on the way out. Back in the tent, he gave Myron the beer and a capsule for his pain. Hokee sprayed the leg injury with a disinfectant and topical pain reliever, then wrapped it in a clean bandage before asking, "Do you know if Shila has eaten tonight?"

"I'm sorry. I do not. Afraid I got distracted. Oh, and I want to buy your wolf."

"Sorry, Myron," Hokee said with a big smile, "but my brother's not for sale. Enjoy your beer. I'll see you tomorrow, and no more speaking until the right moment. Good night."

"Good night, Hokee."

They weren't aware of the impending hell and endless sleepless nights ahead.

Chapter Forty

War begins

With the scotch in hand, Hokee walked with Shila up the driveway and across the flats. It was a balmy evening, and Hokee was enjoying walking with Shila, sipping scotch, when Shila took off chasing a scent or an animal he could have for dinner. A few minutes later, Shila returned without catching anything. Hokee suspected Myron did not think about Shila's dinner, so when they returned, Hokee pulled a rabbit from the porch refrigerator and laid it out for him just in case. Wolves will rarely eat if they are not hungry. Shila devoured the rabbit.

Going into his house, Hokee raided the pantry for something quick and easy. Spotting a can of Scout Smoked Wild Albacore Tuna, a grilled tuna sandwich sounded appealing. Taking a loaf of BAKE-AT-HOME SOURDOUGH BREAD from the package, he threw it in a toaster oven while prepping the tuna. Mayo, relish, and finely chopped celery were added to a bowl with the tuna, along with one fresh egg beaten with a fork which was microwaved. The cooked bread was ready for the spread when he finished making the tuna mix. A slice of extra sharp American cheese was placed on top; then he grilled the sandwich in a cast-iron skillet with melted butter.

After he had eaten, Hokee invited Shila inside to sleep with him on his big king-sized bed, possibly saving the wolf's life.

At 12:15 a.m., Hokee woke to a familiar sound, the faint fast *whopwhopwhop* of a distant helicopter. While getting out of bed, the sound grew louder, *whopwhopwhop,* until it sounded like it was right overhead, *whopwhopwhoop,* then the front half of his house exploded in a giant fireball. Hokee and Shila ran around the lava rock wall Hokee built to separate his bedroom from the underground river. When Hokee built his home, he put his bedroom in that part of his house that was the cave and underground river he discovered on nis nearly fatal vision quest. He next separated the cave from his main living area by another lava rock wall. This wall saved most of his bedroom from the explosive fire, but the heat and smoke filled the room. Behind the wall next to the river, Hokee and Shila experienced little smoke; however, the roaring fire of his burning house sounded like the thunder of a large run-away railroad steam engine loose in his kitchen.

Myron, who didn't initially know he was the intended target, was safe in his tent, which was overlooked in the dark by the helicopter crew and its passengers. The loud helicopter noise woke Myron, who hobbled out of the tent just as the aircraft flew overhead. He saw a big barrel (later, they learned it was a 55-gallon oil drum full of high-octane airplane gasoline) swinging on a long cable beneath the helicopter. Myron watched in horror as the helicopter swung the barrel, dropping it into the front of Hokee's house, which exploded in a giant, roaring fireball. It sounded like an entire Fourth of July fireworks display going off simultaneously. Myron and his tent were safe from the fire, but feeling the heat, he moved away, looking back in shock at the roaring fire that was Hokee's house. Never invited inside the home, Myron was unfamiliar with the underground river and the rock wall separating Hokee's bedroom from his primary living quarters. Tears filled his eyes, and intense pain gripped his chest as he looked at the roaring inferno and assumed Hokee and Shila had been burned alive.

The fire consumed everything he looked at that would burn, so Myron had no reason to hang around. Yet, some instinct, or maybe a feeling of guilt at being spared, or perhaps a macabre desire to see if any remains could be identified as a human being, Myron waited and watched the fire, expecting a fire engine or a police officer to show up. When orange sunlight shimmied down the mountains to the west, and no one arrived to quell the fire or inspect the damage, Myron decided it was time to leave. While gathering his possessions, he was angry that not one of Pocatello's fire engines came to fight the fire; then he remembered the ten-mile driveway into the lava flats and the house was two-hundred feet below the plain. Hokee's house was probably too far away from anyone to hear the fire, and the flames would be barely visible above the lava plain. Hokee purposefully located his home in an isolated area.

How did they get information about Hokee's whereabouts? Hokee said few people were knowledgeable about where his house was located, and why kill Hokee? In Hokee's business, he undoubtedly made enemies, but someone hired a helicopter to burn him alive inside of his house? That seems extreme. And then a BIG thought hit Myron like a sledgehammer to the head.

What if they were trying to kill me?'

A few close associates at the university and more in Singularity Inc. were aware of his vision quest and the name of the shaman he was visiting, but none of his associates knew where Hokee lived. However, it didn't take a high IQ to realize that money can buy almost anything. Hell, murderers go free all the time because they can spend whatever it takes to remain free.

Someone sold him out. In Myron's world, such occurrences never happened,

Myron painfully collected his tent and belongings, stowing them in the trunk of his vehicle. He was in the driver's seat, about to start the engine, when he saw Hokee and Shila stepping gingerly around smoldering hot spots on their way out of what had been a beautiful house.

Shocked beyond comprehension, Myron fumbled his way out of his car and started hobbling towards Hokee and his wolf. Before even thinking to acknowledge Hokee's and Shila's miraculous survival, he yelled.

"They were trying to kill me. They probably thought that I slept in your house. I don't think they even cared if you were home."

Hokee responded immediately with a deadly intensity Myron found chilling.

"Whoever they were after, and whoever they are, they made a fatal mistake."

His soft voice cracked like a whip from outer space and white, laser-like light pierced the night from his eyes while his deadly stone-faced expression left no doubt about his intentions.

"Which mistake is that?" Myron asked, still shaken and unable to see any mistake his enemies made.

In a hard-flat voice declaring war, he said, **"They didn't kill me."**

CHAPTER FORTY-ONE

Planning Revenge

Thinking about why Myron was at his house, Hokee said, "Myron, your vision quest just took an unfortunate step into the Twilight Zone. Let's find someplace to consider our options and plan a way for your journey to resume, considering we are on a different path than the one we happily shared yesterday. We will still address the issues you have regarding your quest, but I concur with your analysis; someone with a lot of money wants you dead."

"I agree, Hokee, but I'm concerned about finding who sold me out."

"We will *find* the Judas. I Promise." His tone left no doubt. "I can easily see another country or large foreign corporation wishing you dead, planning on acquiring your A.I. technology from one of your partners in Singularity, Inc."

"Damn, Hokee, I'm sorry about your house. I'll pay to have it rebuilt." Myron was trying to stand on one leg and appeared ready to fall. Pain distorted his face. His ordinarily smooth forehead had deep creases, and his eyes looked like little deep black holes surrounded by dark shadows.

"Just hang on a minute, Myron. Don't move. I will drive over here and help you get in. We'll leave your car here so people will assume you died in the flames. With my ride missing, they may think I wasn't home, or the bad guys stole it. We'll get a hotel room and put you to bed to rest your leg. By tomorrow, I will have a plan."

Hokee drove them to Hampton Inn close to Hokee's office but on the opposite side of the freeway, signing in under false names. This wouldn't be safe for long, but it should be suitable for one night. After checking in as a single, Hokee drove them to a side entrance normally used by guests after checking in. He didn't want anyone to see Myron, who might know him, and they also didn't want anyone to see his bandages. Bandages get noticed. Hokee helped Myron to his room and got him lying propped up on the bed with pain meds and drinking water nearby.

"Myron, I probably don't need to warn you, but under no circumstances can you use a telephone for talking or texting. Not your cellphone or the room phone. Do not contact anybody. Give me your phone so I can disable it. We want anyone searching for you to think you perished in the fire."

"I got it, Hokee." Myron said, nodding his head. "No contact with anyone."

Satisfied that Myron was set for a while, Hokee said, "I need to get Shila and lock the car, then I'll come back, and we can discuss breakfast."

"Okay Hokee, thanks. I'll wait here," he said, with a grin with, or grimace, waving his hand.

Hokee let Shila out then leaning against the white ash covered Explorer called Grant Olson.

"Hokee, my God man, I've been calling you for hours. I wa.."

Interrupting, Hokee said with an urgency, **"Grant, hold up,** I don't have time for talk, I need a favor.

"What do you need? Anything at all."

"A while back, you offered to provide me with some shooters. Are they still around? What sort of men were they? And how many can you get immediately?

"Sounds like you're in trouble. You know, Hokee, Idaho is the preferred retirement for police officers from California and several other states. We also have several old-fashioned survivalists who spend all their time in the forest training for the next big civil war. Many of the cops are survivalists. I can probably round up at least a hundred well-trained men. I believe we also have a few retired SEALS. The others are not Seal Team Six candidates, but they're competent warriors."

"Grant, I am going to war with some deep-pocket criminals. I don't know whether it's from a country of private industry, but they are truly nasty, amoral, criminal assholes. This will be a dangerous enterprise. I immediately want four qualified candidates willing to risk their lives. To understand the seriousness Grant, the fate of humanity may hinge on the outcome.

"Jesus, Hokee. Can you tell me what this is about?"

"What is your knowledge of Artificial Intelligence, typically known as A.I.?"

"Just what I see on television occasionally. These machines will probably be smarter than humans before long."

"That time is already here. I have a client who has developed an A.I. robot that makes the brightest human being on the planet look like an uneducated idiot. Without controls, these robots will render modern humans obsolete. Several countries and companies are actively working on A.I., and most are not friendly with our government. Tonight, someone tried to kill my client by firebombing my house to acquire his technology. They destroyed my home, but fortunately, my client is safe. Perhaps you realize I live entirely off the grid in a remote location, which is practically unknown. Whoever was responsible had enormous resources. I need to find and kill them before they kill us both. We are hiding and it will be difficult for anyone to find us until this ends.

"Hokee. I'm sure sorry to hear about your home. We'll catch up another time. Let me get busy and see what I can put together. How do I contact you?"

"You can't. I'm ditching this phone and will grab a few burners. I'll call you tomorrow with a new number and an update. Please make sure the interested individuals understand the risks."

"Okay, Hokee. I'll be prayen for ya."

"Thanks, Grant. And don't use my name when talking to any of your candidates, I'm supposed to be dead. And don't mention A.I. We'll brief the participants before they commit. Talk to you later."

The line went dead.

Hokee had Shila jump in and took the Explorer to a drive through car wash to get rid of the ash and soot so it wouldn't stand out. At McDonalds, he bought ten egg-sausage-cheese McMuffins, ten McSpuds and four large black coffees. After breakfast in Myron's room, with Shila getting most of the McMuffins and potatoes, Hokee left with Shila to get both men decent clothes. They needed to dump the smoky ones they were wearing. They also needed shaving kits and twenty burner phones.

Returning with his purchases, Hokee helped Myron shed his clothes, taking the bashful professor to the tub, trying to keep his injured leg and head from getting wet. With Myron settled again with paper and pens for his lists, Hokee took Shila for a drive. It was time to pay Why-ay'-looh a visit. He planned to spend a long time in his mentor's sweat lodge, seeking answers and balance for his anger.

CHAPTER FORTY-TWO

Hokee

Not wanting anyone on the reservation to suspect he was alive and visiting, he parked the Explorer in the Chevron station parking lot and started walking. It was only three miles to Why-ay-ay'-looh's hogan, which took forty minutes with Shila by his side. When he arrived, Hokee was not surprised to see his teacher, mentor, surrogate father and friend waiting for him by the sweat lodge.

"Greetings, my son. I have seen the evils you are fighting and prepared a fresh bowl of water and herbs for your sweat."

"Hello father, I'm sorry to impose on your hospitality, but as you already know, I could use your help. Would you sit with me in the lodge?"

"It will be an honor. The lava rocks are ready for the pit. I'll let you put them inside the lodge when you are ready."

Hokee undressed quickly, leaving his folded clothes in a pile next to the lodge. Why-ay'-looh did the same while Hokee used a shovel to place four white-hot rocks into the pit. With the rocks heating the lodge, Hokee and his master sat down inside, closing the flap. Hot rocks provided the sole light. Both men spent the first few minutes meditating on their quest for this sweat lodge session. When he felt the time was right, Hokee sprinkled dried herbs onto the rocks, filling the lodge with powerful herbal smoke, bringing alive visions and opening powers in their minds. Why-ay'-looh's herbs, selected for this session by the master, put both men into the comfortable realm of non-being. This out-of-body experience differs from that taught by other shamans. In this state, watching the firefighters sift through the ashes of Hokee's home was possible. Next, it was time to travel beyond this realm, which Hokee accomplished by dumping Why-ay'-looh's herb-infused water onto the hot rocks. The steam and smoke sent both men beyond the boundaries of thought, past the deepest levels of semi-consciousness, into the realm of non-local realities.

At first, the sights were confusing. It was like watching a movie running at half-speed; everything seemed jerky and disjointed. Why-ay'-looh spoke for the first time, "watch closely, Hokee; this will go by fast." Now, it felt like the projectionist for this sequence of images ran the movie at two or three times the normal speed. Getting a firm fix on any images was difficult, but a man of Chinese ancestry flipped by several times in a blur. Emerging from the shadows was the face of someone around Myron's age who exuded an intellectual vibe. Hokee's intuition suggested this was the face of the man who betrayed Myron.

Sensing they had garnered everything this sweat will produce, Why-ay'-looh pulled back the flap, letting in light and fresh air. Next to the lodge was the shower. A fifty-gallon barrel on a seven-foot-high cradle was filled daily by young boys eager for the shaman's approval. Attached to the bottom was a hand-held shower at the end of a five-foot-long hose. Why-ay'-looh's hogan was isolated from the other dwellings, providing privacy.

After getting dressed, Why-ay'-looh disappeared inside his hogan for a few seconds, returning with two glasses of a cold herb fusion. "Drink this, my son; it will help drain the poison from your aura."

"Thank you, father. Tomorrow I will ask Zoey to bring Dr. Myron Whittleman here to hide and finish his vision quest if you will do me the honor of completing his quest for me.

"I am aware of its significance." I will do as you wish."

"Thanks, Father. That refreshing drink you prepared is new to me. I want to get the herbs from you after rebuilding my house. I would also like you to keep Shila for me until this mess ends.

"You know I love that wolf. He will be in friendly hands. Go with the spirits who are our friends. I'll focus my energy on you to support your mission."

"Your blessing will be most welcome. I must go now. Thanks for sharing the sweat lodge with me."

Hokee began the forty-minute walk back to his Explorer.

CHAPTER FORTY-THREE

War Preparation

Early the following day, using the telephone in his room, Hokee called Bannock County Deputy Sheriff Robert (Curly) Billingsford, a long-time friend.

"Deputy Billingsford, how can I help you?"

"Good morning, Curly; I didn't get you up, did I?"

"Hokee, what a surprise, my favorite PI, and nope, I'm awake. I suppose you need the sheriff's department's help save your ass again." This was a long-standing joke between the two friends, as Hokee was constantly helping the sheriff's department solve tough cases.

"Yep, this time you got it right, Curly. I need you to go close my office and find a safe place for Hilda to live until I contact you again."

"Why sure, Hokee. It sounds like you bought yourself some more trouble. I guess you ran into more bad guys like those Arabian killers. This sounds serious."

"Someone firebombed my house last night to kill my client. I don't know how they found out where I lived, but until I find those responsible, my office will not be safe."

"What? They burned down your beautiful home?" Curly's voice cracked, and he sounded deeply sorry for Hokee's loss. Although he had only been a guest a few times, each time he was in awe of the spectacular house filled with Hokee's paintings and handmade furniture.

"Yes. I can't go back until I find those responsible. I don't have much time. Will you take care of my office and Hilda right away?"

"Hokee, I don't know what to say. Yes, I'll get right on it. Are you sure I can't help you in this hunt? Do you need a place to stay?"

"Helping me would just make you a target, Curly. I need to maintain the illusion of my death until I can devise a plan. I'm going to be moving around, but I'm getting some burners, so I'll give you a phone number next time we talk. After taking care of Hilda, would you mind getting the firefighters out to see the damage? I may need them to make a visit to satisfy my insurance company. The firemen will look for human bones unless they could have been cremated in the fire. Someone else may be watching as well. Watch out for them. I want the people who burned my house, and they will watch to see what the firefighters discover. My client's car is at my place. See that it hauled someplace safe. The keys are in the car. And watch yourself, Curly, we're dealing with some viscous, dangerous people. I'll call you when I can."

Hokee disconnected the call before the deputy could ask where he was going. His next call was to the Fort Hall Indian Reservation headquarters.

"Good morning. You have reached the Fort Hall Indian Reservation headquarters, Zoey speaking." Zoey Deere, the tribal council's girl Friday, helped Hokee on a human trafficking case last year.

"Hi Zoey, this is Hokee. Please don't let anyone know you are talking to me and don't say my name out loud. Okay?"

"Why sure Ho... kay."

"Thanks. If you are available, I would like you to do me a favor." After their first encounter, Zoey had a schoolgirl crush on the famous detective and could barely believe her romantic interest was asking her for a favor.

"Oh, my yes," she gushed, "anything."

"Zoey, first, I don't want anyone to know that I contacted you, especially Chief Wahvevah. Next, I need someplace on the reservation that is isolated, with no one living close by. It's been several years since I lived there, and I'm sure things have changed. On the reservation map you showed me last year, can you spot any potential locations for me?

"Let me take a quick look," After about thirty seconds, she returned online, "Hum... yes, I can see a great open place north of the Ross Fork Cemetery. There's a..."

"**Stop, Zoey**," Hokee interrupted, "Can you get away for a few hours without telling anyone where you are going?"

"Oh Ho... kay, I can make that happen." Zoey's excitement at spending time with a man she practically worshiped came through the phone. He had known about Zoey's infatuation from the beginning and tried to discourage her interest, but Hokee's present need transcended any concern he had about the young lady and her expectations. Can you meet me at the Holiday Inn Express on the Center Street off-ramp for I-15?"

As soon as he said the Hotel's name, Hokee silently cussed himself, knowing she would get the wrong impression.

"Aha..." (confirming Hokee's thoughts), "it will take a few minutes to make arrangements, but I can be there in an hour."

"Great, and Zoey, bring the map."

"Sure, I'll see you soon." She expected a response, but the line was dead. Next on his list was a call to Grant.

"Good morning Hokee. I've been waiting for your call."

"Morning, Grant. Do you have any news for me?

"Yes, its great news. I stayed up all night making calls and interviewing. There are nearly eighty who initially appear to be qualified and eager to get involved."

"That is good news. If you can spare the time, I would like to hire four of the most qualified candidates to come to the Fort Hall Indian Reservation Headquarters immediately. I need three or four additional people on standby for a few days.

"Hell Hokee, I'm coming down myself. It will be an honor to help you in any way possible. After what you did for us in Tahiti, I owe you my life. Gene can run the company as well as me. I'll take off whatever time is needed to help you get these bastards. And don't worry about paying for anything; I've got more money than I could spend in a hundred lifetimes. I only work because it's so much blooming fun and I don't t have anything else to occupy my time. Now that you've given me something to do that interests me, I'll be there with the men we talked about this afternoon.

"That's great, Grant. I can use your help, which is truly appreciated. After getting the warriors, they will need a couple of motorhomes so they can live comfortably for a few weeks. Hopefully, it won't take that long, but plan for the worst. Then have them drive to the Fort Hall Indian reservation. Don't go onto the reservation property, I'll meet you at the Phillips 66 station just off I-15."

"Okay, I can take care of that."

"Thanks; I'll call later today to see how you're doing and coordinate times."

The call ended, it was time to see how Myron was doing and get ready for Zoey.

Chapter Forty-Four

Xiu

When Draco delivered the helicopter to America and hired its crew, it completed the Chinaman's first phase. Needing another Chinese associate on American soil, Cheng previously contacted Xiu Zoeng, who was familiar with American customs being stationed in Los Angeles and ordered him to assist Draco in completing phase two.

Derick, the snake Ward, lived in Colorado as much as anyplace. The Snake was sought by all in the region who desired someone skilled in the black arts. His reputation for slithering into and out of the nastiest places kept him busy. Xiu's search for a patsy to help finish phase two of the Chinaman's program led him to Derick. Xiu met Snake in a Denver bar, fittingly called The Last Chance, where he was hired for the job.

After the stupid Chinese man bought him several rusty nails, which are primarily cheap scotch, the Snake was all ears when his clever slanty-eyed companion offered him ten thousand dollars to firebomb some half-breed's house in Pocatello, Idaho. The helicopter and crew will be waiting for him in Idaho. All he had to do was locate the Indian's home in the lava flats and determine the target's presence. He had to coordinate the fuel pickup for the helicopter crew and then burn down the Indian's house. Afterward, he was to fly with the helicopter crew to a remote part in the desert, then dispose of the plane and crew. Someone else would pick him up. Ten thousand dollars was more than he usually made in months. *Of course*, he will help burn some Indian's place to the ground.

The People's Republic of China's American Embassy is in Washington, D.C., and the Chinese Consulate General of the People's Republic is in Los Angeles. Supposedly, Xiu Zoeng, who worked out of the Consulate Office in Los Angeles, reported to Mingze Chong in the primary Chinese Embassy in Washington, D.C. However, Xiu bowed to no man and ignored the Washington embassy until he needed money or political pressure that only an embassy could provide. When the Ambassador Extraordinary in Los Angeles summoned him to his office, he was tempted to ignore the invitation, but some sixth sense, some call it intuition, urged him to see what the Ambassador wanted. With his usual swagger, he sauntered into the office, but the Ambassador was absent. Two killers were there instead, Feng Cheng, who he recognized and a taller, fit, swarthy, white-haired man with a pockmarked face and sunken dark eyes. The man looked menacing with a scouring, dry-ice chilling glare. Obviously, another killer. Xiu had never met Cheng, only talked with him over the phone, but he had seen a photograph of him in the past.

"Wipe the insolent smile from your face and act like a man, not some street thug, out to mug a stripper," Cheng addressed the cocky Xiu in soft, flawless English, but the deadly look in the Chinaman's white eyes was enough to bring Xiu to attention. He was used to being the top dog, but everyone knew you never, ever crossed DDyi, the number one Chinese assassin. The other man was even more intimidating.

"What did your man do with the Russian Helicopter?" Cheng asked in a soft, stern voice that commanded attention. It was the soft sound you heard from a rattlesnake getting ready to strike. It was a voice demanding an instant truthful answer.

Xiu was quick to respond. "After firebombing the half-breed's house, the helicopter crew flew the chopper to a remote spot in the Craters of the Moon Preserve we identified earlier. It is a desolate location never visited by humans. The man I hired, Derick Ward, killed the helicopter crew and then set the helicopter on fire with their bodies inside. He reported there was nothing but ashes left at the scene."

Still unknown was the fate of Dr. Whittleman, but Xiu saw images of the burned-down house and couldn't believe anyone escaped the fire. It was only a matter of time before they acquired the 'late' Dr. Whittleman's secret formula for advanced A.I. from Singularity's vice president, Larry Mills. In his mind, Xiu's country would recognize his brilliance and reward him accordingly.

"Excellent. Dispose of Ward, then fly to Pocatello. Mister Vargas will accompany you. I want to have one hundred proficient mercenary fighters staged in Pocatello within the next week. Include as many American warriors willing to kill other Caucasians as possible. Put them up in several hotels. Mr. Vargas will be in charge." He said, pointing at Draco. "I also want you to locate Larry Mills, the Vice President of Singularity Inc. Vargas is dedicated to getting the A.I. secret formula developed by Whittleman. You will assist him as he asks."

Xiu was used to being the alpha male and throwing his influence around whenever and wherever he wanted, but after meeting the terrifying freak with white hair and chilling white eyes, he wisely accepted second place.

Snake met Xiu at a local Denver watering hole called The Post Office to receive his last payment. After collecting his money and drowning himself in enough celebratory rusty nails to float a small boat, he stumbled out of the bar and stood on the sidewalk, remembering where he parked his car. In his drunken haze, he didn't see the monster Peterbilt Truck swerve onto the sidewalk. It was a better death than he deserved, but it cleaned up the playing board for Xiu, leaving no Chinese fingerprint on the firebombed house and the unfortunate death of Dr. Myron Whittleman.

CHAPTER FORTY-FIVE

Zoey Joins the War

Hokee was in the Holiday Inn Express parking lot with Myron when Zoey drove up in her little blue 2007 Fiat 500. She wore a big smile while waving a greeting and parking next to Hokee's Explorer. Before she could exit the car, Hokee was at her driver's side window, accompanied by a handsome young man limping on a bandaged leg with another bandage on his head.

"Hi, Zoey. It's great to see you, but I don't have time for a reunion. I need your help with several items, but first, did you bring the map I requested?"

Zoeys disappointment was instantly apparent. Hokee was unsure whether her solemn frown resulted from them not meeting in the hotel for a romantic interlude or from his question about her memory of the map. "Why yes, Hokee," she answered in a voice filled with disappointment, "it's right here," she added, handing Hokee the map through the car window.

Looking straight into the eyes of the sad girl so she could see the seriousness of the situation, Hokee said, "Zoey, this man by my side is Dr. Myron Whittleman. There are people with a lot of money trying to kill him, so for now, you and I are the only ones aware that he is alive. No one else is to know he is alive except Why-ay'-looh."

Grasping the seriousness of the meeting, Zoey said, "Whew... that's a...hi Dr. Whittleman, It's ni..."

Interrupting the stunning looking shy girl, he said, "Please call me Myron Zoey, and I'm happy to meet such a beautiful young lady, although I wish it were under better circumstances."

"Before you all get better acquainted," Hokee said, reflecting the seriousness of the situation in his voice, "I want you to drive Myron to see Why-ay'-looh. No one else is to see Myron or know he is living there. Last night, someone interrupted his vision quest, and I will appreciate it if my old master continues in my place. Myron has a diary of his progress to date. Make certain that no one sees you take Myron there, and please make sure the master knows how to keep Myron hidden. This time, your desire for excitement will be more than you bargained for Zoey, because if anyone connects you to either Myron or me, your life will be in danger. The killers also think I am dead, and I want them to think that as long as possible. I'm sorry to put you in this situation, Zoey, but there *is* no one else I can trust. You understand why I didn't want you to mention my name on the telephone or inform anyone that you will assist me.

Zoey was stunned as she sat in her fancy little blue car. One look at her face, and even a stranger could see the confusion, fear, uncertainty, and helpless, worried eyes. "Yeah... I mean... I understand. It is a pleasure to assist Myron in meeting Why-ay'-looh. Are you going to be okay?"

"Sometime soon," his voice was soft, but it cracked like a whip. "Thanks for helping us out, Zoey. You really are a princess." Turning to Myron, he continued, "let me help you hop in the car with Zoey, then I want to look at the maps Zoey brought."

Hokee glanced over the maps, mainly to see what had been changed since he left there several years ago. "I can see four roads with access to the wilderness area you initially suggested. Is that your understanding?" He asked Zoey.

"Yes, I know all four roads."

"That's great, Zoey. Now comes the hard part. Between three and four hours from now, two motorhomes will park at Phillips 66 station near the-15 exit to the reservation. I would like you to escort them to the wilderness area. Ideally, no one will see these RVs enter the reservation. You know all the back roads away from small settlements. Can you do all of that without arousing questions about your absence?"

"I can do that, Hokee. I often take off for a few hours when we are not busy. Will I be seeing you later?" The hope in her eyes was hard to miss.

"Yes, Zoey, you will see me later today. Our adventure is only beginning. Please be extra cautious with the chief and the reservation police. No one can see Myron, and it would be better if no one saw the RVs gather at the wilderness site."

"I'll do my best, Hokee." Even though she was disappointed that their hotel meeting was not what she expected, her excitement about helping Hokee and Myron transcended any other consideration.

"I'll see you all later." Hokee waved goodbye as he got into his Explorer and drove away.

Once he left the Holiday Inn parking lot, Hokee called Grant.

"Hi Hokee, we have the motor homes ready to roll. Where are we going.?"

"At the exit from I-15 to the Fort Hall reservation, just south of the reservation, is a Phillips 66 station. A young lady named Zoey driving a blue Fiat will be there to meet the motorhomes and escort them onto the reservation. We have a plan to avoid being seen, which means Zoey will lead the homes on some backcountry dirt roads. Zoey fully understands the importance of secrecy and is trustworthy.

"Thanks, Hokee, I'll see you later today."

Chapter Forty-Six

The Hunt Begins

Hokee returned to the reservation, taking Myron, Why-ay'-looh and Shila, egg, cheese and sausage breakfast burritos from Burger King. As they were eating, Hokee described for Myron the shadowy person he saw in the sweat lodge. Without hesitation, Myron identified the individual and told Hokee where he worked on the university campus and where he lived..

After filling the Explorer's gas tank, Hokee drove to Pocatello's Idaho State University campus, parking illegally beside the science building. Inside, he searched for the computer lab. The large lab on the second floor featured several rows of work benches, with computers about every five feet on each bench. Along one wall were a few enclosed offices. After he entered, Hokee and sought someone to question regarding other individuals in the lab. A young girl close to the door who looked like a freshman with blue sapphire eyes, a silver nose ring and dark brown hair tied in a ponytail was sitting at a nearby terminal.

"Hello, mind if I disturb you for a minute?" He asked.

With a wry grin, the girl looked up from her keyboard, "Well, since you have already accomplished that, what can I do for you?"

"Would you know a Mr. Gunther Klein?"

"Sure, everybody knows Gunny; that's what we call the professor."

"Is he in this building?" Hokee gave the girl his killer smile, showing her he was friendly.

The smile appeared to work. "I believe so," she replied, showing interest, "but I haven't been paying attention to anyone else in the building." The large, handsome, smiling man with a dark complexion was attractive. He looked like an Indian. Not a student. Interesting. "I've been paying attention to my project. If he's there, his office is the second door on the left," she said, pointing the way.

Thanking the young lady whose face betrayed her interest, Hokee made his way to the office the girl mentioned, entering without knocking. Sitting at a desk facing a window sat a young man Hokee thought looked twenty-five, about the same age as Myron. This man wore a casual outfit, blue jeans, an Idaho State University sweatshirt, and leather sandals without stockings. With a cherubic face and long dark eyelashes, most women would call him handsome. As he was sitting, it wasn't easy to gauge his height accurately, but Hokee thought he was about five foot ten. He guessed his weight at around one seventy.

"With a disarming smile, Hokee asked, "Are you Gunther Kline?"

"Well, that depends; who is asking?" The smile was not returned.

With no more preamble, Hokee pulled the Colt 45 from behind his back, shoving it in the man's face. "Okay, Gunny, stand up and be calm. Don't think for one second I would not shoot you. Your friends have already attempted to kill me, and I'm not in a good mood."

With fear in his eyes as he stood up, Gunther said, "What? I don't have any information about anybody trying to kill you.

"Don't talk, Gunther; just walk out of the room and down the stairs as if you were showing a friend around the campus. Now move," he said, jabbing the gun in the frightened man's side.

There was nothing Hokee could do to erase the fear from Gunther's face, but fortunately, the only other person in the room was the young lady who directed Hokee to Gunther's room. She was once again busy with her project and paid them no attention.

Directing Gunther to his Explorer, Hokee looked around and, seeing no one nearby, told Gunther to get in the vehicle.

"What? I'm not getting in a car with you." He had a defiant look on his face.

Jabbing the gun into the man's guts hard enough to make him double over in pain, Hokee said, "Gunther, if you do not get into this Explorer right now, I will put a bullet in your right knee." One look at the fire in those dark eyes was enough for a frightened man to do as ordered.

Five miles northeast of the university campus, a fold in the lava plain created a shield from prying eyes, plus it is far enough away from everything that no one would pay any attention to a gunshot. Hokee parked and turned to face Gunther with the pistol pointing at the man's body. "Gunther, give me your phone and I want you to tell me how you found out where I live and who else you told."

Averting looking at Hokee, he responded, "I am unaware of what you're talking about." After speaking, he looked at Hokee to see if the lie was believed.

"Gunther, get out of the car." Hokee's demand almost sounded friendly."

With a confused look, Gunther asked, "Why do you want me to get out?"

"I don't want to get blood all over the inside of my car. It's hard to get it out of the seat cushions. But give me your phone first."

With a smirk on his face, Gunther uttered his response. "You won't shoot me. I recognize bluster when I hear it.

With no response, Hokee left the Explorer and walked around, opening the passenger door. Grabbing Gunther's arm, he none too gently jerked him outside, dumping him on the hard, rocky ground. With the pistol pointed at Gunther's knee, he said, "One last time, your phone *now*! And who told you where I live and who asked you to find out?"

Believing this was just theatrics, Gunther said, "I don't know what you're ta…"

The gunshot echoed off the lava wall, immediately followed by a scream from the wounded man.

In a loud, wailing voice, he yelled, "Jesus Christ, man, you shot me!"

"Probably the first of many. Now, give me your damn phone and answer my questions."

Stuttering said, "It, it's aaahh, a girl on campus said you rescued her from some kidnappers," as he was speaking he dug the phone from his pants pocket, tossing it to Hokee, then continued with his answer, "she told me she spent a night at your home out in some lava flat."

'Okay, you're doing good for now. Did she also tell you how to get to my house?"

"Yeah. Hey, I need a doctor. I asked her to draw me a map. Okay, you got what you wanted. Now call me a doctor. This pain is killing me."

"Who wanted the directions to my house?" Hokee asked, leaving no doubt that only by telling the truth would Gunther avoid another shot-up knee.

"I don't know him. He said to call him Snake. That's all I remember."

"No, that's not all you know, Gunny. Why did Snake want directions to my home? What reason did he give for wanting that information?"

"God, my knee is painful. Will you call a doctor?" he asked in a strained voice.

"If you want help, answer the damn question. I'm running out of patience with you, Gunny."

"All he told me was that they wanted to talk with Myron to see if he would sell them his formula for A.I."

"And you just told this man, a stranger, where to find my house?

"Well, not right then. I told him I wanted to think about it first, so he offered me ten thousand dollars."

"Weren't you a little suspicious about his reason for directions after he offered you the money?"

Not at first, but he gave me the money, and I didn't expect them to murder him. He said this with a straight face, as though no one would believe they would really kill Myron.

"Did he ask you for the formula?"

"Yeah, but I don't know it. Myron wouldn't tell anybody what he discovered. Now, can I get a doctor?"

"Okay, you can get a doctor after you hobble out to the road and wave down a ride." Hokee started walking around the Explorer to drive away.

"You're not leaving me here, are you?" He whined. "I answered your questions."

"Bless your God, you still get to breathe. I would kill you, but you're not worth the bullet. Your rich ten-thousand-dollar benefactor fire-bombed my house with me inside. If you mention seeing me to anybody, and I mean *anybody*, I *will* kill you. Slowly. Count on it. You cost me a fortune, and I would truly love to torture you to death. So, for those who will ask, you shot yourself by accident." Hokee got in his vehicle and drove away. As he was leaving, he could hear Gunny yell, "DON'T LEAVE ME HERE!"

CHAPTER FORTY-SEVEN

Assignments

After questioning Gunther, Hokee changed his original plan, deciding to meet Grant and the boys at the Phillips 66 station, but first stopped at Walgreens Drug Store for a few items. He arrived two minutes before Zoey, with Grant barely seconds later driving his own custom-built motor home. His four men were close behind in two additional motor homes. Hokee led them all inside the Phillips station for coffee. In his opinion, their coffee was better than Starbucks and a hell of a lot less expensive. The gas station didn't provide college tuition to its employees. This station featured two inside picnic tables, one commandeered by Hokee for a few minutes.

Grant introduced his men to Hokee, who introduced them all to Zoey. All four men looked like the men playing SEALS on television as they admired the pretty Indian princess. Daniel was a trim six-two who weighed two hundred and ten pounds. He looked like a miniature version of Paul Bunyon, with a square face and narrow hips. Noah was only five foot eight with a cherubic face, but one look in his steely blue eyes dispelled any notion that he was a candy-ass. Charles was the joker with gray eyes and almost always wore a smile, regardless of the situation. However, taking his smile for an easygoing man with a friendly disposition would be a mistake. He was built like a fireplug and, of the four; he accounted for the most kills. Lucas had long, stringy blond hair framing an oval face with dark brown eyes, often mistaken for black. All four men were highly trained in martial arts, but Lucas excelled with black belts in four different styles. Grant, a solid six two billionaire business tycoon, still had the firm body of a day worker he started with forty years ago, but his shaggy hair was pure white.

"Okay," Hokee began. "After studying the situation, I have decided different tactics are called for. Grant and the four of you will need cars for mobility. I need someone to spell our sheriff who is sitting at my home, which I am sure Grant has informed you was firebombed the night before last."

All four men said yes, muttering words of damn shame, and we'll get the bastards.

"We refer to the deputy as Curly because of his bald head, despite his name being Robert Billingsford." He needs to be relieved, plus I now believe that location will become of interest to the people behind the attempt to kill the man who was staying at my property. He is only alive because he was sleeping outside in a tent, which the helicopter crew bombing my house missed in the dark. As far as the enemy is concerned, the man is dead. I want to keep it that way."

Grant inquired about the tasks for the men staying on your property.

"For now, Curly is monitoring the fire department, which is sifting through the ashes, looking for bones. They will leave soon, and I expect the enemy to be watching and will then take an interest in my home when the firemen leave. It may not be for a few hours, but when they show up, we will raise hell. Once they know the property is defended, they may mount some offensive action. Whoever gets this assignment should be ready for some serious action. Please be cautious, and if you need help, call. This reminds me: Here are burner phones for each of you. I have already programmed the numbers of the other phones into each one. Do not use your personal phone or a public phone under any circumstance. The enemy has deep pockets and will monitor any phone activity regarding Artificial Intelligence, A.I., or the fire at my house. They will also look for strangers registered at every hotel and boarding house. That is why we will live in motor homes on the Indian reservation. Zoey works on the reservation and will watch for any interest in our activities shown by the reservation police or tribal management. She will also have a burner and can contact us if necessary."

Lucas asked, "Hokee, you have mentioned the men who will watch your property, and I volunteer for that assignment with my partner in crime, Danial, but what about the others?

"Right. Good question. You and Danial will take your motor home to my property where you will live and relieve Curly. I'll take you to rent a car on the way." Next, the company that developed A.I. is named Singularity Inc. The Vice President of Singularity Inc. is Larry Mills. I believe the enemy will contact him to see about acquiring the company's secret computer code for their advanced A.I. I want Grant to find Mills and see who contacts him. That contact will either be the enemy or someone they have hired. I want to know the faces of my enemies.

"Do you have any contact information for Larry?" Grant asked.

"No, but he also works for Idaho State University in Pocatello and should be easy to locate. Singularity owns a building a few blocks from the university where you will find him. You can Google the company's address. We don't want him to know he is being watched. You may have to have help from Team Two. I'm calling the team who watches my property Team One."

Charles asked, "Since we are Team Two, what do you have planned for Noah and me?"

"My house was firebombed with a helicopter flying a barrel full of high-octane fuel. They could not rent a helicopter anywhere near my home without being discovered, and they couldn't fly from where they had their helicopter to my house with a full barrel of fuel. They needed a nearby place for staging within a few miles of my home to acquire the barrel and fuel. Search for that place and see if you can find out who those people are."

Seeing he had their full attention, Hokee continued, "Okay, let's talk about cars. Grant will need a vehicle, as will both teams. Zoey will drive to the reservation, followed by Grant and Team Two in their motor homes. Zoey has made a reservation map, and I prepared copies for Grant and Team Two. After parking the motor homes, Grant and Team Two will ride with Zoey to Enterprise car rental in Pocatello, where they can rent cars. I will drive past Noah and Charles at Phillips station, leading them to the Pocatello Enterprise car rental. We cannot use your real names to rent automobiles; however, in my business, it is often necessary to use an alias, and I have several with full documentation. The Walgreens where I bought the burners has a phone booth where we will get new pictures for your driver's licenses. We'll replace my photo on the licenses with yours. At Enterprise, they rarely look at the license. They only make a copy for their files."

"What will you be doing, Hokee?" Grant asked.

"I will search out where they rented or bought a helicopter and who flew the mission."

"It sounds like we are dealing with some dangerous people, Hokee. I can have another four people here tomorrow," Grant said.

"Let's see how it plays out the next day or two. We may need more men, after all. I'll check back on the reservation tonight sometime and check in with Team One at my home."

"Alright," Grant said. "Let's get moving."

"Noah, you and Charles hang loose for about forty-five minutes, and I will stop back and lead you to my home after Zoey leads the other onto the reservation."

CHAPTER FORTY-EIGHT

Hokee

Zoey left with Grant and Team Two following. When they had their motorhomes parked to their liking, Zoey drove them back to the Phillies station, where Hokee was waiting.

'Zoey, I appreciate your help. If anyone in your office is interested in this wilderness area or what is happening with me, please call me immediately. I'll check in with you each day for a quick chat to stay informed. Will that be okay?"

"Oh, yes, Hokee. I'm happy you trust me to help you. I'll wait for your call each day."

Grant and Team Two rode in Hokee's Explorer for a trip to Enterprise Car Rental, with Team One following. They leased four cars. Grant rented a Lincoln Navigator, and the others opted for Subaru Outbacks. Daniel drove their Outback with Lucas following in their motorhome. Team Two left Enterprise to go searching for a place the helicopter could have parked to load its lethal barrel of high-octane fuel.

When they were parked around the fountain in Hokee's yard and exited their vehicles, Daniel said, "Well, you told us they firebombed your home, and they sure didn't leave you much," he joined Grant and the Lucas gawking at the mess. Lucas commented, "you sure live a hell of a long way from civilization. How did you ever find this place?

"That's a rather long story Lucas, it's best told over a single malt scotch some other time."

Curly walked over to see who Hokee had with him. "Curly, I would like you to meet the men who are going to give you a rest. The gentleman with the mean eyes is Lucas Talbott, and the tall Paul Bunyon dude is Daniel Walker. The handsome, distinguished older gent is my friend, Grant. "Men", he said, waving at them while looking at Curly, "this bald-headed dude in sheriff's clothing is my good friend Mister Robert Billingsford, known throughout the world as Curly."

After greetings and handshakes, Hokee asked Curly, "When did fire people leave?"

"They left about five hours ago. I stopped one of them from looting your bedroom.

"Did we have any unwanted visitors?"

Three cars came down your driveway, two seemed like they were just curious. There was a car with one man who quickly left when he saw my uniform. I had some strong negative feelings about him. You can expect him to be back, probably with a few friends."

"Okay, good job, friend. You can take off now. Lucas and Daniel will camp here for a few days.

"Okay, Hokee. Let me know if I can be of more help. I sure would like to find those responsible for burning down your home and trying to kill you."

"Thanks Curly. I'll be in touch."

As Curly drove away, Hokee turned to Daniel and Lucas, "Alright, men, as you heard Curly, there will undoubtedly be someone coming to check out the situation. They will not be friendly, so be on guard. I have metal gates back at the beginning of the ten-mile driveway. I'll close and lock them, but they probably will not stop the people we are expecting. Here's a key for the lock if you need to leave," he said, handing a key to Lucas. "If you need some help, call me and Team Two immediately."

Lucas said with nonchalance, "Don't worry, Hokee, we won't let you down." Earning his attitude the hard way as a former SEAL, Lucas relished the idea of getting some payback against the evil he sensed was behind the current situation.

With a wave goodbye, Hokee drove off in search of a helicopter and its crew. His first stop was the Pocatello airport, twenty miles away.

Dutch Pastell, the airport manager, was no stranger to Hokee, as the private investigator was a frequent visitor with some interesting requests, especially in the last few weeks. The tower was still buzzing about the large SB-1 military helicopter that had picked up Hokee a few days earlier. Dutch was a solid five-foot-ten former professional boxer in good shape who fought Sergio Martinez for the middleweight championship. He hung up the gloves after losing but kept in excellent physical condition with a daily exercise routine. Hokee found him in his office next to the control tower. "Hello, Hokee, drop by for a few fighting tips?"

"Yeah, Dutch, sort of, in a way. I'm looking for a helicopter and crew who firebombed my house, and you don't need to have that panicked look in your eyes, I never thought your airport was involved. Today I'm just looking for information. The people involved have deep pockets, so they might have bought their own chopper to be destroyed later, but maybe they found one to lease. They would need a crew and somewhere to put high-octane fuel in a fifty-five-gallon oil drum. Do you have any ideas that don't include boxing lessons?"

"Ah, damn, Hokee, I'm sorry to hear about your home. Kick the door shut and let me see what I can find in our files."

Dutch spent a couple of minutes shuffling through files in a desk drawer before pulling out a folder that he placed on his desk. "Okay, we have two outfits here at the airport that fly helicopters for their own customers, but they don't lease their helicopters out, and I'm damn sure they wouldn't fly a helicopter to firebomb anyone's house, even a private dick's house.

"Damn it, Dutch, be polite. I'm trying to get over my dislike for losing boxers."

"Alright, I deserved that. In my files, I have the name of a company in Boise that sells and leases helicopters, and there is another one in Kootenai, which is way the hell up north someplace. Your firebombers probably wouldn't go that far to lease or buy a helicopter."

"You're probably right. Boise seems likely. Can you give me the contact information?"

"Here's their brochure," he said, handing Hokee a copy of a slick sales promotion publication extolling the benefits of using Dewey's Helicopter Company for all your helicopter needs.

Thanks, Dutch," Hokee said as he stood up. "I think I'll go pay these guys a visit. How about getting one of your hotshot charter pilots to fly me to Boise? Can I get there before they close for the night?

"I wouldn't push it. Your best bet is to be there first thing in the morning while they're fumbling around, getting cobwebs out of their heads."

"Good advice, Dutch, Thanks. How about six a.m. for a quick trip to our state's beautiful capital city? Can I get a charter flight?"

"You got it, Hokee. Let me know how it turns out. I hope you find the bastards. They don't call you the state's number one investigator without good reason."

Hokee left Dutch's office at the airport hoping to get some answers tomorrow.

He felt scattered and unfocused, chasing too many trails. Now it was time to check in with his partners in this war. Then he desperately needed another long sweat. The sweat he shared with Why-ay'-looh felt like a distant memory, but it provided him with knowledge about his world. Now he needed to focus his energy and get grounded.

CHAPTER FORTY-NINE

The Chinaman Gets Active

Getting the late Dr. Whittleman's secret A.I. formula was Cheng's highest priority. With so much at stake, Cheng left the Paris embassy for the shithole Pocatello to direct Draco and Xiu firsthand. Cheng stayed at the Red Lion, one of Pocatello's premiere hotels, because of its status and the name. The Chinese people favor red, and the lion is reminiscent of the dragon. Besides, it was not in the busy and noisy downtown traffic corridor where Xiu and Draco were staying.

Hokee randomly chooses a different hotel each night to make finding him more difficult. If the Chinese knew he was still alive, they would undoubtedly try to rectify that situation. It was, therefore, entirely coincidental that he wound up staying at the Red Lion Hotel. He had no way of knowing this was Cheng's headquarters.

Hokee checked in around eleven after visiting Team One and spending time with Grant and Team Two on the reservation. Tired but unable to relax, after taking his small bag to his room, he headed to the bar in an alcove off to the side of the lobby for a Black Label straight up and, hopefully, some soft jazz. He almost missed the Chinaman who was sitting in a booth nursing a baijiu from a bottle he brought with him, as that beverage was unavailable in Pocatello.

Cheng was in the lounge because being in a quiet public place allowed him to better assimilate local customs. Getting a feel for the local people helped him blend and hide.

Hokee sat at the bar where a TV was showing images of a peaceful mountain creek accompanied by a peaceful alto saxophone as accompaniment. Close enough to being jazz that Hokee found it relaxing. With the scotch and pleasing music releasing the tension from his shoulders, something kept tugging at his consciousness. Professionals in dangerous occupations develop a kind of sixth sense, an uncomfortable buzzing in their nervous system. Right brain kind of stuff. It isn't a feeling you get by thinking. Unable to find a reason for this twitching in his brain, he surveyed the room; that's when he saw the Chinaman. It was the eyes. For only a microsecond, their eyes met. Each recognized in the other a formidable foe. The Chinaman's face remained innocent, only the white eyes betrayed evil. A fleeting glance confirmed their shared realization — their enemy was before them. Cheng immediately left the room, abandoning his drink without looking back.

Hokee stayed on to finish his scotch. If the Chinese man wanted him dead, he would give orders to his troops. He had been certain there was some big money behind this war, and he had now seen its source. It was practically a given that the Chinese man did not expect to see him alive, but there was no mistake in his recognition of the man whose house they destroyed.

Cheng didn't have Hokee's picture, but he knew the man they believed killed in the fire was half-Indian and a shaman. He was positive he had seen the dead man.

It must have been one hell of a shock to see the man they thought was dead sitting at a bar drinking scotch. *Well, hell,* Hokee thought, *the damn Chinese can die as well as a half-Indian.*

Leaving the lounge, Hokee found an empty lobby with several soft chairs offering privacy. Alone where no one could hear him, Hokee called Daniel in the Team Two motorhome. A sleepy voice answered the phone. "Hi, Hokee, what's up?"

"Daniel, I need you and Lucas to come to the Red Lion Hotel in Pocatello right now. It's off I-15 on Pocatello Creek Road. I'll be in the lounge off to the left of the lobby."

Hokee's next call was to the Hertz car rental at the Pocatello airport. It was the only car rental agency open all night. He ordered an SUV to be delivered to the Red Lion Hotel immediately. His next call was to Grant in his motor home on the reservation.

"Hell, Hokee. Can't a fella get any sleep around here?" He sounded gruff, but Hokee could hear the smile on his face.

"Good morning, Grant, time to rise and shine. I would like to get the next four shooters here immediately. They will each need a car plus a couple more motor homes. It would be great if they could be here in their cars at the Red Lion Hotel in Pocatello before 5:30. I need to reach the airport by six. Do you think that is possible?

"Don't even doubt it. I'll get the motor homes and extra vehicles and have them at the Red Lion. It's only about a three-and-a-half-hour drive. I'll be there just as soon as I make the arrangements, and you can tell me what's happening. Where will I find you?"

After describing his location, Hokee added, "I'll be in the lounge on the left side facing the front door. I'll see you when you get here."

The line went dead.

Chapter Fifty

The Warriors Suit Up

Team Two arrived at the Red Lion a little after 12:30 a.m. They spotted Hokee sitting in the lounge as soon as they entered. Hokee was still nursing his Johnny Walker scotch.

Daniel and Lucas sat down across from Hokee and ordered coffee from the attractive Shoshone Indian server before anyone spoke. After the waitress left, Hokee started, "Thanks for coming so quickly. Another vehicle should be here shortly, so you can both have wheels. Here's the situation. I spotted the enemy's man in charge across the lounge earlier. By sheer coincidence, he is staying here at the Red Lion, which I chose at random for the night. With a little sleuthing, I found out his name is Feng Cheng. His name suggests Chinese, which is what I saw in my last sweat lodge. What I saw tonight were the deadly eyes of a supreme assassin. Perhaps one of the best in the world. He is undoubtedly here to lead his country's effort in locating and getting my client's Singularity secret. Grant and I gave you a summary of what this is all about back on the reservation and why it is important that we win this battle. If needed, I'll give you more details when we have the time." Hokee paused for a minute and took a small sip of scotch.

"I get why this war we signed up for is important, but what do you want us to do now, Hokee?" Lucas asked.

"I'm getting to that. We can be certain that with the Chinese general on the scene, his staff and warriors are somewhere close, and I don't know the size of his staff. Besides his staff, he surely has a small army waiting to be mobilized. I don't know the quantity of men he has or their nationalities. It's mixed, and undoubtedly there will be some Americans. I want you men to follow Cheng, see where he goes and who he contacts. To ensure he remains unaware of being followed, it's necessary for both of you to have cars. There will be four additional men and vehicles here around 5:30, so with six cars, you will follow Cheng without being discovered. He may organize a hit on me, and it is a certainty that he will be after Singularity's Vice President, Larry Mills. Grant has been shadowing Mills this afternoon and knows his location. A good time for an ambush might arise if they go after Mills. You'll have to decide that on the fly. Grant will be here to help coordinate everything, and you can rely on him to make the correct decision. Questions?"

"Yes," Daniel said. How will we recognize Cheng, and do you know where Cheng's men are staying? Also, where will you be?

"Ah damn. Good questions. Should have thought about that. Grant's excellent choice is evident, just as I expected. I'm heading for Bosie to check out helicopter rentals and I don't know where his men are staying. Cheng is slender, about five-ten or so, weighing about 155, all well-conditioned hard muscle. He moves with balletic grace. Ladies will consider his moon-shaped face to be handsome, and his straight black hair is cut short, below the ears. But the man's most outstanding features and how you will know it is Cheng are his assassin's white eyes. Eyes bright white, with black endless caves for pupils. Those twin black holes radiate malignant evil, like dark ocean waves thrown about by a thrashing killer whale. A frightening man. You will feel his presence no matter who else might be in the area."

"Man. You told us he was the big general. After your description, I would have to agree," Daniel responded.

"Yeah," Lucas added, "you also told us he has the eyes of a supreme assassin."

"You will not have any trouble identifying him when he leaves. I suspect he will have someone outside discreetly watching for me to leave to see where I am going. I am now on his watch list."

"What time are you leaving, Hokee?" Lucas asked.

"I have a flight to Bosie at six o'clock. I'm checking out the helicopter business, but now that I've seen Cheng, I may reconsider that plan."

Grant entered the hotel lobby a little before one a.m. and, seeing the three men huddled together in a corner of the lounge, went over and joined the huddle. "I see my men are drinking coffee, but Hokee, I didn't think you would be drinking alcohol with a war going on."

"Yeah, I know Grant. I ordered this drink two hours ago before realizing the seriousness of the situation. I've been nursing it ever since. Hate to waste a good black label."

At that moment, a man in a Hertz uniform shirt came into the lobby looking around for someone who ordered a car. Hokee left the booth to collect the Keys and sign the paperwork. After telling Hokee the car was in the portico, the man left to catch his waiting ride back to the rental office.

Hokee arrived back at the booth with the keys to a KIA, which he handed to Daniel. The server came as everybody settled in, announcing the last call. Grant and Hokee both ordered coffee, which caused a brief frown. She was hoping for a larger tip since her shift was ending, but she quickly replaced the frown with a dazzling smile. Hokee waited until the coffee arrived and the girl was gone before filling Grant in on everything.

Grant waited until Hokee finished with his narrative before responding. "I think you are right about someone waiting to follow you. I saw a couple of suspicious people in the parking lot around the corner from the portico, watching the hotel traffic.

"Damn. I guess my flight to Boise got canceled. Well, it's what I expected, but... maybe not this fast. That means Cheng will leave before long. I better go draw off his dogs, watching for me to leave. Wait a couple of minutes; then Daniel will take the car in the Portico and park it in an inconspicuous spot to watch for the Chinaman to leave. Lucas can watch the exit from here and can call Danial on the burner to say Cheng is on the way. Grant needs to stay here and direct the other four drivers. They will all need burner phones to stay in contact. The Longs Drug Store is about a mile away, and they deliver twenty-four-seven. I'll call and order more phones as soon as I leave. Grant can collect the phones and program in all our numbers for the new men."

"God, Hokee. This is getting hot fast. I will call for more help."

"It wouldn't hurt to have another five or six on call. Let's see how things shape up in the next few hours and review the situation." Hokee stood up to leave, tossing a hundred-dollar bill on the table for the attractive Indian girl. He left his unfinished scotch and the coffee, which he barely touched. "Okay, I better leave and draw away my watchers. I'll stay in touch."

"Watch yourself, Hokee. Don't want you getting killed." With a worried expression, Grand watched Hokee leave the table. The concerned look you see on a face when a valued friend leaves your side, walking away into an unknown danger.

Chapter Fifty-One

Feng Cheng

Cầo!!! Cầo. Cầo. The damned American half-breed. He was supposed to be dead. Maybe the scientist, Whittleman, is also still alive. How did they survive the fire and how, in the name of TAO, did that ignorant savage find me? Being one of the world's top spy-assassins, Cheng didn't believe in coincidences. *I thought they called the Indian shaman. A shaman, like a sage, an old wise one. Perhaps not as ignorant or savage as I initially believed. I saw pictures of his burned-out home. It is inconceivable that he is still alive. He is an investigator, someone who uses his power to locate individuals. That's undoubtedly how he found me. That makes him a formidable adversary. I saw his eyes. The eyes of one with extreme power. Not someone we can afford to underestimate.*

True to his assassin's nature, Cheng spent several minutes meditating on the situation before acting.

Picking up a burner phone, he called Xiu.

The phone rang only once before it was answered. "Xiu."

"Have Draco in your room in ten minutes."

The line was dead.

Repacking his small carryall, Cheng surveyed the room to make sure he had everything, then took the stairs down to the lobby. He glanced over to the lounge, looking for Hokee, but saw only two tired-looking men talking together; one was older, the other one about thirty, drinking coffee. The lounge was closed for business, and the men seemed half asleep. Still, Cheng was careful leaving the lobby, looking for Hokee or someone else who might be watching for him to leave. Cheng saw nothing suspicious but kept a close watch on the parking lot in case Hokee arranged for somebody to follow him. Monitoring his rear-view mirror watching for a tail, he didn't see anybody. He arrived at the Holiday Inn Express where Xiu and Draco were staying confident that he had not been followed. During his ten-minute drive, he saw only three vehicles on the road with him. All three vehicles were different from each other, and only one followed him onto I-15, and that vehicle did not exit when he did.

Xiu had been waiting nervously for Cheng to arrive, and the door to his room opened before Cheng could knock.

Chen began addressing Xiu forcefully, albeit in his soft, menacing voice, without a greeting. "You told me the Indian and scientist were both dead."

"I saw pictures of the house burned to the ground," Xiu responded quickly, hoping to avoid a confrontation. There was no time for those inside to leave, as the front of the house was where the firebomb had been dropped. Draco saw the burned-out house. No one could get out of that fire, right, Draco?" Xiu was clearly uneasy. While his answer was the truth, there was still something burning in the dark pit of Cheng's frightening eyes. It wasn't a pleasant sight, and Xiu was afraid of the assassin.

"That's right," Draco responded, and unlike Xiu, he showed no fear of Cheng. Cheng's fierce look did not bother him. "I went back the next day to watch the firemen sort through the ashes. One man left the ruins with something wrapped in a blanket when a deputy sheriff made him take it back. I don't know how a blanket survived the fire, but if a blanket survived, then who knows? The scientist's Cadillac never left the place, so we assumed he died in the fire. If they did not die from the fire, the smoke should have killed them, and the fire would have cremated their bones. However, that blanket has me concerned."

"I saw that Indian not two hours ago having a drink in my hotel," Cheng told the pair. It looks like your suspicion is correct, Draco. We recognized each other. It's in the eyes. If the Indian survived, the scientist might also be alive. Have you found Larry Mills?"

Xiu was relieved to see the dangerous look on Cheng's face soften as he asked a question Xiu could answer. "Yes, it's about four miles from here, near the University and Singularity headquarters."

"Do you know his schedule?"

"I have a local detective watching Mills house, and he reports to me every few hours. Mills has not left his house in two days."

"We will go visit him at eight o'clock when it's fully light out if your detective reports Mills is still in the house. If Mills doesn't know the formula, he may know if the genius is still alive and where he is hiding. Did your men follow the Indian when he left the Red Lion?"

Xiu was relieved to get a question he could answer. We haven't seen the Indian yet, but we're ready to follow him once he leaves the hotel.

"Good. I want to know where the Indian goes and who he sees. We may have to force him to tell us where the scientist is hiding. Don't let the Indian know he is being followed."

"The men waiting for him to leave understand that," Xiu responded.

Draco, who appeared to be bored with the conversation, announced, "I'm going to catch another few hours of sleep. I'll meet you in the lounge at seven for some coffee." In silence, Cheng and Xiu watched as the other man with fearful eyes left the room.

CHAPTER FIFTY-TWO

First Blood

Hokee knew he was being followed, but looking for information, he drove slowly, allowing the dark blue Subaru to maintain visual contact and easily follow him. When a white Chevrolet took the Subaru's place three hundred feet in the rear, he had to smile. The two vehicles played hopscotch behind Hokee all the way to his driveway. An amateur surveillance job by men unused to following someone in a vehicle. Unlocking his gate, Hokee drove through and then relocked it, forcing the men behind to walk if they were going to continue their surveillance. Stopping at the beginning of the slope down to his house, he saw Daniel and Lucas both standing at the bottom of his driveway, holding M4A1 automatics pointing up the slope. Hokee gave them a few seconds to recognize his vehicle, then slowly drove down to the waiting men. They watched him get out and speak before pointing their rifles at the ground.

"Good morning, men, I'm sorry to interrupt your sleep, but I'm happy to see you. I led some enemies here from my hotel. They are in a dark blue Subaru and white Chevrolet Blazer. I'm not sure how many men are in the cars, but. I will guess two men in each. It's almost certain they have been following me to see where I'm going and who I am seeing. The Chinese want me dead, so that could be their aim. Our war became active. Others are undoubtedly searching for Larry Mills. Team Two and Grant are watching their actions. I shut and locked the gate, forcing those following me to walk down the driveway. What if you guys hide at the top of the driveway to greet them? Do you want any help?

A unanimous "NO!"

"Great. In that case, I'm going to be busy for the next few hours and don't wish to be disturbed unless it is necessary. I'll be in the sweat lodge. Don't kill all of them unless it is necessary. I'd like to question at least one. When I'm done, I'll help dispose of the dead bodies."

"We have a few minutes, Hokee. Do you need any help with your preparations?" Daniel asked as Hokee started walking away. Ready for battle, both men had a serious focused look on their faces. It reminded Hokee of the intense stare of a mountain lion on a tree branch, moments before it leaps onto its target.

"No, but thanks. I've got it covered." Without uttering another word, Hokee walked over to his sweat lodge. Made of lava rocks, it did not burn in the fire, nor did his mesquite logs stacked between the lodge and the 200-foot-high lava wall surrounding his little oasis. Already in a meditative state, Hokee methodically built a fire and then placed lava rocks in the fire pit to get hot. After undressing, he placed his weapons and folded clothes outside of the opening to the lodge to have them handy. Hokee took a cold shower to wash away most of the negative energy clinging to his aura, followed by a sage smudge, an eagle feather for and aura sweep and then after homage to the gods of fate with tobacco offerings, he was ready for his sweat. A glazed clay pot resembling a large cookie jar held the herbs used inside Hokee's sweat lodge. A red-glazed clay water cup decorated with gold-colored earth symbols was also inside the pot. The water cup was used to soak cedar, sage, and eucalyptus chips.

Finished with the preparations, he put four of the glowing white-hot lava rocks in the sweat lodge pit, then crawled inside, pulling a blanket over the opening for the most intense sweat of his lifetime.

At 5:10, Grant's four new recruits arrived at the Red Lion. Once his men were in the parking lot, Grant used his burner to make plans for following the Chinese. He assumed Cheng was visiting his senior staff and discussing their forthcoming visit with Larry Mills. By the time Grant gave the men burner phones with the numbers of everybody's phones and made plans for tailing either one or more cars, it was nearly 6:15. They had almost a two-hour wait.

Daniel and Lucas hiked up to the top of Hokee's sloping driveway, looking for places to spring their ambush. The undulating lava plain was reasonably flat, but between mounds of solid lava, thin bubble layers hid wicked cavities below for the unwary. The hole in which Myron injured his leg, and the nearby depression caught Lucas's attention. It was low enough to provide concealment as it was behind an outcropping of lava rocks. Signaling Daniel, he positioned himself to surprise those creeping down Hokee's driveway.

It took Daniel another five minutes of searching on the other side of the driveway before he found a similar depression deep enough to hide his body. Both men settled in to wait.

The cars following Hokee had to stop at the iron gates at the beginning of his ten-mile-long driveway. From the lead car, a passenger stepped out to examine the gate, only to discover it was locked. Signaling the others, the four men were soon standing in front of the gate holding automatic AK-47s. Two men were Caucasian, one was Asian, and one man appeared to be from the Near East, maybe Egypt. They were all about six feet tall, close to two hundred pounds, and in excellent physical condition. They wore camouflage denim pants and jackets with pockets full of extra magazine clips for their rifles. Black baseball caps without lettering covered their heads.

They looked at each other, searching for options besides walking down a long, dark driveway disappearing into the black night. They could not see a reasonable alternative their leaders would accept other than to follow the road. Their only choice was to creep down the driveway with their senses on full alert. To reach the driveway on the other side of the gate, they were forced to walk into the lava fields around the gate posts. Two men circled the gate from each end. The Asian man in one team went around the post first and stepped onto the thin dome of an enormous bubble, eleven feet across. He tumbled down twelve feet before landing on the rocks below. He lay at the bottom, crumpled like an old beggar's laundry sack, moaning through clenched teeth. Although badly bruised, with patches of skin weeping blood, the only broken bone was the hand holding his rifle as it banged against the wall. It took all three of his companions ten minutes to get him out of the hole without falling in themselves.

When all four were ready to edge down the driveway, two men crept down the middle with a man on either side walking carefully on the outside edge, hoping to avoid another lava bubble. It took the stalkers roughly three hours to reach the ambush site.

The stalkers reached Daniel's hiding place first, but he waited until all four men passed Lucas's hiding place before standing and yelling in an unmistakable stern voice, **"hands up! Do not turn around."** Both Lucas and Danial were now behind the intruders.

As Daniel gave his command, Lucas instantly stood up, ready to fire on the men in the driveway.

Xiu's four men, battle-tested survivors of many fighting years, chose an action with little chance of succeeding, but to these men, a little chance was still a chance, one they were forced to take. Instead of obeying the command, which would have saved their lives, each man dropped into a crouch, spinning around, spraying gunfire as they turned. Bullets glanced from rocks spraying sparks like fireworks until the six automatic rifles fell silent, almost at the same time.

In the silence following six ear-pounding rifles, Daniel and Lucas waited to see if any of the downed me were moving. They were as motionless as the lava rocks surrounding their bodies.

"Well, sheiit," Lucas mutters, taking off his hat and shaking out his hair. "The boss man ain't gonna be happy. No one is alive."

"Nope," Danial agreed, "he ain't. But they give us no choice." Coming together, the men fist-bumped, celebrating being alive. An afterglow on the faces of two warriors who survived another gun fight.

"Yeah. No choice, Lucas agreed. But if there was gonna be first blood, I'm glad it's not us."

"I better call Grant," Daniel said, thinking out loud. "This might change their plans."

"Good idea. Think we ought to bother Hokee?" The tone in his voice suggested that Lucas didn't think this minor affair rated such an action, but he asked in case Daniel disagreed.

"Nah. Leave him alone. What he is doing is doubtless the most important action he can take. The war will wait until he is ready."

CHAPTER FIFTY-THREE

The Sweat

For the rare time he used a hallucinogen, Hokee kept a couple of magic mushrooms in the herb pot. He only used mushrooms once before, when his mentor, Why-ay'-looh, took him on a trip somewhere outside of our universe. It became abundantly clear that this was a dangerous journey, only to be undertaken in dire times. And this qualified as a dire time. Only shaman masters used hallucinating drugs in sweat lodge ceremonies, and then only on rare occasions. Hokee began his meditation outside, which only set the stage for the beginning of a long-distance voyage.

The two mountain grown mushrooms were soaking in the same jar as his herbs. Once seated inside, Hokee took three long, deep breaths, exhaling slowly. After giving thanks to the gods in each of the four directions and asking his spiritual masters for guidance, he chewed the mushrooms. Then he dropped the soaked wood chips and sage leaves onto the red-hot coals, filling the lodge with healing aromatic smoke. Hokee breathed the smoke deep into his lungs, then started a ceremonial ritual of intense Sumerian chanting. The mantra used in this chant is older than time, handed down by medicine men and shamans through millenniums.

After five minutes of chanting, the mushrooms started kicking in, putting Hokee in an alternate universe, ready to blast off into the completely unknown. He dumped the herb-infused water onto the glowing rocks, instantly filling the sweat lodge with intense, hot, aromatic steam. That physical shock, combined with the mushroom effect and the fusion instilled steam, was the last physical sensation his body experienced. From that point on, it was entirely in the mind. Our experienced reality isn't lost by losing bodily inputs to the brain. Senses continually send electronic impulses to our brains, creating the physical sensations our brains record. Losing conscious contact with his mind, Hokee's brain sent him into overdrive, flashing images and lights behind closed eyes at blinding speed. Sounds from all frequencies were roaring in his head. He experienced the simultaneous melting and freezing of his body. He alternately experienced hunger and starvation, with a tongue experiencing every taste imaginable. And finally, with canines smelling capacity, he experienced the memories attached to scents, and, ***then he didn't exist.***

The next thing he experienced was blinding, burning, white light. Yet his physical eyes were closed. The brilliant light overwhelmed every other mental sensation. There was only the painful light. No present. No past. No time. Nothing but light. No thoughts, no thinker present. Then, after what felt like an eternity, a thought emerged from the depths of Hokee's mind.

Who wanted Myron dead?

*Who **was** Myron?*

Suddenly, he could think. His body did not exist; he felt no pain, and he had no frame of reference to define *here.* But he could order his mind to obey certain commands. Mushrooms expand space to infinity, whereas LSD expands time to infinity. Space and time are proven to be equivalent by Einstein and in a euphoric sweat lodge experience are interchangeable. According to ancient scripts used in Taoism and Confucianism, all is one. Hokee was now in infinity, where all was one.

When he asked who Myron was, his brain took him through his entire experience with Dr. Whittleman, beginning with his desire for a vision quest. The question of A.I.'s role in humanity's future dominated his thinking. Hokee saw an apocalypse in which machines ruled the earth, much like the portrayal in Matrix. The answer Hokee was seeking came through.

Protect Myron's A.I. from destruction and ensure its constant advancement over unfriendly A.I. robots. A friendly, smarter, more advanced machine is man's only answer to protect themselves from other advanced A.I.s capable of destroying humanity. Warrior robots made by our enemies.

While in this infinite time/space state, Hokee had no physical body. There was no alternative but to wait for this journey to end, hopefully with an intact mind.

Since he could now control his thoughts, Hokee began asking questions about who was behind this war for A.I. control and what he could do to end it? He was sure the Chinese were behind the attempt on Myron's life, and when in his trance, he saw Feng Cheng's Paris meeting with Draco Vargas; he knew for certain. Everything is energy, and energy can never be destroyed, and Chen's Paris meeting was recorded in the Akashic Chronicles. Easily discovered by one with Hokee's ability.

The damnable aspect of taking magic mushrooms along with the sage and herbal smoke and steam was that you were left outside of space and time without a physical 3-D existence. And there was nothing Hokee could do to make it appear faster. Although adrift without a frame of reference, he was not afraid of being lost. Everything is one. And in remembering this, Hokee relaxed in being, letting his mind drift until his own universe began reforming.

It was almost seven in the morning when Hokee left the sweat lodge and headed for a shower. The long mushroom-fueled journey was hard on his body, and he was dehydrated and famished. He was drying off when Daniel came by with the news of their evening's activities. After learning about the four dead men who had been trailing him earlier, Hokee called Grant.

"Morning, Hokee."

"Morning Grant. I guess you heard we had a little excitement here last night. Your Team One men were exceptional. I came from my sweat lodge these guys told you about, and I can confirm the Chinese burned my house to murder Myron. There are only a few Chinese nationals involved; the other killers in his little army are mercenaries from all over the world. China is keeping a low profile but is serious about acquiring Myron's work."

"We're set up to follow Cheng and his men when they leave their hotel," Grant responded. "I was planning on an ambush when they got to where Mills is hiding. Shall I execute or wait until later?"

"After my sweat and given the four dead men from Cheng's army, I believe it might be better to let the Chinese question Mills. He knows nothing important and cannot do us any harm. He believes Myron to be dead. The Chinese will want Myron if he is alive. Since Cheng saw me at my hotel, he may wonder if Myron is also alive. "I'm inclined to set a trap for Cheng and his warriors. But I need to talk with Myron first. How about keeping Cheng and his men under discrete surveillance until later today?"

"We can do that."

"Great, and thanks." The line was dead.

CHAPTER FIFTY-FOUR

Myron

Hokee drove Daniel and Lucas out to the gate to bring the dead men's cars back to his yard. Then, while waiting for Grant's new recruits to arrive, the three men ate breakfast in Team One's motorhome.

Lucas, the one with the scary dark eyes, volunteered to cook breakfast. Slabs of ham steak with roasted red potatoes, scrambled eggs and cheese, and lots of toast. They assumed the four new men would also be hungry, so for a few minutes, the small kitchen looked like a cookhouse for lumberjacks. Lucas might not be Julia Child, but the food was satisfying, and the men all had seconds. Stuffed with the breakfast Lucas prepared, and two gallons of orange juice later, the men were ready to deal with the dead.

Grant showed up in his vehicle with the four new men driving another SUV just as the three men finished eating. Team Two was left to keep tabs on Cheng and his men. Team One's motorhome pantry was getting low on food, but there was plenty of coffee. The men stood around drinking coffee while Grant, Hokee, and Team One discussed plans to deal with the Chinese problem.

After debating various options, Hokee had a plan. "Grant, it would make it easier if Myron stayed dead. Right now, only a few are aware he survived the fire. Besides us and our men, only Zoey and Why-ay'-looh are aware he is alive. I need to discuss this with Myron, but if he agrees, could we find a new home for him where he can continue with his work under an assumed name? I can supply him with the documentation for a new identity.

"Hell, I have five acres and a lodge on Lake Coeur d'Alene. It's private, with no close neighbors. We rarely go up there anymore. The house could easily accommodate half a dozen people, and we could build him a modern computer lab and more houses if necessary."

"That sounds perfect if you don't mind letting it go."

"Given the situation, the property couldn't be used for a greater purpose. Idaho is attracting more than retired law enforcement people. Several high-tech start-ups are locating in the state. Another one would not bring unwanted attention. He couldn't advertise his A.I. projects, but computer services are needed, which he could use to camouflage other activities."

"All right, let me run this past Myron. He may have some personal conflicts. Wife, kids, parents, and so forth. I am not familiar with his situation. We were focused on his vision quest. I'll have to get back to you later. I've been thinking, why don't we load the dead men in their cars and park them at the hotel where Cheng men are staying?"

"Well, yeah, we could do that. But why? What do you have in mind?" Grant wasn't seeing Hokee's plan.

"Several reasons Grant. I want to rattle them. They won't know exactly what happened for their men to get killed or how many men they are facing. The appearance of four dead men at their hotel informs them we know their identification. Since they were following me, they will think my place is our staging spot. It kind of makes sense since, supposedly, this place is vacant. The Chinese government cannot allow anyone to be informed about their killing an American citizen on American soil. Certain countries and corporations will assume that the Chinese, like themselves, will kill anyone in their way to own the most advanced A.I. technology in the world. However, they must not be caught doing the killing, especially in a foreign country."

"When the Chinese find the dead men, they will assume I had some help. To limit their exposure, I believe the Chinese will mount a full-scale effort to eliminate the opposition who knows who they are. That's us. If they take the bait, Cheng may order an all-out attack on this place to eliminate me and whoever else might be here. I like the idea of having the battle out here on the lava flats, which would not endanger the innocent people in Pocatello."

"Okay, but these guys aren't idiots, Hokee," Grant argued. "They won't start a war without doing some reconnaissance. Maybe use a drone. A helicopter. Both."

"I'm counting on that. We need one man to follow the vehicles hauling the dead men back to their hotel to pick up the two drivers. The four new men will go pick up the other motorhomes from the reservation. While they're running errands, I'll pick up some army surplus tents to make it look like a major battle encampment. Maybe a few cooking fires with men hustling around. Make it look like a serious army. We could use those other men you talked about, not only to make it look real, but to provide more firepower. Those extra men could be here before dark. I don't expect the Chinese to make any moves for another day or two. They have to gather intelligence and make plans. I wouldn't be surprised to see helicopters with armed men rappelling down here and maybe some military-grade drones with armament. The Chinese will employ every weapon and technology they can lay their hands on to kill us in their war."

"You're right," Grant agreed. "Go meet with Myron and see what you can arrange. I'll stay here and start planning our defenses. If the Chinese plan a major attack to kill us, they'll need to get creative because of the single road leading here. Your attack drone scenario and helicopter drop for warriors make perfect sense."

It was after eight in the morning when Hokee pulled up to Why-ay'-looh's hogan. Shila almost knocked him down as soon as he was out of his vehicle. Standing on his hind legs with both front legs on Hokee's shoulders, the wolf licked his master's face, grinning like a four-year-old child on Christmas morning looking at the haul Santa Claus left. After this greeting, Hokee knocked softly on the hogan's only door and waited for it to be opened. The door swung open and Hokee entered, closely followed by Shila, who refused to let his master out of sight. As he shut the door behind him, Hokee greeted the two men inside.

"Greetings father, Hello Myron." Both men were standing, and his mentor mirrored the big smile on Hokee's face. Myron looked especially pleased. Why-ay'-looh wrapped his arms around his adopted son, giving him a gigantic hug. Hokee embraced the man who gave him life and then greeted Myron with a handshake.

Before Myron could speak, Why-ay'-looh said, "Coming this early must mean you have some important news."

"Yes, father. But before we get into that, how about a cup of your famous tea, and we all sit down?" The hogan was small. Why-ay'-looh slept on a WW II army cot that also served as his chair. Myron slept on the floor as Hokee once did for eleven years. Today, Hokee sat on the floor with Shila's head on his lap, leaving the cot for Why-ay'-looh and Myron."

"Myron, how goes the vision quest?" Hokee asked while Myron sat on the far side of the cot.

"Great, Hokee. Yesterday I had my first sweat lodge experience with Why-ay'-looh. It was fantastic. Mind-blowing to use a hackneyed phrase. But true. A real eye opener."

"I'm happy for you, Myron. Did you come to any conclusion regarding your quest?"

"I certainly did. The questions you asked me to write every day have truly paid off. Ultimately, I am fully aware that I cannot relinquish the advantage I possess in the A.I. universe. Civilization needs a superior A.I. to combat warrior machines unscrupulous countries and companies are sure to develop. Building superior A.I. warriors will be too tempting to resist."

"Perfect." Hokee was relieved that he didn't have to persuade Myron. "I was sure that would be your decision. Did you see and interface with your spirit animal?" A wry grin appeared on Hokee's face as he asked the question. It was like he already knew the answer.

"Oh man, Hokee. You must let me have Shila. He was my spirit animal, and in that hallowed space outside of time where we met, the wolf promised to always direct my thoughts to the good."

Hokee almost burst out with a laugh while Why-ay'-looh had a sly smile. "It seems your lodge experience and vision quest has been a success, Myron, but you can't have Shila. He was a gift from my father here," he said, nodding at Why-ay'-looh who was making the tea. "But once you get settled, I promise to find you a wolf."

"Would you? Can you? And what do you mean when I am settled?" Panic momentarily clouded Myron's eyes.

Before Hokee could respond, Why-ay'-looh turned from the bench he worked on, handing both men tea in tin cups before sitting back down beside Myron on the cot with his own cup.

"Myron, the world believes you are dead. Aside from the three of us and Zoey, plus a few men who are helping me battle the men who killed you, no one else knows you are alive. If I could provide you absolute privacy with a beautiful home on a lake, and a lab with all the equipment you desire, a new identity complete with birth certificate, driver's license, and SS card, is there any reason you cannot stay dead?"

"WOW! Jesus! Are you serious? Stay dead? You mean like having a funeral for ole Doctor Myron Whittleman while letting the estate pick apart his life's work like patents, work products, life insurance, bank accounts, investments, and so forth? That the kind of dead you're talking about?"

"Well... yeah. That kind of dead." Hokee glanced over at Why-ay'-looh, who exhibited a big smile on his old, weathered face, and couldn't help but grin in return.

"Shoot. I've already been dead now for what, three, four, five days? I've lost track of time between living in a tent and staying inside here. This old blue ball still seems to keep on spinning around the sun in my presumed absence. My apparent death hasn't had a calamitous effect on the world. My parents and associates already believe me dead. Right now, they are grieving, and while it seems a little cruel, they don't need to know I am still alive. They need not be involved in my A.I. battle. So, yeah, I guess I could stay dead. But that won't stop me from building you a new house.

'Okay. I'll let you." Myron's acceptance of his fate was a great relief to Hokee, which was apparent as the muscles in his face relaxed. "And so you know, my tastes ain't cheap," causing both Myron and Why-ay'-looh to grin.

"Thanks, Hokee. For everything," Myron replied. 'You gave me life, and there is nothing I will not do for you. Now, how about our war? What's happening?"

Hokee gave both men a full recap, including his plans to end the war. After speaking for several minutes, silence filled the small hogan. Every man pondered the A.I. battle and their role in the future fight.

As an old wise shaman, Why-ay'-looh fully appreciated the possibility of a singularity event if control of A.I. got out of hand. Like the other men with him in the hogan, he understood an advanced A.I. like the one Myron possessed might be the only weapon humanity has to stay in existence.

Chapter Fifty-Five

Mills

Cheng was drinking green tea while Xiu had coffee with two creamers and three sugar packages when Draco entered the hotel's breakfast room. Draco's arrival received no acknowledgment from Cheng, but Xiu couldn't help but make a snide comment. That the scary man with deep-set eyes, pock-marked face, and snow-white hair ignored him and seemed impervious to Cheng's lethality rankled. "How *nice* of you to join us, *Mister* Vargas," he uttered in a sneering tone; the words, nice and Mister Vargas, sounded like he was eating raw lemon. Xiu simply could not hide the venom in his voice. Earlier in Xiu's hotel room, Draco said he would meet them in the lounge at seven. It was six-fifty-nine, one minute before his announced arrival time, and for Draco, Xiu's insulting comment was unworthy of an answer. That Draco completely ignored the insult, only made Xiu more frustrated. He was about to say something else when Cheng gave him a scathing, watch yourself look. The look you will see on your father's face when you have done something foolish and are about to compound your stupidity. Cheng saved Xiu from getting his ass handed to him at the end of a table leg by asking, "Is your man still watching Mill's house?"

"Yes." Sounding almost normal with an effort after recognizing that his arrogance almost got him in serious trouble. The look in Chen's eyes caused Xiu to rethink his words. Aggravating China's foremost assassin would not be smart. In a more subdued voice, he continued, "My man informed me fifteen minutes ago that Mills had not left his house. The absence of lights suggests he's still in bed.

"Are we positive that Mills is in the house?" Cheng was being cautious.

"Our man has been watching him for the last two days. After entering his house two days ago, Mills has not gone outside. His car is parked in the driveway, and he has had no visitors."

"Alright. let's eat and then pay him a visit."

During breakfast, at Cheng's insistence, Xiu made two other calls to the men in charge of the army he assembled. Feeling like events were about to escalate, Cheng wanted everybody ready for instant action. After seeing Hokee in his hotel's lounge, Cheng's sense of danger had him on a razor's edge. His guts, using the Americanized slang, made him one of the most successful assassins in the world while keeping him alive. With his guts clamoring to be heard, Cheng aspired to be one step ahead in the forthcoming war. His leaders gave him no options. China must have the most advanced A.I. capability in the world regardless of the price or lives lost, and there was only one answer for failure, death to those who failed to deliver.

That they had not heard from the four men following Hokee concerned Cheng. Their last communication was when they were standing outside of the gates to Hokee's driveway, discussing their options. His guts also told him his men were led into a trap, and they were now dead or in prison. Probably dead. He had not warned them that the Indian was a deadly opponent, as it should not have been unnecessary. If his soldiers died at the Indian's home, maybe that's where the war should be fought.

Larry Mills lived in a single-story red brick house with white shutters and a single-car garage. Realtors had several names for this kind of house: the newlywed's home, a starter home, or a retirement home, depending on the age and makeup of their clients. Mills purchased the house three years earlier after marrying Julie Westover, his high school sweetheart. Not long after they were married, Julie discovered Mills was already married to Singularity and had little time for a wife or family. She dumped him two years ago. Given his salary, Mills could afford a much grander house, but with little free time, changing his address would have to wait until later. It was a few minutes past eight a.m. when Cheng and his men parked on the street near the driveway of Mill's house. Xiu exited the vehicle first to confer with the detective he hired to keep track of Mills. After confirming that Mills was still in his house, Xiu paid the detective and told him to leave, as his services were no longer required.

As the detective drove away, Cheng and Draco also got out of their vehicle and joined by Xiu, began walking up the cracked cement sidewalk toward the house. The front yard had once been grass but was now a dry, untended weed patch ten inches high. The walkway led to a rain-stained porch littered with dead leaves, bird droppings, and old junk flyers. It wasn't the sort of house and yard you will expect a wealthy entrepreneur to live in. The house and yard screamed neglect. Xiu rang the doorbell, and all three men heard the chimes inside. Two minutes passed with Xiu tapping his toe on the soiled front porch. Cheng and Draco stood like statutes. After two minutes, Xiu rang the bell once more for several seconds, followed by pounding on the door with his fists. After another full minute, the three men heard movement inside.

"Who is it?" A raspy like that of a smoker asked."

Xiu looked over at Cheng. They did not anticipate the question and were not prepared to answer. Seeing and hearing nothing from Cheng, Xiu rang the doorbell again as though that answered the question.

"Who is it? What do you want?" Besides sounding like a barfing dog, the voice also sounded pissed.

"Business associates." Draco's voice was not loud, but it still sounded like thunder.

For whatever reason, that seemed to work. "Okay, give me a minute. I wasn't expecting company." This time, the voice sounded almost normal, albeit somewhat gravelly.

The three men waited on the porch for another five minutes, unaware that they were observed by Team Two parked on top of a large lava mound a half mile in the distance. Both watchers had Steiner model 2675 military-grade binoculars, allowing them to see the sweat under the arms of Xiu's white shirt. Charles couldn't help but comment. "It looks like one of those

Chinese men is a little tense," Noah said to his partner. "I guess ole Mills is making him sweat."

"Maybe the dude with the white hair is making him sweat," Noah responded. "I would be sweating if he was standing by me."

"You make a point. The other Chinaman seems calm, but the white-haired man is sending out all kinds of vibrations. He could be a problem if we get into a fight."

"Maybe. But not today. We're just observers. Oh, the door opened. I guess Mills is home. I'd love to hear their conversation."

"Speaking of sweating. I think our old buddy Mills will be sweating blood before long."

"I hope they don't kill him, but the son-of-a-bitch deserves to die. Regardless of what the Chinese do to him, his days as an officer in Singularity are finished." As the three men on the porch went inside the house, Charlie and Noah lowered the binoculars, giving their eyes a rest.

Larry Mills looked as haggard as his voice sounded through the door. He was unshaven with bloodshot eyes, and while he was dressed, his clothes looked as if they had been slept in for days. Once the three men were inside, Draco assumed control.

"We want Doctor Whittleman's formula for advanced A.I." Not only was Draco's appearance daunting, but his soft voice cut the air like a meat cleaver. Looking at the menacing trio, it was not a command to be ignored.

"I knew you would come," Larry whined. "Gunny called me. He said that half-breed son-of-a-bitch shot him asking about Myron's formula. Gunny said he wasn't supposed to tell anybody about the Indian, but he told me anyway. He didn't know the formula; none of us do. We asked Myron for it, but he wouldn't share."

Draco was certain that Mills was not familiar with the formula.

"Where is Myron hiding?" Draco asked. This question couldn't be ignored either. It was a question for which only the truth will keep Mills breathing.

"What? Myron is dead. You guys killed him when you bombed the Indian's house. He got cremated." Draco and Cheng were both sure that Mills thought Myron was dead.

"Since the Indian is still alive, maybe Myron also escaped the fire." Cheng's tone of voice was also commanding, and like Draco's, it was not loud.

The three men he was facing obviously frightened mills. He was aware of the danger to his life. Sweat covered his face, and his voice wavered as he said, "he doesn't answer his phone." No one has seen him, and he hasn't contacted anyone from Singularity or the university. Substitute teachers are covering his classes. If he was still alive, he would have contacted someone."

It was obvious to the three men that Mills believed Myron was dead. It did seem rather odd that no one saw or heard from Myron since the fire, but that doesn't mean he is dead. There must be someone Myron trusted who would know the truth. But regardless, they will learn nothing from Larry Mills. As one of the traitors, his future was not promising. Without Myron, Singularity will cease to exist and in the world of advanced technology, traitors will find it difficult to find other employment.

Charles and Noah watched the three men leave the house. Looking through their binoculars, they saw frowns on all three faces as they stalked down the sidewalk.

Cheng stopped by their vehicle but didn't enter. Addressing his companions, he told them the Indian was the sole individual who knew if the scientist was alive or dead. It won't be easy to get him to talk. Maybe impossible. Let's go back to my hotel and discuss the situation. We will have to teach that savage how the oldest civilization on earth deals with inferior people."

Their resolve intensified when they found the four dead men who had been trailing Hokee.

CHAPTER FIFTY-SIX

Preparation

Before leaving Why-ay'-looh and Myron, Hokee cautioned them to keep Myron out of sight until they could prepare for his future. Myron seemed eager to visit his new home and resume living a somewhat normal life. They discussed various possibilities for his new name, but Myron wanted to give it more thought. It isn't every day you assume a new identity, one that can't be associated with your current life. One issue he thought about was the title of doctor. While having a PhD after your name has certain benefits, Myron wondered if he would be more invisible without the title. Hokee told him to take his time and talk about it with Why-ay'-looh. He said he would visit them as soon as he could, but warned them it might not be for a few days. "Sorry Myron, but you get to sleep on the floor a bit more. I promise it won't kill you. It was my bed for a few years. He said this with a sardonic grin, lighting his handsome face.

Hokee had been sitting on the floor with Shila's head on his lap before he got up to leave. At the doors to Why-ay'-looh's hogan, Hokee said, "Shila, ready to go home, pal?" Shila almost knocked Hokee over as he rushed through the door to Hokee's Explorer. Thanking his mentor/father for taking care of his friend, Hokee opened the passenger door for the one true love of his life. Shila preferred riding in front whenever he was invited. Giving Shila a hug and scratching his head, Hokee took his brother back home. The name Shila does mean brother. And in different ways, they *were* both wolves.

When Hokee reached his driveway, he was surprised to find the gates unlocked. He decided that if any unwanted visitors were to come, they would be met with an unfriendly reception, so he opted to keep them unlocked. He had driven a little over a mile when he saw a caravan of large dump trucks heading towards him. When he built the ten-mile road to his house, Hokee made a wide spot at every mile for cars to pass. During the eighteen years he lived here on the lava flat, he never once passed a vehicle coming in the other direction, so the turnouts were overgrown, making them difficult to spot. With no listing on the county register, only a handful knew about his home, resulting in minimal traffic on his driveway. These big trucks heading his way were a surprise, and he frantically looked around for one of his turnouts. Hokee drove slowly, looking for a turnout, and he didn't have to wait long before spotting one of the wide weed-covered spots. Hokee parked his vehicle, then stepped out, signaling the truck driver to halt. With a wide grin on his bearded face, the truck driver with the name **Iron** stitched on his blue-collar shirt—Hokee wasn't sure if it meant a job title or the man's name—informed Hokee that he and those coming behind were employees of the Olson Construction Company from Nampa and were hauling away the ashes and ruins from a house, "I guess that's was yours," he finished with another big grin.

Yesterday, as a surprise for his friend, Grant called Bosie and ordered the trucks, front loaders, plus twenty construction men to come down to Pocatello, load up the dead ashes and fire debris so he could begin working on Hokee's new house. Hokee thanked the driver and wished him a good day, then stood by as five more large dump trucks drove past, hauling away a life that ended in a roaring fire.

Arriving at the slope leading to his big yard, there were so many vehicles, campers and tents Hokee was forced to hunt for someplace to park. Shila jumped out of the vehicle trotting around the yard, sniffing everything and everybody in the entire two-acre site, getting a sense of the environment and people. For every scent receptor a human has, a dog has around fifty. Their sense of smell is 10,000 to 100,000 times more acute than man's. Being the protector, this is one way the wolf prepares for danger if it ever approaches. Cataloging scents. That was the other reason for Hokee bringing Shila back home. The main one is that he enjoyed Shila's company.

Hokee stood by his vehicle, looking around at the men and equipment Grant brought to clean up the mess caused by the exploding drum of high-octane fuel. The ruins of his old house were gone, leaving only the lava wall that separated his bedroom from the rest of the house. With a broad smile, Grant walked over to a stunned man, "What do you think, Hokee? You came back before I could get it rebuilt."

"Ah, man, Grant. I have no idea what to say. The thought of cleaning up the mess was discouraging, and I came back to find the place all cleaned up. I guess thanks will have to do."

"Hell, Hokee. This little clean-up job isn't nearly payment enough for saving my family. I'll build you a damn mansion after we get the plans."

"I really appreciate having a friend like you Grant, but friends don't do friends a favor for a reward. However, if you feel the absolute need to build me a new house, you will have to fight with Myron over who pays for it. I left him with Why-ay'-looh's and he made me promise to let him build me a new house. I told him it would not be cheap. You guys can split the bill."

"We'll figure it out. I threw away everything in your bedroom. Too much smoke damage. I found your underground river where you and Shila escaped the fire. It's a wonderful setup for your power and water needs. I'd like to study your electrical system when we get a chance."

Once upon a time, that water saved my life. I loved the isolation, the river and the cave, so this is where I built my house, out here in the middle of nowhere. An engineer from the university designed my electrical system and helped me locate some of the equipment. The design was lost in the fire, but we can back-engineer the components and draw a new set of plans. It is an awesome system."

"It's a sweet little setup, Hokee. Your own oasis and privacy. When we build your new mansion, I'll pave your driveway."

"That would be appreciated, but before we get all giddy about the building project, we have a war to fight. Speaking of which, can you ask your buddy at Mountain Home AFB to supply us with one of those fancy drones the military uses?"

"Why sure. The commanding colonel who provided your thrilling plane ride still owes me. He won't let me have their classified drones, but the military has several other advanced models I can borrow. I'll make a call right now."

"Before you make the call. We could also use some 50-caliber rifles and a couple of cases of ammunition. And *thrilling* doesn't even begin to describe that plane ride."

"I'm ahead of you this time, Hokee. I have ten 50s on their way. Do you think we need more?

"We need men up on the plain to watch our flanks and fight helicopters. I think one or two more would be useful."

"Got it. They'll be here before dark."

"Thanks, Grant. I'll see you later."

Hokee went looking for Daniel or Lucas, but before locating them, his phone buzzed. It was from Charles.

"Hi Charles, what's the news?"

"We watched Cheng, and his two henchmen visit Mills. When the three men left his house, they all had sour looks on their faces. They drove straight to Cheng's hotel and immediately spotted the dead men's cars. One man stayed with the cars to make a call, while the other two entered the hotel. Their body language suggests some pissed-off men."

"That's great, Charles. Work. Thanks for the report. Please keep watching Cheng. I think he's getting ready for war, and I want to always know his location. Don't get caught.

"Got it, boss. We will be careful."

CHAPTER FIFTY-SEVEN

The Chess Game

Back in his hotel room, Change was enraged. The discovery of the four dead men who were trailing Hokee caused him to reconsider his plans. In a calm, clear voice full of fury, he said, **"Cầo! Cầo! Cầo!"** Emphasizing every syllable like the words were excrement. "I knew that fucking Indian was trouble. He knows we are behind the fire and are here for the A.I. design. He will have other men with him now, and they will all be aware of China's involvement. Before they involve the American authorities with evidence of Chinese involvement, we need to kill every one of them. Xiu has over put together one hundred fighting men we can field immediately. We need pictures of the Indian's place and the immediate area so we can make plans to disappear the Indian and those with him. I want the Indian alive if possible, so he can tell us where Whittleman is hiding. The doctor must be alive. Draco, you watched the Indians place after it burned to the ground; what did you see?"

Cheng regarded Draco Vargas as an associate with lethal capabilities equal to his own, but the man with a chilling glare and pox face always wore blue denim pants and ridiculous boots, the clothing of an inferior man in Cheng's opinion. While Draco's choice of attire influenced Cheng's negative opinion of the killer, Cheng was certain that his thoughts remained hidden.

Vargas, however, was fully aware of what the clever Chinaman thought of him, but such macho bullshit couldn't bother him. Cheng had gathered a little information about his life, but no one on earth knew the real Draco Vargas. Some people knew a little about one small segment of his life and assumed they knew him. Other people saw a different aspect of him, and they also believed they knew who he was. These tableaus were repeated several more times in multiple facets of Draco's life, to the extent that he often wondered which part of him was real. He knew there was no one on earth more lethal than himself and that this created a dangerous persona that was apparent at some level to every person he met. Cheng did not know one-tenth of who Draco was, and his feelings of superiority almost made Draco smile. But that would be telling.

Draco responded to Cheng's question in a calm voice, free from any anger. "The Indian lived in a basin on a lava flat surrounded by several thousand acres. The lava plains look formidable. Hugh black rock ripples in ten-to-fifteen-foot swells and humps, making crossing it difficult and dangerous. No one else lives anywhere close to him. No lights were visible for miles around his home when I visited at night. His closest neighbors are at least fifteen miles away, maybe farther."

"Can we approach his residence across the lava flats with using the road?"

"I don't know. It will be a tough hike, but I didn't see any serious impediment."

Xiu knocked on the door while Draco spoke, and Cheng let him in. "Ah, just in time." Pointing at Xiu, Cheng said. "Find us an advanced drone and some heavy artillery. Right now. And several 50-caliber guns will be needed. We also need six large helicopters that can carry eight to ten armed men. Something like a Sikorsky CH-53E Super Stallion or the CH-53K King Stallion. You must make sure that a Chinese person is not seen buying this equipment; the drones, artillery, or helicopters and these items will be purchased from different dealers around the country. We want everything here within the next two days. Money is not a problem."

As Xiu went towards the bedroom to order equipment, Draco asked, "I have been told you have over a hundred fighting men available. Is that true?"

"Yes," Xiu snarls. He didn't like Draco and disliked being questioned by the man.

"We need to see the men and their weapons as soon as possible." As Draco talked, Xiu looked like he wanted to strangle the man he also considered an inferior being.

"This will have to take place somewhere private where we will not be observed," Cheng added. "Are you aware of a place like that?"

"Camelback Mountain is eight to ten miles west and is isolated," Xiu said. A hunter or hiker may be around, but we can handle it. It will be an excellent staging location."

"That sounds perfect. Arrange for your men to be there this afternoon or early tomorrow. Draco will serve as the primary contact once the men are assembled. I don't want China to be associated with the men or their assignments. Draco, you will evaluate the men and organize them into teams of eight to ten men each. Be sure to have a man familiar with 50-caliber guns on each team."

Xiu was furious that Draco would be responsible for the mercenary army he put together but understood why he could not be involved. He located and hired his fighters using a British SAS mercenary. He damn well wanted to inspect the men who all commanded large up-front payments.

Cheng saw the look on Xiu's face and understood the reason. "Xiu, we'll observe and study the men from afar. I imagine Camelback Mountain has a secluded spot to observe without being seen."

"Yes, I believe so. I'll locate a topographical map we can study."

***

Little by little, Grant's men gathered at Hokee's place. Hokee arranged the parking of motorhomes so those with collapsable awnings could roll them out, giving the camp a larger footprint. He assumed that Cheng would soon have drones flying overhead if they were not already deployed. They set up four large campaign tents and a dozen small four-man tents in strategic locations to give the yard a military-style appearance. Vehicles, motorhomes and tents were arranged around Hokee's stunning fountain.

Hokee was sure that Cheng would bring as many fighters as possible without arousing unwanted attention. Life for the Chinese is cheap compared to owning the world's dominant A.I. Cheng could throw as many warriors at Hokee as he desired, limited only by the number of soldiers they can field without drawing attention from the local authority.

Hokee would not have nearly as many fighters as the number of mercenaries he expected to face. But he had several advantages, starting with the terrain, which gave his fighters a serious home-field advantage. Plus, his men were fighting to save humanity, whereas Cheng's mercenaries were only fighting for money.

A few hours later, the 50-caliber rifles arrived with over a thousand rounds of ammunition. An hour before dark, the small army received early Christmas presents. Grant's friend, Air Force Colonel Lawrence Ogden, sent four advanced drones from Mountain Home along with four highly trained drone operators. Besides being drone operators, they were all elite warriors, with only a few months or weeks of service remaining on their enlistment. After their last deployment, they chose stateside duty at one of the military bases for the time remaining on their commitment. The colonel gave these men who *volunteered* to accompany their drones only one command. *"Don't get killed!"*

After everybody got acquainted, the drone operators explained to the other fighters that each drone carried four high-resolution cameras with military optical capabilities, including infrared lenses. Their ceiling is 10,000 feet, with a one-hour flight time before needing a new battery. Each drone came with two batteries, so one battery can be in a charging station and available with a full charge when the other battery needed replacing. The entire group of men stood near the drone operators, who were demonstrating the drones capabilities. Sophisticated laptop computers with high-resolution color image screens displayed the cameras views. Using the computer, drone operators can control every aspect of the flight, such as camera focus, view area, and resolution. The operators considered themselves drone pilots. Their exceptional training and experience as warriors were also a special bonus, as Hokee's small army needed all the professional help it could get. Next, the men checked out the 50-caliber guns. When everyone was settled, Hokee decided to brief everyone on his thoughts and plans using a surprise appearance.

No one in the group knew Hokee Wolf, except for Grant, and their relationship had been mostly business and infrequent. Grant knew one thing about Hokee for sure: he always delivered. However, when Hokee began speaking, it is safe to say not one of those present ever witnessed a more deadly man. While he had a commanding voice ringing with authority, his appearance shook these fierce, experienced warriors from their campaign hats to their toes tucked into their high-top laced combat boots.

Shamans rarely reveal their true nature. Whether meeting with friends or people doing business, they display a normal appearance in harmony with the situation. Everyone on planet earth wears a mask, shamans included. But unlike most people, a shaman is conscious of the mask he wears. He never wears a mask to deceive or to make himself more appreciated. Their masks are for illumination and to assure those they are with that they are normal people with special knowledge. Their masks are to help people accept them as regular folks. For the men seeing Hokee this afternoon, it was like watching a stage magician who looks normal and then, in the blink of an eye, either disappears or is seen hovering in the air in a glass cage. As Hokee spoke, his appearance changed to become that of an all-powerful, frightening giant. The men witnessed an unusual sight: a shaman without a mask.

This rarely occurs. However, Hokee, fully embracing his warrior role, wanted these men, who were risking their lives, to see who they were fighting alongside. Unless the men he faced were already familiar with him, this unmasked Hokee would have been too terrifying.

Hokee's body doubled in size and appeared to be made of light blue tinted marble with a hint of violet around the edge. Everyone has an energy body surrounding their physical one, which is often referred to as an aura. Few observe auras, but all can practice to see them. Most of the earth's inhabitants never heard of an aura, or if they have, they don't believe it exists. Auras appear insubstantial. They are basically light energy. A shaman can project his aura, so it appears substantial. Hokee's super large body appeared solid; it gave the look of being harder than steel.

While his body transformation was frighteningly spectacular, it was his face that made chills run down men's spines. His face was as white as a freshly calved iceberg and just as deadly as icebergs are to polar bears trapped on their surface. His features were a composite of the granite heads on Mount Rushmore and images of Genghis Khan. The Khan who did unspeakable things to his enemies. Our eyes convey our identity. Windows to our souls. Those witnessing Hokee's transformation saw in those carbon black holes in his eyes the entire history of Earth and all mankind, projected through a deadly, blinding-white light.

In an ice chilling voice that rang like a granite boulder being struck with a sledgehammer, he began, "Men, let me explain what I believe we will be facing and then decide how best to meet the challenge. A Chinese man named Feng Cheng is here in America to steal or buy the designs of an A.I. that far transcends the combined intelligence of all the brightest humans on earth. The Chinese intend to use this A.I. to rule the world, despite its impact on all life forms. We know Cheng has two men on his staff; one is another Chinese assassin, and the other one is a mercenary assassin with skills matched only by Cheng. They now have several other mercenaries waiting for orders. In all, about one hundred trained killers. China was behind the firebombing of my house to kill my client. I was only meant to be collateral damage."

Grant, with the strain of seeing and hearing his friend, needed to catch a breath and couldn't help but interrupt with a nongermane comment. "Hokee, you can't die before we drink a single malt scotch together in crystal glasses, after I build you a new home."

"Perish the thought," Hokee jested, trying and failing to speak in a friendly tone, but he grinned for his friend, attempting to present a brief hint of the Hokee Grant worked with in the past. But the white fire in his eyes did not diminish, and the small smile cracked the glacial-white face, exposing momentarily red-hot creases. An already terrifying look grew even more frightening. Not exactly what Hokee intended.

"China has avoided leaving evidence of its actions, except for two minor events that can be explained without implicating them. Daniel and Lucas killed four men here earlier, one was Chinese, but one or two foreign nationals can always be explained. I believe their mercenary army is ready to assault this place, hoping to capture me for information or kill me to eliminate the threat I pose. I stand between them and the man who owns the technology they are willing to risk a war over. They also don't want to leave anyone alive who knows that China is behind this war and will kill anybody who is here and stands between them and their intent." Hokee paused to assess the men's reactions to his words. They were standing ridged, in awe of the shaman, listening as though their lives were at stake, which they were.

"My guess is their mercenaries are special-force operators from all over the world. The Chinese want to remain invisible. Their warriors will be much like you, undoubtedly highly proficient, but they will have had little time to work up teams and attack plans. In addition, they are only fighting for a paycheck. They didn't come here to die. Whereas we are fighting for something more significant than our lives. The lava plains surrounding this oasis present a significant challenge for ground troops. It would be insanity to sneak across those flats in the dark, even with night vision goggles. During daylight, there may be men crossing the flats. These lave flats are treacherous and will eliminate those trying that route with no help from us. After seeing comrades seriously injured or killed crossing the plains, those still active will more than likely retreat."

Hokee paused in his assessment, allowing anyone to comment on what he had said so far. No one spoke.

"Okay. I believe sixty soldiers will come in by helicopter to rappel down attempting to overwhelm us with their numbers. I'm guessing ten men for each copter, so six helicopters. These helicopters will have to cross as least fifteen miles of empty lava flats regardless of which direction they choose, and they will certainly come from several directions, making us split our defense. They will not fly in formation from their staging area because that would attract unwanted attention from local authorities. Six helicopters flying together would be too noticeable. Believing themselves to have superior numbers and highly skilled soldiers, they do not expect the fight out here to last long. At least they have *that* part right."

This brought a laugh from the men who were becoming used to Hokee's appearance and voice. Hokee was pleased to hear the men laugh, as he was aware of how intense he seemed. It was time to relax a little. Shila was sitting by his side, unafraid of his master's appearance, so he got a head rub, bringing a smile to the wolf's face.

"We need to fight up on the lava plain, not down here. Tomorrow, we will hike around this oasis, looking for places we can fight from with minimum risk. We will stagger fighters around this oasis in a large circle, facing every direction. There are fifteen of us, and eleven will have a 50-caliber gun besides their regular weapons. The presence of full-time drone operators will simplify our tasks. We need to shoot down the helicopters on the flats before they reach here, and we need to stop those walking across the flats if they haven't turned back."

Michael Archibald interrupted with a question. "I don't suppose we can find any antitank or antiaircraft missiles," Asked Michael, a well-built blond warrior of Swedish descent and one of the drone operators.

Hokee looked at Grant for an answer. "I don't know," Grant replied in thought. A homing missile would be nice. With the 50-cal rifles, we can't shoot at the helicopters until they get within seven thousand feet. And then we must pour a ton of lead at them to knock them down, and they will be going fast. Getting every copter to crash before their mercenaries can rappel to the ground will be difficult. I better make a call to my favorite colonel."

"Shoot. I will find a missile or two." This came from Valance Ortega, another drone operator. Ortega was a former SEAL and a proud fourth-generation Mexican.

"A missile will be a welcome asset," Hokee responded. "See what you can do. I received a call from Charles. The mercenaries the Chinese brought here are being organized into groups on a nearby mountain. My guess of about a hundred men is close. Team Two will keep us informed. I will get a drone out now to check them out from ten thousand feet, so they won't know we're watching."

"I'll put mine in the air," Archibald volunteered.

Hokee, satisfied the men had seen and heard enough, returned to his normal form. The men witnessed Hokee's light and eye beam vanish as his appearance returned to normal. The shaman disappeared, and the men began checking their weapons. With Shila at his side, Hokee said, "Come on boy, let's get Grant to fix our dinner."

CHAPTER FIFTY-EIGHT

Spying

Grant drove a giant luxury Mercedez motorhome, but it was crowded with Hokee, Shila, Grant and team one, plus Archibald with his drone computer tablet. Dinner was frozen TV meals; Grant didn't cook. Each person chose and microwaved their own dinner. With the utilization of Bluetooth, Archibald projected the drone images from his tablet onto Grant's 44-inch flat TV installed above the passenger seat. It was still light outside, so the images were clear and bright. The drone was two miles high, but Archibald used the drone's zoom lens to provide close-up views of Cheng's armed encampment. Once the full camp was in view, they froze the image to get an accurate take of the men and their equipment.

After watching the video feed from the drone for a few minutes, Hokee called Noah on team two. "Noah, can you describe where you are on Camelback Mountain and the location of Cheng and his lieutenants?

Hokee put his phone on the speaker, so Archibald could hear Noah as he described the information needed for zooming in on Cheng's observation spot. The drone image showed Cheng and another Chinese man they had not seen before, plus three other Caucasian men. They were huddled over a tablet monitor lying on the hood of an SUV. Next to their vehicle sat a small blue drone with four two-foot-long rotor blades.

"It looks like we're going to be on TV," Grant suggested. "You said they will do that, Hokee. Let's keep our guns and the other drones out of sight."

"I believe you're right, Grant. We need to get our weapons and men undercover. No reason to give away our hand."

"I'll go take care of that," Charles volunteered.

"Thanks, Charles. Noah," Hokee said, over the phone, "What information do you have about the other Chinese man with Cheng?"

"His name is Xiu Zoeng. We believe he was Cheng's frontman, who has been here for a few weeks, perhaps even months. His reputation is that he is exceptionally dangerous."

"I'd like to ask how you are aware of that," Hokee quipped, but it can wait. "Your team reported trailing three men. Cheng and the other Chinese man. Who is the other man and where can he be found?

"We don't know his name. He appears to have equal status with Cheng, and he looks even deadlier. Right now, he is down with the mercenaries. It appears he is in charge. We overheard part of an earlier conversation between him and Cheng. He spoke as though he was on your property watching the fire fighters digging through the ashes of your house."

"Thanks. Yes, we see him now from our drone. You guys are doing a one-hell-of-a job. Do you need anything? Want us to spell you? You've been watching those guys for quite a while."

"Not right now. We take turns watching, so we're getting a little rest. We stocked up on food and water before coming up here. We're good."

"Great. We'll talk later." Hokee put the phone away. He saw all he needed from their drone, so he told Archibald to bring down, but not to their location. They did not want the Chinese to know they also had a drone, so Hokee volunteered to drive Archibald a few miles away to retrieve his plane. Taking Shila, he drove them a few miles past his gate to another open spot where they could land the drone. When they returned to the motorhome, the other men had eaten and scattered, except for a satisfied Grant, who watched as Archibald chose the Thanksgiving turkey dinner and Hokee chose two Swanson five-piece Kentucky-style fried chicken dinners for him and Shila.

***

Up on Camelback Mountain, Cheng stood transfixed, looking at the images from their drone. Clearly visible were the remnants of Hokee's house and the military-style encampment in his yard. He couldn't see many men, but the motorhomes and tents suggested a small force of around forty or fifty. While the setup appeared to be a military style encampment, the setup seemed arranged, and Cheng smiled. "It's like I thought," he said to Xiu. "That clever Indian wants us to believe he has a significant military force, but he has no military experience and no known military ties. I don't think he has many men."

Xiu had been muted until his phone buzzed. After a brief conversation, he addressed Cheng. "We have news on the helicopters. Our buyers found five Sikorsky CH-53E Super Stallions and one CH-53K King Stallion. The five Super Stallions will be tomorrow. The King Stallion is being fitted with a 50-caliber machine gun and will be here the day after. You wanted everything here tomorrow, but I thought having the King outfitted with the machine gun was worth an extra day."

"Excellent. We can afford the extra day if it means eliminating that cunning Indian bastard. Let's have our drone keep their camp under surveillance to see what preparations they're making."

It needs battery changes every fifty minutes, but it will only take seconds and then it can be back on site. Xiu was delighted to have Cheng's approval and was happy that the white-haired freak was busy down below with their mercenary army.

Cheng stepped back from the hood of the vehicle and said to Xiu, "Call Draco and have him take an inventory of our grenades. I want to dump a few on their camp before the fighting begins." Xiu didn't enjoy talking with Draco, but it will feel good giving him an order for a change.

A few phone calls later, Xiu was happy to tell Cheng. "Draco said they have no grenades on hand, but one of the Germans said he can get a crate of high explosive fragmentation grenades here tomorrow. He wants a million U.S. dollars."

"Fine, see to it." Cheng had seen enough for today. "Let's go back to the hotel. We'll have Draco stop by for a report when he returns,"

Chapter Fifty-Nine

Battle Stations

After dinner, Hokee strolled around the yard, trailed by Shila. He spent a little time talking to each small group of men, reminding them to assume they were under surveillance and to stagger their movements in the open to keep the Chinese guessing about their actual number. Returning to the motorhome, he found Grant sitting with Ortega, their Mexican American drone operator.

"News, Hokee," Grant was happy to provide. "Ortega scored an anti-tank missile. It will be here tomorrow."

"When we got back to the States from our last deployment," Ortega chipped in, "we had some unused ordnance that mysteriously didn't get turned back into stores. One of my buddies had an anti-tank missile. He wanted ten grand; I offered five." He was beaming like a first-grade school child whom the teacher had praised.

"That's great Ortega. I am concerned about their helicopters. Your missile will take care of at least one for us. And I have an idea about eliminating another three or four so we can concentrate our 50-caliber guns on the remaining one or two. That raises my confidence level significantly."

Grant scratched his head with a workman's fingers made thick with years of heavy labor before striking it rich in the construction business. "You don't suppose Cheng will lead his mercenary army, do you, Hokee?"

"I think it is highly unlikely. First, he doesn't want his warriors to know they are fighting for China, and second, he wants an escape if they lose the fight."

"I guess that's why Team Two is keeping a watch on him for us," Grant surmised.

"Yes. I don't want him to escape. The bastard destroyed my home attempting to kill me and Myron." Hearing the tone in Hokee's voice, Grant glanced over at his friend just in time to catch a brief glimpse of the shaman.

The next morning, after breakfast, Hokee and Shila walked up their long, sloping driveway to the lava plain. For the next three hours, Hokee hiked around the rim, circling the camp below, looking for places where his fighters could fire on the helicopters and ground troops without overly exposing themselves. He wanted Daniel and Lucas out by the gates on the road to his driveway to keep Cheng's mercenaries from using it. The pair had already proven to be a lethal combination. With Grant and Hokee, that left twelve shooters to distribute around the rim with approximately 30 degrees of separation between fighters depending on the terrain. In a small notebook, Hokee drew a map of the rim, marking off likely spots he picked out to place the shooters. He also made notes about treacherous spots to avoid when going to their battle stations. The plan was to bring the men up on the rim after dark when Cheng's drone was less likely to see what they were doing. They aimed to prevent Cheng's mercenary army from discovering the fighter's location.

That afternoon, Cheng's fighters received their first five helicopters with battle proven pilots. Draco was so pleased with the machines Xiu purchased he decided to take one for an early evening flight. Picking up three of the high explosive fragmentation grenades, he had his pilot fly over Hokee's camp using the same path previously used to firebomb the house. Draco stood in the open cabin door with a live grenade in each hand, ready to throw them down on the camp below. If there was enough time, the other grenade would be tossed down. He ordered the pilot to fly slow enough that the men in Hokee's camp could get a brief look at him, but fast enough so no one on the ground would have time to grab a gun and shoot him. The helicopter speed was too fast to allow Draco any kind of accurate toss, but Hokee's camp was large enough that any grenade thrown in its midst was bound to cause damage, perhaps even kill a few.

The first grenade rolled under one of the team's motorhomes before exploding. When the grenade exploded, it took out the propane tank, destroying one home entirely and damaging two others nearby. Fortunately, no one was inside of the home that exploded and those in the other two houses escaped with ringing ears. Not so fortunate were the three men sitting on the wall of Hokee's fountain drinking beer. The second grenade bounced against a large lava rock Hokee used as a step up onto his large deck. While the deck burned with the rest of the house, the rock remained. The grenade exploded against the rock that acted like a blast door, sending grenade fragments and rock debris back toward the three men by the fountain. Each man receiving several large cuts requiring stitches and large bruises; one man had a dislocated shoulder, another was knocked unconscious, resulting in a concussion, and the third man who faced the exploding grenade head-on was temporarily blind from rock fragments. He wouldn't lose his eyes, but would be out of commission for a few days until his vision returned.

After inspecting the camp and reviewing the damage, Hokee and Grant were relieved they didn't suffer more damage or lose any lives. Not that their small army needed any more incentive, but they all swore to avenge this cowardly attack. Two men took their positions on the lava flat with 50-caliber rifles to prevent future attacks.

Hokee felt responsible for the attack since he assumed they would not be at war until tomorrow or the day after. He should have posted two guards out by the gates. The attack demonstrated that the Chinese intended to kill all of them. From now on, their fighters would not hesitate to kill any mercenary soldier caught in their sight

After his attack on Hokee's compound, Draco visited Cheng, who had moved to a different hotel to remain difficult to find. Cheng wanted to avoid any further personal encounters with Hokee or his men. Xiu and he were enjoying baijius when Draco knocked on the door.

Once inside, with adrenaline still in his system, Draco started talking sounding almost cheerful, which for him was about as eager as he ever allowed himself to feel. "I dropped a couple of grenades on the Indian's camp. What a rush. Not sure about how much damage we caused, but they made one hell of a racket. I saw at least one motorhome blow up. Not sure if I killed anyone, but it got their attention. From what I observed, they won't be much of a challenge when we repel sixty warriors down on them. I didn't see many men around. Their camp gives the illusion of housing more people. The drone operator showed me the pictures from today's flight. The Indian doesn't have many people."

"Did you think it was smart to stir up the hornet's nest?" Xiu sneered.

Ignoring the tone of the unpleasant little Chinese man, Draco responded, "I wanted to see their camp for myself and get a feel for their readiness. They pose no threat. Hell, they didn't even have any guards posted. After we get our gunship tomorrow, we can kiss the Indian and his men goodbye."

"Don't forget Draco; we want to take the Indian alive if possible. We will torture him, making it quicker to find the missing scientist. I know you are a master of interrogation, but you may be surprised by some of the techniques China has developed."

"It may not be possible to capture him alive, Cheng," Draco said. "However, I have an idea about that scientist. I want to collect the last big payment you offered for delivery of the design." After this speech, Draco turned to go, leaving Cheng and Xiu to wonder what he had in mind. Cheng had a parting comment.

"Killing everyone who knows China is involved in this unholy mess takes priority over capturing the Indian alive. However we still need to find the missing scientist. It would simply be a bonus for us if your idea pans out." Tilting the bottle, Cheng took a sip of his baijiu like it was making the point for him.

CHAPTER SIXTY

Chief Wahvevah

Chief of police on the Fort Hall Indian reservation, Wahvevah was usually content to sit in his oversized office chair dressed in a ridiculous custom-made chief's uniform he designed that looked like a cross between what a San Francisco drag queen will wear on Halloween eve or a low budget western comedy sheriff's costume. He wore white custom-made cowboy boots featuring red roses on the front, into which he tucked black denim pants with a purple silk tuxedo stripe running down the sides. In addition, he added a creamy white silk shirt and a Holstein calf hide vest with a silver sheriff's badge the size of a small salad plate, which flapped about when he walked. A turquoise gem bolo tie topped off the ensemble. On a nearby hat rack perched a pure white ten-gallon Stetson. He almost always sat at his desk looking at porno magazines while playing at being a police chief, but today he was upset with Zoey, the reservation greeter, receptionist, and secretary when needed, which was almost never.

For the past few days, she behaved suspiciously. First, she took off for several hours, providing no explanation, and then someone reported they had seen her drive by the station several times. Then she hovered around the receptionist's desk, although there was nothing to keep her there. The chief had grown used to getting his own coffee as half the time Zoey was out of the building. Every time he left his office to grab a fresh cup, she sat at her desk, rarely leaving except for a bathroom break. Something was not right, and the chief was determined to discover the problem. She didn't use to hang around all day doing nothing. Zoey had no romantic interests he could find, even though she was a beautiful young lady. The police station had few visitors requiring her attention, even though it featured an outstanding display of Indian artifacts. Her entire behavior was mysterious, and the chief could find no reason.

Until.

The chief was refilling his coffee cup in the break room next to Zoey's desk when he heard her on the telephone. He only caught one word, but it was enough to grab his attention. Why-ay'-looh. Everyone on the reservation knew the medicine man. Why would Zoey be interested in his activities? As soon as the handset was returned to the receiver, she left the station with the chief close behind. Ever since that telephone business with the Paris police officer when he revealed Hokee's office location which led to the attack on Hilda, Zoey had shown him disrespect, and the chief wanted to find her doing something illegal or wrong so he will feel better about getting Hokee's office gal carved up. It was common knowledge among everyone on the reservation that those Arab killers nearly murdered Hokee's secretary after he confirmed the detective's identification and hometown. If the chief could catch Zoey doing something bad, he could even the score.

The chief followed Zoey to Why-ay'-looh's one room hogan, parking his Lincoln Navigator out of sight in a nearby reservation market's parking lot. From his vehicle he watched as Zoey knocked on the door, which was opened by a young, pleasant looking white man with a bandage on his head. Why-ay'-looh has no telephone, so the call the chief overheard did not originate here. Who was the man in the bandage? What was he doing in the hogan? Why was Zoey here?

The news of Hokee's house fire spread widely, but nobody had any information on how the fire originated or if Hokee survived the fire. And no one on the reservation except for Zoey knew Myron was the target or that he was now living in Why-ay'-looh's hogan. Knowing Zoey was keeping secrets, the chief returned to headquarters, waiting for her to return so he could get answers to his questions.

She was obviously being sneaky.

It was almost dark when Chief Wahvevah returned to police headquarters to wait for Zoey. A stranger was admiring Indian blankets in one of the display cases when the chief entered the lobby. Observing the readily identifiable chief's entrance, the stranger introduced himself.

"Chief, Wahvevah? Did I pronounce your name correctly?" Although the man had unusual features, some might say frighting, he was polite and posed no threat.

"Yes. Waa-vay-ah. You said it perfectly. And you are?"

"My name is Draco Vargas. I have been informed that mister Hokee Wolf lived here on the reservation at one time."

"Yes," the chief beamed. "It has been a source of pride for our small community to call the reservation his proper home."

"Does Mister Wolf maintain a residence here on the reservation?" Vargas was especially polite with the chief. One quick glance at the chief was all it took to recognize a monstrous ego.

"Oh no. He lived with our medicine man, who taught him all he knows." Young mister Wolf had no family and no money when he came to live here." The chief seemed pleased to share this information with the strange-looking man. And the man was exceptionally polite, showing great interest in what the chief had to say.

"Does mister Wolf visit here often? Come by to see his old teacher?"

These questions would normally seem unusual for a stranger to be asking, but the chief was more than happy to answer the polite man's questions. "Well, I hardly keep track of Mister Wolf's visiting schedule. He is rather busy with his investigator's practice. Just recently, someone burned down his house." The chief acted pleased to share this tidbit with his visitor.

"Yes. I heard about that. They say he almost lost his life." Vargas also seemed pleased to share his information with the chief.

"Oh, I never heard that. No one I spoke to appears to be well-informed about the fire. I don't even know where his house was located. The chief seemed perturbed that this stranger knew things about Hokee that he didn't.

"Yes. Well, I am with First Casualty Fire Insurance, and we are looking for Mister Wolf regarding the loss of his house. Do you know where he is?"

"No, but I'm certain he will be happy to see you." The chief looked confused about the stranger's visit. "You didn't expect to see Mister Wolf here, did you?"

"No, I was hopeful you might have information on his whereabouts or any tips on how I can find him?" Vargas almost appeared to plead.

"Mister Wolf doesn't keep in touch with anyone on the reservation except for the medicine man he calls father. He is the only one here who might have information about how to contact him. " The chief's disappointment at not being able to tell this polite man where Hokee was reflected on his face like it was a television screen.

"And can you be so kind as to tell me where I can find this... medicine man?"

A beaming smile replaced the chief's earlier disappointment, "You betcha! I just arrived from that place, and I am certain that mister Wolf is not present, but another young white man is present, and one of them must have information on where he is staying." The Chief didn't tell the stranger that his secretary was also just there. The chief suspected Zoey had a crush on Hokee and that they had spent time together in the past. As he thought about it, he wondered if Hokee had something to do with her visit to the medicine man. "Here, I'll draw you a map," he said. Going over to Zoey's desk, the chief grabbed a pencil and, on her notepad, drew a brief map of the surrounding area, noting the location of Why-ay'-looh's hogan.

Thanking the thoughtful police chief, the polite man left to go visit the medicine man, passing Zoey at the door on her way in. Seeing the chief at her desk, she asked, "Who was that man?"

"Some insurance man looking for Hokee. I sent him to see Why-ay'-looh and the white man staying with him. And now that you're he..." was all she heard before whirling around and bolting back out of the door, leaving the chief to wonder what was happening.

She raced to her Fiat and floored the gas pedal on the way to Why-ay'-looh's hogan, hoping to beat the stranger there. Zoey desperately wanted to call Hokee for help but was afraid there wasn't time, and she needed her full attention in the present. After driving a half-mile, Zoey passed a late model black SUV going slowly, looking for signs. She assumed it was the stranger going to kill Myron. *That stupid fucking chief.* After another fast two miles, she skidded to a stop, barely missing the hogan. Rushing inside, she grabbed Myron, screaming, "We must leave here RIGHT! NOW! He's coming to kill you!"

Myron never hesitated. Saying a brief "thank you" on the way out, he grabbed his notes and followed Zoey to the little blue Fiat 500. She left the hogan by a different road, so they wouldn't pass by Draco on his way to see Why-ay'-looh. Now she could call Hokee for help.

CHAPTER SIXTY-ONE

Zoey and Myron

Zoey kept anxiously looking in her rear-view mirror, watching for a fast-moving black SUV, but fortunately, the traffic was light, and it was easy to see that no one was chasing her down. Before they even hit the freeway, she had Hokee on the phone.

"Zoey, what's happening?" After talking with Zoey a few minutes earlier, Hokee felt something awful must have happened for her to be calling him back so quickly.

"Hokee. Thank God," she cried with relief. "I'm on the road with Myron, staying alive. Chief Wahvevah discovered Myron was staying with Why-ay'-looh. He wasn't sure it was Myron, but he told a scary stranger with white hair that a young white man was with the medicine man and even made him a map. I was on my way inside the station when I passed the stranger going out and then I saw the chief at my desk. When I asked him about the stranger, he told me the man was from your insurance company looking for you hoping Why-ay'-looh will tell him where you are. I beat the man back to the Hogan and grabbed Myron. I am sure the man was looking for Myron to kill him, just like you told us." During this little speech Zoey took an off ramp and stopped at the first place she found. After finishing with her explanation, Zoey sat in her seat shaking, listening to Hokee.

"All right Zoey. You're doing great." Hokee could hear the distress in her voice and knew she was having trouble coping with what had been a harrowing experience. "Where are you now Zoey?"

"I took 91 south and just now pulled off at the trading post parking lot."

"Do you believe you have been followed?"

"No. I left Why-ay'-looh's by a different road, so we missed the man looking for Myron. I have been watching carefully, and no one was following us."

"Okay. Thanks. Do you remember the Holiday Inn parking lot where you picked up Myron?"

"Yes. I know where it is."

"Meet me there. I'll be waiting for you there when you arrive. If you see anyone following you, please call me immediately. I'll be on the road as soon as we stop talking."

"Oh Hokee. Thanks, I knew we could count on you. See you soon." Hokee felt the shift in Zoey's energy after their brief conversation.

Turning to face Grant, he said, "Come with me Grant. We need to be on the road, and I want to discuss something with you. Let's go Shila. The wolf didn't need any prompting."

On their way to the motel's parking lot, Hokee explained Zoey and Myron's situation. Then he added, "I'm afraid Zoey cannot return to the reservation. Their police chief is a buffoon who tells everybody anything they ask. By now, the man looking for Myron has talked with Why-ay'-looh and learned that Zoey just picked him up. He will return to the police station where the chief will tell the 'insurance man' everything he knows about Zoey, including where she lives, what kind of car she is driving and who she might have gone to see. The Chinese will not stop looking for Myron and they will go through Zoey to get him. They need to hide someplace away from here. Is there any way in which they can go to that property you talked about up north?"

"Why shore. I'll have Gene meet them in Nampa right off the freeway. He can take them right to the house and make sure they have everything they need. Gene will get them new transportation and get rid of her car and phone. No one needs to know where they are. Will they be alright together for a spell?"

"Thanks Grant. It sounds like you thought of everything. No wonder you're the best contractor in the world." Grant puffed a groan and Hokee grinned, then continued. "I saw the way Myron looked at Zoey when they first met right after the fire. He can be quite persuasive. She'll feel lucky, and who knows? So yah, I think they'll be okay together."

"Great. I'll call Gene and get the ball rolling.

"Preciate it."

They drove in silence, Grant softly talking to his son and Hokee thinking ahead, then chastising himself for not being present, then chastising himself for forgetting that he could be present *and* planning the future... concurrently. When they reached the Holliday Inn, Hokee parked the car to observe the entrance for Zoey and Myron. Grant was still on the phone when they parked. Hokee got out to stretch his legs and let Shila out to sniff around and check for enemies. He and Shila were standing together when Zoey drove into the parking area and, seeing Hokee, drove up next to his vehicle.

Zoey beat Myron out of her car, but not by much, as they both rushed up to Hokee, wrapping him up in a tight embrace. After this greeting, Hokee explained the plan he and Grant came up with. Zoey already figured out that with that blundering idiot police chief Wahvevah, she was no longer safe on the reservation.

"My God, Hokee. You're a blessing. I am beyond sorry..." Myron choked up for a moment, then with tears in his eyes, "for the grief I brought into your life. Thank you with all my heart."

Sensing that the mood was too heavy for a constructive exchange of thoughts, Hokee joked, "Oh, I'm not God," he grinned, "well not Thee God of the entire universe and everything, just plain ole God Hokee." Then, glancing down at Shila, he gave a signal, and the wolf jumped up on his hind legs, placing his front legs on Myron's shoulder and licking him on the face, wiping away his tears.

"Oh, Shila, how I love you. I wish I could take you with me, pal." The love Myron expressed was visible on his face, with bright moist eyes and a dreamy smile, and at that moment, Grant joined them in the parking lot.

"Okay, kids, listen up." Grant also had a smile on his face, which was explained as he continued speaking. "I got off the phone with Gene, my son. He is going to meet you in Boise, right off the freeway. You will take the Highway 55 exit off Interstate I-84. There is a Holiday Inn right off the exit. Gene will be there with a new car for you and lead you to your new home." Grant pulled out his wallet and gave Myron one thousand dollars in hundred-dollar bills. "This will tide you over until you get settled. Get rid of your old credit cards until you get settled and apply for new ones under your new names."

"Mister Olson, I can't thank you enough for all your help. When I can make arrangements, I will repay your kindness."

"Myron, if you keep your advanced A.I. machine ahead of the bad guys, is all the reward I need."

"Look, you guys need to get on the road," Hokee warned. "You will be okay in your car for the next few hours, Zoey. It will take the Chinese some time to arrange a search for you and your car. You will be in Bosie with Gene in about four hours with new wheels. He'll take care of your car so it will never be found. Gene will make sure you are set up in your new home. You can always call me, and when this mess is finished, I'll come up there to check on you. Myron, I'm sorry we didn't get to complete your vision quest together, but I'm sure Why-ay'-looh finished it for you in grand style."

"My God Hokee. Yeah, I said that already, but you never cease to surprise me. And yes, my vision quest is complete. I can never let anyone buy my design and I will have to work diligently to make sure I am always ahead of the competition. Please extend my gratitude to Why-ay'-looh. I didn't have time to give him a proper thanks."

"No problem. That old medicine man knows who you are and what's in your heart. But I'll stop by and thank him for both of us."

"Hokee, promise you'll come to visit soon. I already miss you." With those words, Zoey threw her arms around the big man she swooned over for one last hug, then grabbing ahold of Myron's hand, she tugged him towards her car.

Hokee and Grant stood in the parking lot watching the hunted man who might one day save the world as Zoey drove him out of sight.

"Let's go see how our boys are doing, Grant," Hokee suggested. "Come on, Shila, let's go home." The wolf was ready and jumped quickly into the Explorer.

Chapter Sixty-Two

Final War Talk

When Hokee and Grant returned to the camp, they assigned two of their fighters guard duties to man the main gate with 50 caliber guns and watch for another helicopter. With that assignment taken care of, Hokee led small groups to the lava plain for a walk around the perimeter, assigning men to the places for concealment he picked out earlier.

Once the assignments for the shooter's placements were finished, Hokee set up a rotation of fighters to man the gate. He then looked for Valance Ortega, the drone operator who arranged for the delivery of their anti-tank missile. Once found, he asked him to round up the other drone operators for a conference.

When they were all together, sitting around the fountain with Grant in attendance, Hokee started with a question. "Ortega, what time will that missile be here tomorrow?"

"Somewhere around ten in the morning. Do you want it to come sooner?

"I don't know the Chinaman's schedule, but they probably will not begin their assault tonight in the dark, but it would be great if we had the missile before sunrise."

"I'll make a call. They were planning on stopping for the night, but they could be here in about six hours."

"Great, thanks. How much experience does someone need to fire the missile accurately?"

"Theoretically, anyone who is physically able and can read directions could fire it, but without a little experience, hitting a moving target will be tricky."

"Are you aware if any of our fighters can fire it accurately?"

"We haven't discussed it, so I don't know, but Oliver can torch her off. He's one of the men bringing us the missile. He's a real pro. One of the best in the business. I think he has a little Spanish blood." Ortega grinned like an idiot. He couldn't help himself. He had to make a joke. "Anyway, he'll be happy to get into an actual fight. Oliver's like us Mexicans, he loves to fight." Another big grin.

"Okay, that's settled. Your friend Oliver, soon to be *our* friend Oliver, will be assigned one helicopter, and I want you four men to knock down four others with your drones. Is that possible?"

We will want to keep one drone flying to watch their camp's preparations?" Michael Archibald, an operator, suggested."

"Yes," Hokee responded. We will do that. I'm not sure why the colonel sent four drones, but we need all the help we can get. My question is, is it possible for a drone to knock a helicopter out of the sky?"

"Yes," Archibald answered. "But, you have to hit it from above, diving through the blades."

"I agree." Jake, another operator, said. "The tricky part is timing it exactly right. If the helicopter is flying on a straight course and at a constant speed, it's easy. But if it is circling and changing speed, it gets complicated?"

"I believe the helicopters will come at us from different directions. We saw five Sikorsky CH-53E Super Stallions, and they may have some others by tomorrow. Each Super Stallion will haul ten men and equipment. Our 50 caliber guns will take out one or two, but any more than that will be pure luck, and I hate to count on luck. Regardless of which direction they come at us from, the last three or four flight miles will be straight and at a steady speed. They will be loaded with fighters ready to rappel, so I don't think they will fly at a high speed."

Grant spoke up. "We need to decide which drone will be responsible for which direction, which helicopter the missile targets, and where we focus our rifle fire."

"Picky, picky Grant. You mean we can't wing it?" Hokee couldn't help but grin, tease Grant, and put a little life into the group. "I suggest we assign one drone to each of the four cardinal directions."

"So, smart ass, where do the rifles aim and the missile?"

"What, do I have to make all the trivial decisions? How about we have the world's most successful contractor, who is also one of the smartest men alive, make those decisions? Once you figured that out, tell me which direction to point *my* rifle. I'll be standing at the top of the driveway with Shila and our new best friend, Oliver, who will have the anti-tank missile."

"That's rich Hokee. When it comes down to the most important decisions, you farm it out to the hired help." Like Hokee, Grant was lightening the mood to help the men relax.

"Hey, my best friend in the world, who is also a successful manager, once told me to hire competent people and assign them responsibilities. So, stop the bitching, Grant, and do the damn job." Hokee couldn't stop laughing as he said that last line joined by Grant followed and then the entire group. The situation didn't seem that funny, but tensions were heightened, and the laughs served as a relief. The momentary relief came with a welcome touch of adrenaline.

"Keep me informed if you need any help or have questions." I'm going to grab a rifle and walk out to the gate with Shila. I'll be back in a few hours. Don't start the war without me." After making this last statement, which brought another reluctant chuckle, Hokee invited the wolf for a walk. "Come on, Shila, let's go for a walk." Hokee hiked up the driveway with a happy Shila loping ahead.

Long walks were a form of meditation for the shaman, and under a star-studded sky, the meditation took on a serious undertone felt throughout his body. Hokee worked at staying outside of his body, so the sensory inputs to his brain were stored for future examination but were otherwise ignored. This left him free to dwell deep into the subconscious, looking for threads, feeling the energy of the immediate surrounding universe. If anyone had been watching Hokee and Shila walking down the ten-mile road, they would have seen a man and a wolf playing together, with no idea that the man's body was on remote control simply following a set of memorized instructions, much like we first learn to walk, and then we pay no more attention to managing our muscles. Hokee could feel the unhealthy energy force originating several miles away, and he sensed the end drawing near. Almost certainly tomorrow. By the time they met Lucas, who was manning the gate, Hokee was relaxed and enjoying being himself.

"Hi, Lucas. How's the watch going?" Hokee asked, leaning against the gate.

"Howdy big boy," Lucas said, kneeling and rubbing the wolf's head before answering Hokee. Then, speaking in a soft voice, almost like a praying whisper, "It's quiet. But I feel the danger. It's close,... soon."

Hokee was amazed that while standing guard, Lucas arrived at the same conclusion he felt while walking with Shila. "How much longer do you have on this guard post, Lucas?"

"Only about thirty minutes. I'll be back out here with Danial at sunrise, and I want a little rest before then."

"I expect one truck full of ground troops to try for the road," Hokee told Lucas. "Probably about four or five fighters, maybe more. They may have grenades, but we didn't see any heavy artillery in our drone's images. If you and Danial set up in the swells outside of the gate, you will get the drop on them without getting yourselves killed." Although the topic was serious, Hokee gave Lucas a smile when he added the part about not getting killed."

"Thanks, Hokee. Your faith in us is inspiring." Lucas responded with a smile.

"All right then. Shila and I will take off. If you see more than one vehicle coming at you on the road tomorrow, call me. I'll rush out some more help."

"Okay, Will do. Goodbye, Shila, see you soon, ole boy," he added, giving the wolf a last head rub.

On the walk back to the camp, Hokee thought about their preparations and how they could make their defense more secure. When he reached Grant's motorhome, he concluded they would have to live or die with what they already had in hand. Although dying was not an option he considered.

Chapter Sixty-Three

War

No one at Hokee's camp got much sleep that night. Everyone knew a battle was at hand, and tensions were too high to allow any rest. Men spent the night checking and rechecking their weapons, making sure they had quick access to spare ammunition and plenty of water. Men wandered around between checking equipment, telling macabre jokes. The anxious warriors listened to ghastly jokes told by retired military members.

"My friend is so successful! He is a general, does surgery, and was recently knighted by the Queen. We call him SirGen." That got a big ugh.

And another joker: *"I was about to lose my job in the Royal Navy unless I make some drastic changes... I have to take a course in anchor management."* This one only brought a groan.

Another attempt: *"My dad said he joined the Royal Navy out of spite. He was a petty officer."* When no one responded, the terrible jokes stopped. Men fidgeted, squirmed, strolled, did pushups, and drank copious cups of coffee.

Just as the sun rose over the Caribou mountains in the east, Ortega had his drone flying over the enemy's camp. The other drones were staged, ready to take over after forty-five minutes, giving Ortega plenty of time to retrieve his drone and exchange batteries. Ortega's friend Oliver arrived to welcoming arms just as the drone left camp to hover over Cheng's army. Hokee phoned Curly, warning about an imminent war with loud explosions. He didn't want the sheriff's department or Pocatello police coming out in the middle of a war.

Over the next few hours, Hokee and Grant, along with rotating members of their small army, saw the enemy getting ready for combat. The enemy loaded rifles and cases of ammunition into vans and helicopters. Cheng's men were gathered in small groups, waiting for action. Jones, whose given name was Wallace but everyone called him Jones, was the fourth drone operator with his drone over the enemy camp when the King Stallion CH-53K Helicopter arrived, armed with GAU-15/A machine guns mounted on each side. Hokee sent someone to gather everyone under Grant's awning.

"Okay, everybody. New battle plans. Oliver, you get the King Stallion. That machine must not reach this camp, or we are dead. Are you confident about taking down the helicopter?

"Mister Wolf, if that missile here will light off," he answered, patting the long army green tube, "I can guarantee you a dead bird."

"Super. Now, let's check the other assignments. Michael," he said, addressing one of the drone operators, "would you get with the other three drone operators and make sure everyone is clear on who aims their drone in which direction?"

"Sure, no problem." Michael grinned, pleased to be given this responsibility.

"Let's assume the enemy has a drone spying on our camp, so let's stay hidden until after their helicopters take off, which should be shortly. Jones, how much longer can your drone remain flying?

Looking down at his laptop computer, he answered, "Thirty-five minutes, give or take a minute."

"Let's watch the time remaining. How fast can you descend the drone accurately?

"Time wise, about three minutes to the ground, speed-wise, around 150 mph."

"I want to hit four of the copters three miles from here. The guys with rifles can only hit targets up to about one and a half miles away. That gives them one or two minutes to zero in on the remaining helicopter, or helicopters, if one of the drones misses."

"Perish, the thought," said Jake, an operator, grinning, as he made a play on the expression Hokee spoke during his 'shaman' speech.

"All right, Daniel. Tine for you and Lucas to take charge of the gates. Take your car and send the two you're replacing back here."

"We're on our way," Lucas said, waving at the group as he and Daniel got in their car.

Hokee's phone buzzed just as he was about to speak to the group. Recognizing the number, he answered, "Hi Charles, are you men, okay?"

"Yes, thanks, Hokee. I'm calling to make sure you see the enemy activity with your drone.

Thank you for the call to confirm. Is Cheng down there now? We cannot get a clear picture of everyone at the same time."

"Yes, he is with his two ass-wipes."

"Now, now. We must play nice." Hokee couldn't keep the smile from his voice. "Regardless of what happens to the men below you, or down here by us, I want you two keeping track of Cheng. He is not to leave the state. And I will prefer being the one stopping him."

"Understand Hokee. We'll do our best to keep him alive."

"Thanks, Charles. Don't forget that he is an exceptionally lethal adversary. Do you men need anything?"

"No, we're fine. One of us is always on watch.

Turning to his small army, Hokee said, "Okay, that was Charles calling with an update. I wa..." **"Hokee!"** Jones yelled, interrupting him, "five of the helicopters took off with ten armed men on each one. Wait, the sixth chopper, the gunship, took off."

"Everybody heard Jones. Let's get to our battle stations." He was about to say, "Launch the drones," but the operators were already taking that on themselves, and the suggestion was left unsaid.

Everyone took off for their designated battle station. Hokee and Grant, each carrying a 50-caliber rifle, ran to the top of the driveway with Shila, who stood by Hokee's side panting, with a grin on his face. "The wolf seems to think this is going to be easy," Grant observed.

"He's a smart boy. Sure hope he's right. I've got a feeling, Grant. I don't believe the ground troops we saw leaving in the vans will do much walking on the lava plains before giving up. If we knock down the helicopters, this war will be over."

"Your mouth to God's ears," Grant said, grinning.

"I didn't know Olson was an Irish name." Hokee joked.

"I'm feeling lucky, and that's enough Irish for the likes of me."

"Oh lordy, Grant. Listen to us joking around like we didn't have a care in the world."

"Yeah. Ain't it great? It's been years since I've had this much fun.

"It feels good to let off a little steam," Hokee said. "The past few days have been a little tense."

"A *little* tense, he sez. Hey pal, I wus here too, ya know."

"Yeah, I know, and I'm eternally grateful for your help, and especially thankful for your presence."

"My God, Hokee. This is trivial to what I owe you, and as I said, and if I didn't say it, I meant to, I wouldn't miss this for anything."

"Let's hope it works out, Grant. I'm eager to see my new house."

"We'll look at some plans as soon as we get rid of this Chinese gang." As he was speaking, they heard the helicopters off in the distance."

"It's about to start. Do you want to find a rock to sit on Grant, or are you okay standing up?"

"This will end soon, regardless of who wins. I'll stand."

"Me too. Oliver will fire his missile first. We will hear it launch anytime now."

"There it goes!" Grant almost yelled. His anxiety was showing as he began stepping side to side. Then they both watched the fireball when the helicopter exploded. The blast sounded like a hundred WWII cannons firing simultaneously. "One down, Hokee. We don't have to worry about that gunship anymore. Our new friend Oliver came through."

"Let's pray that our drones are equally effective," Hokee added.

During the next five minutes, the two friends watched as first one drone downed a helicopter, then the second one hit, and finally, the last two drones hit their target helicopters simultaneously. A minute later, everyone, including Hokee and Grant, began firing their 50-caliber guns at the one remaining helicopter, making so much noise it was deafening, like thunderclaps directly overhead.

And just like that, the war was over. Cheng's ground troops never showed up. Whether they came and were dissuaded by the long march ahead, or they began the march and experienced the difficulty as they watched the helicopters crash, they backed off and left for home with their advanced payment. Hokee and the troops were never certain what happened to them. As soon as the last helicopter crashed, Hokee called Charles.

"What's Cheng's status, Charles?

"He watched the helicopters disappear on his drone's laptop computer, and now he and the other Chinese man are getting into their vehicle and heading out. They are going to their hotel to checkout and then disappear."

"What about that Caucasian who was with Cheng?"

"Oh, he flew in the gunship. He must have died in the explosion."

"Damn, I wanted to kill him myself. Well okay. Stay on Cheng. I'll meet you at the hotel."

Hokee's next call was to Curly telling him the war was over and asking him to keep visitors away.

"My lord Hokee, it sounded like a war for a few minutes. People were not sure where the sounds came from and no one saw the explosions, so you may not have any visitors. I'm only five minutes away from your gate and I'll stop anyone who is curious from coming in."

"Thanks Curly."

"Grant, I need to go find Cheng and make sure he doesn't escape. Would you see to the men for me? If they can hang around another day or two, I would like to throw a victory bash.

"I'll be happy to Hokee. You go get that Chinese bastard. And you can bet the men want to hang around and savor our victory."

"Come on Shila, let's go for a ride."

The wolf didn't require coaxing.

CHAPTER SIXTY-FOUR

Cheng

Cheng watched in disbelief as his helicopters were blown out of the sky one after the other. *Where in the hell did that Indian bastard get a missile and all those damn drones?* Turning to Xiu he said, "let's got back to the hotel. We're done here."

Their latest hotel, The Black Swan, features luxurious theme rooms. Some rooms are two stories high with gigantic fireplaces plus the Royal Suite, chosen by Cheng, whose interior was based on Louis XIVs Palace in Versailles. Cheng found peace in all the red velvet furnishings. Back in his room, DDyi opened a bottle of baijiu for himself, handing another one, unopened, to Xiu. "We need to stay here for a few days. There's also plenty of room here for you. Undoubtedly, that fucking half-breed has us under surveillance. We'll stay out of sight for a while and wait for them to tire of watching for us to appear. After a time, an opportunity will come when we can sneak out without drawing attention."

Xiu, who assembled their mercenaries, watched their deaths in horror. He was not agonizing about the loss of their lives, but by losing his warriors, any chance to get the A.I. information China wanted was lost. That was his anguish. Familiar with Chinese customs, he was trained to know that failure typically meant death. He also knew that Cheng was DDyi and had also failed China. Would Cheng execute him here, then return to China and meet his own fate? The question was paralyzing, freezing the blood in his veins, keeping his mouth shut. He heard Cheng speaking, but was it lies or the truth? Watching Xiu struggle with his uncertainties, and knowing China's ruthless actions when someone fails, Cheng understood why Xiu might have problems. Cheng was certain that if Xiu returned to China, they would kill him, slowly. He was not sure how their leaders would treat him. As the country's most proficient assassin, being DDyi, might buy him another chance. It was impossible to predict his own outcome.

"Xiu, relax. I will not kill you," Cheng said in a silky-smooth voice. We are both aware of how China treats failure. If you return home, they will kill you. They may do the same for me, but over the years, I performed a few favors for our leaders. Whether that will be enough to save me, I don't know. You cannot leave here until the situation changes, but after we sneak out, you are free to go your own way. Knowing America, it will be easy for you to assimilate."

Filled with relief, Xiu felt the tension leaving his shoulders and his jaw relaxed. While he opened and drank his baijiu, Cheng paced around the suite like a lost child. Just as Xiu drank the last swallow from his bottle, DDyi, walked behind the now unsuspecting affiliate, put the muzzle of a silenced Walther 22-caliber pistol to the back of his head and pulled the trigger. An obsidian 9 silencer makes almost no sound, and the bullet stays in the victim's head, leaving no messy blood to worry about. In Cheng's case, this was especially important as he wanted to stay in his room for a while longer, and blood on the carpet or walls would be noticed and that might mean the authorities.

As Xiu crumpled, Cheng caught the empty bottle before it hit the floor. He dragged Xiu's body into the bedroom, then used Google to find a business that sold wardrobe trunks, the kind theatre productions used to pack costumes for road shows. After ordering the trunk to be delivered to his room at the Black Swan Inn, Cheng opened another bottle of baijiu and sat in a recliner to wait for the trunk to arrive.

The trunk was delivered to Cheng's room thirty minutes later. If the men who delivered the trunk wondered why a hotel resident will need such a large sea chest, they didn't question the Chinese man with frightening eyes.

After the delivery men left, Cheng called one of his DDs in Paris with an order. It took nearly six hours before the moving crew arrived with an embassy shipping document addressed to the Chinese Consulate General of the People's Republic in Los Angeles, California. No return address, although the shipping manifest will identify Pocatello, Idaho, and the Black Swan Inn as its origination. The crew loaded the dead Xiu into the wardrobe trunk, then secured it with an embassy padlock. With real shipping documents stolen from a UPS truck, in the unlikely event anyone questioned them, the crew took the crate down the freight elevator to a waiting truck idling near the hotel's freight loading door.

Chapter Sixty-Five

The Black Swan Hotel

Hokee met Noah in the Black Swan Hotel parking lot. Noah told him Charles was sitting in the lounge nursing a beer where he could watch every exit except the freight door in the rear. He was in the parking lot where he could watch the freight door in case Cheng slipped past Charles in the lounge. Cheng still had to get into a truck or car for transportation, either his rental or someone picking him up. Maybe an Uber. Noah was watching in case Cheng chose one of these options.

As Hokee and Noah were shaking hands, Hokee asked, "How's it going, Noah?"

"No sign of either Chinese man since they entered the hotel," He responded. "Charles is inside the lounge watching the exits. He can't see the loading dock, but I can get a glimpse from here."

"Okay, thanks. I'll go inside with Charles for an hour or two, then one of us will come to spell you. This could be a long wait unless I kill the bugger in his room. It might come down to that if I can figure out how to do it and not get caught."

After giving it some thought, Noah said, "Charles or I can do it with little risk, you stand out in any crowd. However, I am aware that you want him for yourself."

"I really do. But seeing his dead body will be okay. I need to make sure the bastard is dead. I'll see you later. Shila, you will stay here with Noah for a bit. Okay, pal?"

"Come on Shila, help me keep watch," Noah teased the wolf every man on the team wanted to adopt. Shila grinned, whipping his long tail in agreement.

Inside, Hokee made his way to the lounge and found Charles. The lounge looked like the inside of an old sailing ship wrapped around tasteful fine furniture, colorful wall hangings of mythical sea creatures, including two mermaids and the nude figurehead from the prow of a ship which the decorator situated making it look like the ship was behind the wall. These decorations alone were worth several million dollars. A gorgeous east Asian server wearing a bright red form fitting Cheongsam saw him arrive and sit before approaching his table for an order. Her dark looks reminded Hokee of the server in his old hotel. Reading her shy smile, he could see her hoping that this guy will drink a little faster than the guy in the booth. He also saw she enjoyed looking at him while being looked at herself.

"Can I get the fine gentleman a cocktail?" It never hurts to butter up the customer. She had a winning smile that lit up her face and eyes. Hokee also noticed the accent confirming her as a lady from Pakistan or India. Long dark hair, smooth oval golden face, brown eyes and a model's body. The red name tag was almost invisible against the Cheongsam, but fortunately, the name Leia was in white letters making it easy to see.

"Leia, my friend still has his beer, and I will appreciate a double Johnny Walker Blue straight up." "We may camp out here for a few hours and we won't be drinking much, but I could use some food. Taking out his wallet, he handed her five hundred dollars. This is to pay for your time, so you won't feel you're getting stiffed on tips. We'll signal you when we want something. I'll pay for the drinks and beer later if you will keep track."

"Wow!" It was hard to believe there was ever a happier smile. Leia couldn't believe her luck. That was more than she made in most weeks. Pocatello isn't a big tipping town. "I'll get your drink right away and a menu for our food."

"Thanks Leia. Greetings, Charles. You men did an excellent job keeping a watch on Cheng and his boys. Have you seen anything interesting lately?

"No, it's been muted. Just me and my beer."

"Super, that's what I wanted to hear. I don't mind a little downtime. I'll sit here with you for a while and then one of us will go spell Noah."

Hokee stretched out his long legs and leaned back into the soft cushion, relaxing for the first time in days. Before long, Leia brought him the scotch and a menu.

Hokee ordered a ham and Swiss cheese sandwich and a glass of water. After finishing his meal and scotch, he was about to signal Leia for another drink when his phone buzzed.

"Yeah Noah, what's up?" Damn, just when he thought he could take it easy for a spell.

"Hokee, you may want to come to the back of the Hotel. Some guys came outside with a heavy wardrobe trunk. Maybe our friend Cheng found another way to exit the hotel."

"I'll be right there. Don't let them load that crate until we see what's inside."

"Noah may have something, Charles, but just in case, keep watching in here. It could be something innocent."

Hokee walked through the lobby to the rear of the hotel in search of the freight door. It was past the *rest stops*. What else would a classy hotel call their toilets? As he exited the freight door, he saw Noah holding three men at gunpoint.

They wouldn't stop loading the chest until I pulled the gun on them," Noah explained,

"Thanks Noah. Good job. Now then, gentlemen, if you would let us look at what is inside of that large trunk, you can be on your way."

"Look, asshole, this is a sealed diplomatic shipment and no one outside of the Embassy is authorized to see its contents. We don't even have a key to the embassy lock on the trunk."

"No problem. Watch out for ricochets," Hokee said, pulling out his trusty Colt-45.

When the embassy crew saw Hokee's big gun, and knowing he meant business, they quickly jumped behind the large trunk. Hokee shot off the lock, making one hell of a noise which was sure to bring someone, or a crowd, to investigate what was clearly a gunshot.

Removing the damaged lock, Hokee lifted the lid, and seeing the dead Chinese man, quickly pull the lid shut while saying, "let's leave here Noah before someone shows up. It wasn't Cheng, but the other Chinaman I wanted to kill." He quickly stepped back through the freight door, followed by Noah. What the moving crew would do now was not a concern. It was unlikely they will inform the man inside who asked them to ship the trunk to the embassy. By smuggling a corpse out of the hotel, they would be reluctant to have anyone else witness their actions. If they were lucky, they would have that trunk inside of the van before anyone showed up to investigate the shooting.

Back in the lounge, Noah and Shila joined Hokee and Charles at their booth. If anyone had objections to an enormous wolf in the lounge, they had the sense to keep it to themselves. "I don't think we have to worry about ole Cheng slipping out of the freight doors for a while," Hokee said. "You may as well join us for a drink, Noah."

Leia was happy to see Hokee return with another customer and was quick to service their table. Leia gasped, and nearly screamed when she saw Shila, but the wolf had an enormous smile and was wagging his tail, and he *was* with the fine, high paying gentleman. She cautiously took their orders. Lucas ordered a Coors Light and grinned at their server's discomfort. "It's okay, Leia," he said, reading her name, "our wolf only eats people late at night." Then turning to the others added, "Nothing like a stakeout, is there? Damn, but this sure beats the crap out of sitting on top of a hill all day."

Hokee let Lucas explain the events out back. It happened on his watch, and he earned the right to boast. Besides, he had mixed feelings about Xiu's demise. He felt glad the man was dead, but unhappy for missing the opportunity. Oh well, there was still hope for Cheng. However, the shaman part of him was satisfied that someone else did in poor Xiu, undoubtedly Cheng, China's premier assassin. And the shaman would be happy if someone else did the same thing to Feng Cheng.

Nothing else happened all night, and after giving the men back home time to have breakfast, Hokee called Grant.

"Grant, we, meaning all of us, may be here for a while. Cheng's companion Xiu met the fate of China's other failures. By Cheng. I require four men present here 24/7 to keep an eye out for Cheng. It may take a few days. Team Two and I need to be spelled. Would you please handle this for me.?"

"Be happy to Hokee. You guys are at the Black Swan, correct?"

"Correct."

"Okay. Someone will be there shortly."

Once he had eaten and rested, Hokee sat with Grant, working on the design of his new house. Their men horsed around on full pay, reliving their victory and more than happy to take turns guarding the Hotel. They sat outside in four cars doing four-hour shifts, watching the hotel doors.

Several days passed before Cheng made an appearance. While waiting, Grant organized work crews to examine the helicopter wrecks for human body parts that needed to be buried. Hokee made sure the men wore sturdy boots, and he led them to the first crash site, showing them how to walk across the lava without losing their legs or their lives.

CHAPTER SIXTY-SIX

The Chase

Cheng sat in his hotel room for five days, ordering in-room service, leaving the room only to wait in the hall while the maid serviced his room. He was never informed about the incident by the freight door, nor did he hear from Los Angeles.

After five days, it was time to move. DDyis do not sit around waiting forever. The enemy would be as unsuspecting now as they would ever get. Cheng checked his Walther 22-caliber gun to ensure it was loaded, plus the Steyr-AUG machine gun he picked up at their camp. The machine gun came with five clips, but Cheng only took one. Hell, if he ever had to fire it, he would not need more than one clip. While the 22 was a successful assassin's gun, it wasn't much use at a distance unless you hit the opponent in a small triangle between the eyes and nose. It is almost impossible to hit that spot with a high level of accuracy on several moving men. Hence the machine gun. But he took the Walther in the slight chance he lived to resume his profession. As an assassin, he was in a class by himself, but in open warfare, his assassin's skills didn't serve him any better than those of any other professional warrior.

It was time to take the field. No matter how long he stayed here, they would be waiting when he left. He may as well take his chances here in Idaho. No telling what would happen to him in China, but if he had to die, it is less shameful to die fighting here. If they were to kill him in China, they will dishonor his name. He was a warrior. It was wartime.

He waited until three a.m., a time when boredom slows reflexes, and the body feels sluggish. Before entering the lobby, Cheng ordered his vehicle to be brought to the portico by a valet. When he saw his Navigator near the front door, he bolted through the lobby straight to the SUV. He wasn't out of the parking lot before he was certain that he was followed. He expected this. Now the run for life began.

By the time Cheng hit I-15 headed north, he was certain there were four cars on his tail. He assumed one man was in each car. Two men per car watching a hotel door would be excessive. However, the man in each car would be a high paid mercenary. But four warriors were a manageable number. He needed a little luck, but DDyis make their own luck. Now to find the right ambush spot.

Cheng drove north on I-15 towards Idaho Falls and then Boise. Having studied maps before embarking on this suicide run, he exited I-15 onto desolate Highway 26 at Blackfoot, heading towards Atomic City. From his maps and Google Earth, he earlier identified an ambush sport fifteen miles out of Blackfoot, where a deep gorge crossed the highway. Cheng planned on heading his Lincoln into the gorge, slowing down enough to allow him to jump out of the vehicle without severe injury while the Lincoln crashed into the ravine below. The four cars following him would have to slow down when he did, giving him time to machine gun their vehicles, killing all four men. Hopefully, one of their cars would still operate and the other three would go into the gorge. That was the plan. Risky, sure, but with a little luck, doable.

When Chen Cheng darted out of the hotel lobby and jumped into his Lincoln Navigator, Oliver, who joined the team as one of the watches, was covering the lobby. He immediately followed in pursuit while calling first his friend Ortega, who brought him onto the team, then Jake and finally Lucas, who called Hokee.

"You're on I-15 heading towards Boise, right?" Hokee was being Hokee, checking everything.

"Yeah," Lucas answered. "We're about ten miles north of Pocatello, traveling 80 mph."

"Damn, at that speed I'll never catch you without finding a cop on my tail. Okay, you men will have to handle it. Are you okay with that?"

"Sure Hokee. Oliver is in front. I don't have much familiarity with him, but he appears to be squared away. Michael, I am familiar with, and Ortega; they're both solid. We will be okay. I'm expecting some kind of ambush. With his reputation, I believe Cheng will go out fighting, and we know he's good at killing. We'll be on guard."

"Don't get yourself killed! Grant and the Colonel would never forgive me. Be cautious, but not fearful."

"Perish the thought." They both smiled at the old joke.

Lucas got the other three drivers on a conference call telling them about his talk with Hokee. He emphasized how lethal Cheng was, repeating what they knew about the man's reputation. He told them his thoughts about Cheng going out fighting and to expect an ambush of some sort ahead. When they exited I-15, Hokee warned the men this highway was a desolate road, something he knew from experience having learned how to track people and animals in the surrounding desert.

Lucas said to his friends, "Cheng studied this area on a map and has something planned. Be on the lookout, Oliver. Don't get yourself killed. Hokee would never forgive you." This brought a smile to the other three men, helping to ease the tension.

Ten minutes later Oliver reported to the others, "I think this is it, there's a gorge right ahead, and he's slowing down."

"**Do not slow down**," Locas yelled. That's *the* trap. You go faster, **RIGHT NOW**! We're behind you and we'll go slow enough to catch the action, but you get out of harm's way."

Oliver was surprised when the Lincoln almost stopped, and going fast he had to swerve sharply to avoid hitting it, causing him to miss seeing Cheng drop out and immediately jump back up. Ortega, who was behind Oliver, slowed enough to see Cheng jump out of his vehicle, so he hit the brakes. Hard! Lucas and Jake, in full attention mode, immediately slammed on their brakes to avoid running into each other. Cheng was standing seventy-five feet away, holding his machine gun on full-auto with a 60-round clip capable of firing all sixty rounds in less than one second. He was in his assassin's clothes, black denim slacks, white turtleneck shirt, and soft black loafers. Yet he stood in hesitation while hearing his vehicle hit the gorge.

Caio! His ambush failed. The lead car had gone by him before he was ready to shoot, and the trailing men were too far away in their cars to ensure their elimination. He might get the first driver, but not the two behind before they got into action. Then there was the man who just passed him. He had to watch his six and wait to kill all four, **up close**. *How in the name of TAO do I do that'*

While Cheng stood there, the three men quickly exited their vehicles on the side, away from him. With their rides between them and him, he didn't have a shot. Oliver and Jake quickly ran to Lucas at the rear of the last car. "What do you think, Lucas?" Jake whispered.

Whispering back, "We've got to get him in a trap. With everyone involved, including Oliver. We cannot go one on one with his machine gun. And we can't stay close together. I'll run across the highway and work toward the gorge. One of you remain here, and in a minute, the other one crosses the highway where I did. We'll have him boxed in." With that, he crept behind his vehicle to the driver's side, then in a flash bolted across the highway and into a ditch before Cheng caught his movement and got his gun into action.

Cheng saw the man dash across the road and immediately recognized their plan. Get into the gorge, surround him, then attack. Highly trained warriors. Elite. He will be lucky to kill even one. Knowing no better fate was in store, he began walking down the middle of the highway towards their vehicles. He began a silent long forgotten Hindu chant, *'Om mani Padme hum, Om mani Padme hum'* watching intently with his head on a swivel, ready to fire instantly. He never saw the shot that killed him. Before Cheng's body hit the pavement, three other bullets slammed into him while his automatic sprayed the ground in his body's last reflexive actions.

"Hokee's gonna be pissed." Lucas said once the echoes all died away and silence returned.

"Oh, somehow I don't think that old shaman will be sorry he missed the show," Jake pronounced.

"Yeah, I agree Oliver said. I heard your stories about the shaman, and I believe they're true."

"What do we do with his body?" Jake asked.

"He was a true warrior and deserves a warrior's treatment," Lucas said. "Let's haul the body out to the lava plains and find a decent spot."

They didn't call Hokee. The shaman would already know. His war was over.

CHAPTER SIXTY-SEVEN

Myron and Zoey

Zoey and Myron rode in silence until reaching Blackfoot, where Zoey had to stop for fuel. Their silence was mostly because of nerves. That they escaped from men who wanted them dead was enough to rattle anybody, not to mention the awkward situation they were forced into and the growing attraction they felt for each other. While getting gas, Myron broke the silence by offering to buy them dinner. They began chatting like old friends over dinner and between Blackfoot and the Highway 55 stop in Bosie; their awkwardness vanished while they became slowly infatuated with each other. Zoey had an old crush on Hokee, but Myron was attractive, rich and he was genuinely taken with the Indian princess, and he was here now, and Hokee was in the past. Myron dreamed of this breathtaking beauty from the first time he saw her, and during the last few hours, was already deeply in love. Gene met the couple at the Holiday Inn parking lot off Highway 55 in Bosie. He had a new gray Lexus LX, a premium SUV, with a documented registration and title for Mr. Arlo Walker, the new name for Dr. Myron Whittleman. Arlo was an Idaho native born in the St Luke's Medical center in Nampa, Idaho. After introducing himself, Gene told Myron his new name and handed him an envelope containing his birth certificate and driver's license with his actual photo obtained from the internet. He told Zoey her new name was Princess Zoey Walker, giving her the same sort of documents given to Arlo.

"I hope your last name is okay, Zoey," Gene replied. "Since you will live together, at least for the time being, I thought having the same name will simplify your arrangement. If I made a mistake, I'm sorry and I will make the change." Gene prayed he had it right. His father didn't give him much to work with.

"No!" Myron declared before Zoey could respond. "I mean, it great, maybe it's the shaman's gift," he added to the puzzled man, "but it's perfect." He added gushing. After our ride, I think we will make it official. Right, Princess Zoey?" He looked at Zoey, hoping he hadn't made a fool of himself.

"Oh, yes," she said, blushing, which only added to her beauty.

"Swell, here's the key fob for your Lexus, Arlo. It's right over there next to my red pickup, "he said, pointing. I hope it suits," Gene said, handing Arlo the gray keyless fob. "My friend Joe will be along shortly to dispose of your Fiat."

"My God Gene, this is truly awesome. It seems like you thought of everything. For all that you and your father have done, my gratitude is beyond words. I'm praying for his safety in the war I feel responsible for causing. I hope someday to return the favor."

"From what dad tells me, you've already paid that debt. And besides, from what my dad said, the war was not of your doing, and he *is* with Hokee. Nothing bad will happen to dad while that dude is around," he added with conviction. "I *know* the man; he saved the life of my wife. Oh, I'm in the red Ford pickup over there," he said, pointing unnecessarily as he pointed it out previously. "It's a seven-hour drive to your new home and you need to rest before making the drive. I've booked you into the Hilton Hotel, two Suites. But you can change that at the desk if you desire," he added with a grin. "The Hilton is an excellent hotel and close by. If you follow me, I'll take you there and tomorrow we'll go to your new home

"Thanks Gene. Zoey can park next to the Lexus while we load our meager belongings."

"Oh, yeah, I almost forgot. Before getting you settled for the night, I made arrangements with the manager of our local Walmart Super Center to open for us so you can buy clothing and whatever else you need. Go shopping for more luxurious items later. Follow me."

The lovers spent nearly an hour selecting clothing, footwear and the necessaries for now and the winter, which Gene told them could be brutal. Later at the hotel, Myron, next to a blushing Zoey, asked the the registration clerk to cancel one room.

The next day Gene met them for breakfast in the hotel restaurant, then led them on a scenic seven-hour Thomas Moran landscape tour to their new home. When Gene drove onto the long driveway towards their new home backed by the large sparkling blue Lake Coeur d'Alene surrounded by tall Easter White pine trees, Zoey couldn't believe this was their new home. Living on a desert reservation in a clapboard house did not prepare her for a billionaire's retreat beside an enormous lake of water. The magnificent two-story Pioneer Log style manor was something out of a Hearth Stone dream book, and when Gene handed Myron the title to the five-acre property covered with pines, it was too much for Zoey. She broke down in tears and even Myron had a lump in his throat when he expressed his thanks. Perched on a small rise fifty feet above the lake, the house looked fantastic. Myron could not have designed or wanted a more magnificent dwelling.

Gene handed Zoey the keys to the door and stood by while she opened the door with all the excitement of a six-year-old girl on Christmas morning unwrapping her first present, then Myron carried her across the threshold. The interior, with the aid of a professional decorator, was equal to or exceeded the exterior in every way. Inside the twin eight-foot cedar doors with stained glass side windows, the atrium soared to the roof with wall hangings from around the world. Polished teak floors with exotic hand-woven Tibetan Gamgchen rugs were in every room with open space architecture. Gene stopped at the entrance.

"I'll say goodbye here and let you two love birds explore the house by yourself. Take your time and have fun. On the Kitchen counter are the instructions books for the appliances and electronics. Everything you need should already be here. Maps for the local area showing the locations of food markets, clothing stores and restaurants are by the instruction manuals."

He held out his hand to Myron for a handshake, but a blubbering grateful scientist grabbed him in a big bear hug, mumbling his gratitude with a tear strained voice. Zoey didn't settle for a hug. She wrapped her arms around the big, tall, handsome man and gave him a wet, teary kiss. Gene left the two wet-eyed lovers and softly closed the doors. It was a long ride back home. On the way, he called his father with the status. It felt fulfilling to help Dr. Whittleman, now Arlo Walker, and his gorgeous Indian Princess. He felt the glow all the way to the highway.

Chapter Sixty-Eight

Hokee

Hokee was in the yard with Grant supervising their men in the lava fields searching for body parts or helicopter debris, when the four men returned from chasing Cheng. They confirmed Hokee's feelings that the war was truly over, and not one of their men died in the battle. There were a few injuries from the grenade, but nothing life threatening. It was celebration time.

Hokee called his friend Lawrence Big-Foot, (a nickname earned because he adamantly believed in Big Foot) Herrington, at Blackhawk BBQ Catering to bring their smoker and fixings for a baby back ribs feast with all the trimmings plus a full bar with cases of beer. Lawrence was an exiled Canadian whose commercial smoker had been stolen. Hokee found the smoker in a makeshift deer hunters camp in an old, abandoned barn above Inkom. Eighteen drunk men and fifteen half-naked women were having an orgy and would have fought Hokee for the smoker but were in no condition to put up a determined resistance. Hokee returned the smoker to a happy relieved caterer in time for him to serve the Western American Authors Writers Conference. That was the most profitable Blackhawk BBQ festival for the entire year, and it meant saving the company and the workers' jobs. While waiting for Lawrence and company to arrive, Grant sent a team to Home Depot for picnic tables and another team to Albertsons grocery store for party supplies. The Albertson team returned first with picnic fixings plus two cases of Coors Light to get the party started. By the time Lawrence arrived with his catering truck and big smoker, the men were already in the party mood. The warriors appreciated how lucky they were to avoid being killed, putting them in a celebratory mood. If only Lawrence had brought more than two gorgeous female workers who loved to tease but were much too busy to pay the horny men much time.

Hokee and Grant sat in aluminum patio chairs under the awning of his Outlaw Wild West Edition motor home drinking single malt scotch for Hokee and Blanton's Buffalo Trace bourbon for Grant. They watched as Lawrence fired up the smoker while his men set up a makeshift bar with liquor and beer. The two ladies helped another crew set up a table for appetizers.

Grant was wearing blue jeans, a colorful Hawaiian shirt covered with bright red hibiscus blossoms and leather sandals relaxing his six-foot plus body with his legs resting on a stool. "Hokee, why don't you take a vacation while I get a crew down here to build you a new house now that we've agreed on the design?"

With Shila lying at his side, Hokee sat close by with his back against the side of Grant's motor home. He wore his traditional levies, black cotton shirt, black Tony Lama boots, black Stetson, and a doeskin white leather headband holding back his long black hair. "That could be arranged. I promised Myron a visit when this conflict ended, and this would be a good time to make it happen. I'll take Shila for a nice long ride."

"Sounds good," Grant replied, taking a sip of his expensive bourbon. "We can have a new house built in a few weeks. Some of these guys want to hang around and help, and I'll have Gene send me down our specialists for the rock and concrete work. You will have to get your own furniture."

"I'll go shopping when I get back from my trip."

"Okay then. I'll be staying here until we finish your house. Hell, Gene will hate it when I return. Maybe I'll take Joy on that Cruise she's been bugging me on for years."

"Great. I shouldn't be gone more than a week." Hokee reached down, giving Shila a head scratch and getting a large canine grin in return. Taking a sip of Macallan single malt, he told Grant, "I better call Curly and Hilda. Curly should be here for the celebration, and Hilda too, although with this rowdy group, she might be in trouble."

Curly and Hilda arrived half an hour later to join the festivities. Hokee sat down with Hilda for a talk about their future. His office manager-lady Friday was enjoying a glass of some unknown brand of chardonnay and was delighted to see her boss alive and relaxed.

"Hilda, I'm going to take some time off from this P.I. business for a while. We'll keep the office for now and have the telephone transferred to your home if that is acceptable. I'm going to give you a pay raise for working at home and a substantial bonus, so you don't have to worry about the future. We will only be interested in finding missing college kids for a while and that usually happens have only once or twice a year. Will that be acceptable?"

"Oh, my Hokee. That sounds wonderful, but when will I see you?" Hilda was in an attractive, colorful, long-sleeved butterfly print sheath dress covering the scars she received from the Saudi Arabian butchers. The sheath accentuated her full figure, making Hilda the center of attraction for a group of sex starved men.

Hokee saw the men's interest in his attractive office partner and noticed Hilda's interest in more than one of the more attractive men, especially the smooth talking six-foot two Danial Walker. He wouldn't be surprised to see them leave together before the day ended. "We'll Hilda, you don't have to worry about that." Then added, "I will miss my beautiful lady Friday too much if I didn't stop in to see you regularly." And to add a note of levity, he continued. "I'll call first, so I won't interrupt something important." They both understood what he meant by something important. Hilda blushed with a little red creeping up her neck.

"I hope you mean two or three times a week by regularly and you don't have to call first. I'm always available for you." After speaking, Hilda realized how the last statement sounded, and quickly added with a deeper blush, "for your work."

"Well, maybe once a week, unless someone calls you with a case we must take. And we may open the office again after my retirement break."

"I will like that." Hilda was a widow with time on her hands and managing Hokee's office filled a void in her life. She was serious about wanting to reopen the office.

"We'll talk later Hilda. Go back to the party and flirt with the men who keep gawping at you. I'm going for a walk with Shila."

Hearing his name, the wolf looked up, and seeing Hokee standing, was quick to be at his side. "Grant' I'm going for a walk with Shila. You get to hold the fort all by yourself."

"Be happy to. Don't get lost," he said with a chuckle.

"I was lost when my mother jumped off a high cliff with me in her arms," he answered, as he took off walking up the driveway with Shila at his heals.

This was the one and only time Hokee ever mentioned his mother's death. Grant heard the words, wondering what he meant, and how *he* survived the fall.

Chapter Sixty-Nine

The Trip North

For the next two days, the entire crew helped one of Grant's Nampa building crews unload cement, lumber, roofing tile, and wallboard. Plus, white quartz rock, heat fused red rocks so smooth they looked like expensive molded plastic and large smooth black quartz boulders that looked like obsidian. Each boulder could make a hundred tomahawk heads or a thousand arrowheads. With the yard cleaned up, the Nampa crew was ready to start the foundation and laid out the materials in the order they would be needed. Six of the mercenaries returned to their homes in northern Idaho after receiving a hefty paycheck and bonus from Grant.

No one was surprised when Danial was one of the men who decided to hang around. The Cheshire grin on his face told the story, and Hokee was thrilled for Hilda. If his lovely office mate found love again, it would be a burden he could let go of permanently. Hilda could still be his office girl Friday, but with another man in her life, Hokee could stop worrying about her emotional well-being.

"With his team one partner hanging around, Lucas also stayed on as a grunt to help. He was a temporary hod carrier, an eighteenth-century name originally given to black men who mixed mortar for men who lay brick and cinderblock buildings. A hod carrier must keep the masons continuously supplied with fresh mortar they had to make between running a ready supply of bricks to the masons. As the walls grow higher, the job becomes a nightmare of hard work with no breaks. Carrying heavy mud–the gunk holding bricks together–in five-gallon buckets and a lode of bricks up rickety scaffolding, makes this one of the most taxing jobs in the world. Daniel's job was easier, keeping the building crew supplied with lumber and wallboard.

Leaving Grant to do his business, Hokee bid him and the crew goodbye as he and Shila left for a long drive to northern Idaho, made even longer because of a promise made to Myron before the name change. A little west on the outskirts of Kalispell, Montana, is a kennel that specializes in raising wolves. Hokee learned of the kennel from one of Curly's deputy friends.

Kalispell is 470 miles north of Pocatello, about an eight-hour drive. With no need to hurry, plus getting a late start, Hokee drove at the speed limit going north on I-15. At a rest stop an hour north of Idaho Falls, Hokee stopped at 4:30 to give Shila a drink and do some stretching. Back on the road, they stopped at a Holiday Inn in Butte for dinner and a bed. Hokee checked in alone, leaving Shila in the car until he registered. He told the receptionist he had a service animal in his vehicle. Not an untruth. Shila served Hokee in many ways. Service animals may stay in their owner's rooms without charge and the hotel cannot refuse to let the animal stay with its owner. Hokee didn't claim Shila to be a service animal to avoid paying extra for the room, but because it saved a lot of explaining. Despite anything he said about Shila being friendly, a hundred-and-eighty-five-pound wild wolf scares the hell out of most people. He discreetly sneaked Shila in later through a side door to avoid encounters.

After a leisurely breakfast with a side order of five sausage patties and ten bacon strips for Shila, Hokee set out for Kalispell, arriving at the kennel just before noon. The Big Sky Kennel was a 20 by 40 steep-metal roofed cedar log building sitting in an emerald-green pasture with six heated kennels for wolves. Colter Gustafsson, the breeder, had only four three-month-old wolves, three males and a bitch. When Hokee and Shila drove into the wide front yard, four young wolves came barking and trotting over to the fence for a close look at the intruders.

Their barking brought Colter out of his house next door to see the cause of all the commotion. Seeing Hokee and Shila getting out of the Explorer, Colter walked over and introduced himself.

"Hi Colter, I'm Hokee, he said leaving off his last name. He felt like saying his last name Wolf sounded a bit much. Are these cubs ready for adoption?"

"Yes. We sometimes let them go as early as six weeks to people who know what they're doing, but after three months, the age of this pack, they're all good to go."

"I need a wolf for a friend of mine who wants my fellow," nodding at Shila, "which he can't have." Hokee let Shila run free after getting the go-ahead nod from Colter. Shila raced over to the fence to sniff and greet his new potential friends.

"That's a beautiful fellow you have there," Colter admired. "What's his name?"

"Shila. Come back here and say hello to this pleasant gentleman."

The wolf came trotting back, observant of his master's wishes. Stopping in front of Colter, Shila held out his paw.

"Well, I'll be damned," Colter said with glee, kneeling and shaking Shila's hand. "It sure is a pleasure to meet such a smart, friendly young wolf like yourself."

"Colter, I came to buy one wolf, but I will make that two. Would it be alright if Shila joined your whelps?"

"Normally, I will be compelled to say no because of insurance regulations and my customer's safety, but after meeting you and your beautiful Shila, sure. Come on, I'll let both of you into the run."

Shila and Colter's young wolves played the games friendly dogs have played for centuries, maybe millenniums. The wolves all ran with tongues swinging from ear-to-ear grins."

"Shila's an unusual name," Colter suggested. "What does it mean, or where does it come from? I'm always looking for more wolf names."

"Shila means brother in the Navajo language." Hokee spoke in a friendly tone, watching Shila interact with the other wolves. He refrained from getting too personal.

Looking at Hokee, it was impossible not to see a handsome, confident Indian man. Colter, living with wild animals, was exceptionally well attuned to the feelings and deepest thoughts of others. While curious, he would never ask. It would be a good puzzle to work on some time.

Neither man spoke as they watched the wolves playing. "What are their names?" Hokee asked.

"The bitch is Sable. Alaska and Apollo have light gray tints at the end of their tails. Apollo's is the one with the longest tail. The one with a wild look in his eyes is Akela. The look is deceptive. That look hides his cunning. He's dazzling in his abilities, highly intelligent."

"I will like Sable and Akela. It looks like Alaska and Apollo have a strong affinity for one another. It will be a shame to separate them."

"Ya know, you're right. I've been thinking about retiring; maybe I'll keep them for myself."

Hokee laid the backseats down, giving Shila, Sable, and Akela plenty of space to lie or sit. Back on the road again, the three wolves were at ease with each other and, like all wild things, lived in the moment. With their fellow birth mates out of mind, Sable and Akela were happy with Shila. Without Shila, the other two might have felt abandoned. They would be at Zoey's and Arlo's new home in about three hours. Perfect.

CHAPTER SEVENTY

The Vision Quest Ends

Hokee stopped at the long entrance to Grant's old retreat and let the three wolves out to run for a few minutes and do their business while he stretched out his long legs. Per usual, he wore moccasins while traveling. Not only did it give him a better feeling for the foot pedals, but when he got out of his vehicle, like now, he was able to get a better feel for the energy in the ground. The sun, an hour before slipping behind the Panhandle National Forest Mountains to the west, cast long shadows across the land and breeze driven lake waves were lit like sparkling diamonds riding on their crests. The ground almost felt hallow, like it had once been the site of Indian ceremonies and powwows. Although that was possible, Hokee didn't believe that was the reason the ground felt sacred. Although Idaho settlements began around 1860, there were less than one million residents until 1999. Idaho features one of America's largest wildernesses preserves with many regions in the state still sparsely populated. The ground beneath Hokee had never been trampled by men in war, not even the Indians. The land had known only peace and love. To Hokee, it felt like home.

Calling the wolves, Hokee loaded them back into the Explorer, then drove down the driveway to the house and lake. In front of a giant Redwood log portico, the crushed red rock driveway circled around a stunning fountain with water running from white vessels held by three naked Greek nymphs. He drove around the fountain, stopping under the portico near the twin double-teak front doors. He barely exited the Explorer before being engulfed by two happy, laughing, crying souls wrapping him tightly in four loving arms.

"Oh, my God, Hokee," Arlo blubbered, laughing and crying at the same time. "We never get visitors, so when you stopped at our driveway, it caught our attention. We both saw immediately it was you, and we couldn't wait for you to drive down here."

"Hokee, it's so darn good to see you," Zoey squealed, "Now that I'm a happily married woman, I want you to give me the kiss I've been waiting years for. Myron got the loud hint and unwrapped his arms from around Hokee, allowing Zoey to pull Hokee's head down, giving him a kiss that nearly rocked him out of his moccasins.

"Damn, Zoey," he teased, "If I had known you kissed like that, I never would have introduced you to the doctor here."

When Zoey finally released Hokee, Arlo put his arms around the shaman's broad shoulders and said, "I can never repay you for all that you have done for me Hokee and putting me in the beautiful Indian Princess's hands increases the debt beyond my ability to ever adequately express thanks."

"Hold that thought," Hokee said with a grin and a twinkle in his eyes, "because your debt is about to be compounded." While saying that, he opened the vehicle's back door, and three wolves came bounding out. Shila promptly approached Arlo and, standing upright on hind legs, placed his front paws on the man's shoulders, affectionately licking his face. With emotions already off the scale, this added touch with Shila brought tears to Arlo's eyes and a lump in his throat prohibiting speech. Patting the wolf's head, he mumbled something, but it came out sounding like "yaouus aaahh gruuunat fraaiiid." You're a great friend.

After the Arlo-Shila love fest, Hokee said, "I promised you a wolf, and that little lady over there," he said, pointing to the pup busy sniffing the fountain, "is Sable, she's yours. Since you've set up housekeeping with the breath-taking Indian princess Arlo, I thought a female wolf more appropriate than a male."

Finally able to speak, Arlo said, "Oh man. I'm cried out, and without words to express my feelings. Let's go inside and have a drink. I have a bottle of Johnny Blue with your name on it. Will the dogs be alright inside?"

"I wouldn't trust the pups just yet. Let's leave them outside for now. Shila will baby-sit for us. Sable and Akela, the other pup, will not stray far without Shila and the big fellow will stay close to the house."

They settled down inside with Johnny Blue straight-up in a cut-glass Waterford tumbler for Hokee, and Lafite Rothschild Cabernet Sauvignon in Waterford crystal wine goblets for the lovebirds. Hokee talked with them about training young wolves inside and outside the house. "You have a wonderful location with privacy, and Sable will not only be a successful 'watch dog' announcing visitors, but when she is fully grown, the lady will provide high-level protection." Hokee didn't need to sell either of them on the wolf, but for Zoey's sake, who was used to living with familiar neighbors, he wanted to emphasize the protection she could expect from Sable.

Hokee told them about the battle, sparing them the grizzlier aspects, but he mentioned the drones and how effective they were at downing the helicopters. The Chinese were confirmed as the ones responsible for the attempt on Myron's life and destroying Hokee's home. They also funded the war, attempting to locate Myron and his A.I. design. While Hokee described the past few days, Arlo and Zoey sat on a soft earthy brown leather love seat holding hands, looking dazed.

"Myron, excuse me for using your old name, but it is necessary for completion. Your vision quest turned out to be rather significant, wouldn't you say?

"Lord Hokee. You saved me in so many ways; **SIGNIFICANT**? Hell, yes, it was significant. Between you and Why-ay'-looh, I learned where I live. Here. I mean this earth. Life, living. All of it. Humans will have no place in a world dominated by A.I. Cyborgs and robots. My life will now be devoted to Zoey and keeping ahead of the competition, so when the inevitable happens, we will have something better on our side. Zoey is going to provide us with a genius to continue my work. Grant has agreed to build a totally shielded laboratory here where I will reinvent Singularity Inc. with a new name on a smaller scale. The shielding will prevent any of my advances from leaking into the A.I. world. My vision quest was a success. Thank you."

"That was one or the reasons for this visit. To make certain you achieved your goals. Plus, of course, my promise of a wolf. Your quest is over. And with that, I will bid you a good day, or perhaps a good evening."

"What? No!" they both shouted. "you've got to stay for dinner, and we have scads of extra room, complete suites," Zoey continued.

"Thank you for the offer. But no. You saw the male pup outside. I need to continue his training in a vehicle, and you have Sable to contend with. Her training will go smoother without our distraction. It's better if I leave now. But I promise to visit again, and now that the war is over, you might travel down to Pocatello. Zoey will want to visit her folks and Grant's building me a new house with a guest room that has Arlo and Zoey's names on it."

Finishing his speech, he reached the front door with Arlo and Zoey close behind. "I'm still going to pay for rebuilding your house, Hokee," Myron said.

"You will have to fight Grant for that privilege, Arlo," Hokee replied with a smile.

They went outside together to say goodbye. All three wolves came running when they heard the door open and their masters come out. Hokee opened the rear hatch for Shila to jump in, then picked up Akela, setting him down beside Shila. Hokee closed the hatch, then turned to face his friends. Turning to Arlo and Zoey, Hokee said, "Sable will miss her friends, but when you shower her with love, she'll soon forget."

They engaged in a mutual three-person hug in silence. Breaking the hug, Hokee said with a big smile lighting up his handsome face, "Don't you dare kiss me again Zoey, I'll never recover."

He got in and started the Explorer while lowering the driver's door window, "I'll call you after I get back with a new permanent phone number," he said. Arlo and Zoey, with tears in their eyes and lumps in their throats, nodded their understanding. Hokee drove off, not looking back. The vision quest was over. Life was ahead.

ABOUT THE AUTHOR

Clark's background includes living at times in most of the settings in his novels. Like Hokee, he also studied with a shaman but became someone else—engineer, entrepreneur, and author. He's been a singer, actor, and makeup artist. Later, he worked as a rocket designer at Cape Kennedy and spent time in Vietnam during the war. His work for the CIA, helping to design spy satellites, was in a top-secret black ops program known to less than a hundred people. His experiences living and working worldwide serve as valuable content for his novels. Clark presently lives in Utah with his loving wife, Kim.

NOTE FROM CLARK VIEHWEG

Word-of-mouth is crucial for any author to succeed. If you enjoyed *Hohee Wolf IV: The Vision Quest*, please leave a review online—anywhere you are able. Even if it's just a sentence or two. It would make all the difference and would be very much appreciated.

Thanks!
Clark Viehweg clarkviehweg07@gmail.com

We hope you enjoyed reading this title from:

BLACK ROSE
writing™

www.blackrosewriting.com

Subscribe to our mailing list – *The Rosevine* – and receive **FREE** books, daily deals, and stay current with news about upcoming releases and our hottest authors.
Scan the QR code below to sign up.

Already a subscriber? Please accept a sincere thank you for being a fan of Black Rose Writing authors.

View other Black Rose Writing titles at www.blackrosewriting.com/books and use promo code **PRINT** to receive a **20% discount** when purchasing.